BIRTHRIGHT

blood enemies
abominations of cerilia

Written by: slade
Development & Editing: Steven E. Schend
Creative Direction: Roger E. Moore
Cover: Jeff Easley
Color interior illustrations: Denis Beauvais, Charles Lang, William O'Connor, & Arnie Swekel
Monochrome interior illustrations: Randy Asplund-Faith, Adrian Bourne, Alyce Bücker Cosart, John Dollar, David MacKay, Tony Szczudlo, & Susan Van Camp
War card art: Douglas Chaffee & Les Dorscheid
Backdrop painting and art frames: Dee Barnett
Graphic design & development: Dee Barnett & Renee Ciske
Cartography: Diesel
Art coordination: Peggy Cooper & Paul Jaquays
Typography by: Nancy J. Kerkstra
Electronic Press Coordination by: Tim Coumbe
Special Thanks: Rich Baker, Carrie A. Bebris, Anne Brown, Colin McComb, Ed Stark

TSR, Inc.
201 Sheridan Springs Road
Lake Geneva
WI 53147-0756
United States of America

TSR Ltd
120 Church End
Cherry Hinton
Cambridge CB1 3LB
United Kingdom

3101XXX1501

table of contents

D.B.
'95

The world of Cerilia is unlike any other ADVANCED DUNGEONS & DRAGONS® game world. Player characters of a BIRTHRIGHT™ campaign are now the rulers, and their focus is no longer on themselves but on those they rule. Many would believe this allows the players an easier time in fighting monsters and keeping everything safe. That is a false assumption, however, for the monsters are no longer simple sword or spell fodder. Just as the PCs rule over their domains, some monsters have also become rulers, and these beasts are far more powerful than any creatures that roam the other AD&D® worlds.

The divine right of kings that courses through the player characters also flows through that of the monstrous rulers known collectively as the *awnsheghlien* (awn-SHAY-len, an elven term that translates into "blood of darkness"), though they are sometimes simply called abominations. Like the

introduction

heroes of Cerilia, the power of the awnsheghlien traces back to the battle at Mount Deissmar, and their bloodlines are all tied to the evil might that was once Azrai the Shadow. Unlike the heroes' bloodlines, Azrai's taint gives his evil scions power at great cost: To use the power of Azrai is to lose personal identity and humanity. Many abominations were once human, but are now corrupted in body and spirit by their very powers. A glimpse inside this tome reveals the awful changes wrought on these creatures' original forms.

Bear in mind that this is not a complete catalog of those whose power is tied to Azrai, nor is it an exhaustive list of every being considered an awnshegh. This is a collection of awnsheghlien who are regents and rulers of their own domains in Cerilia, and it provides notes on a few others who draw power from Azrai. For centuries, these beings have wielded powers and hungered for more; it is easier to guard power in secret and remain hidden until they can strike and gather more from unsuspecting heroes of the blood. Fool and king alike must beware the shadows. . . .

how to use this book

Outside of this introduction and the appendices needed for readers and players, the *Blood Enemies* book exists as a "real" manuscript under the title of *Daznig's Libram on Those Enemies of the Blood*; Daznig, a sage and explorer, maintains the original bound sheaf of parchments himself, and has provided copies of it to the libraries of the prince of Avanil, The Mhor, and the Royal College of Sorcery in the Imperial City.

Below, "Daznig's Introduction" explains itself and the book's inner construction as it appears to natives of Cerilia. In short, each of the main entries in this book is laid out in the following pattern: an autobiography or interview with the awnshegh (if it has enough intelligence to be interviewed at all); Cerilian sages' conceptions (some incorrect) of the creature based on ancient tomes, personal accounts, and the many rumors and legends surrounding the creature; and finally the statistical information needed for the AD&D game, including information on realms should the awnshegh be a ruler or major power in part of Cerilia.

With three or more forms of data given for the awnsheghlien, it can be difficult to determine which information is accurate and which is inaccurate. For the DM's sake, only the AD&D game statistics for the awnshegh and the realm information are absolutely accurate. The remainder of the information provides color for use in a game. The interviews give DMs a roleplaying aid, showing how the creature speaks and thinks. Daznig's notes give more information and legendary details, many of which can be false rumors to throw off the players. DMs are encouraged to use the information as they see fit, taking what they like and ignoring the rest. In this way, a particular awnshegh in one DM's campaign differs slightly from that in another.

Note: Throughout this book, the *DUNGEON MASTER® Guide* is abbreviated as *DMG* and the *Players' Handbook* is abbreviated as *PHB*.

awnshegh statistics

Each entry provides the same facts as those in the MONSTROUS MANUAL™ tome, though the format of statistics and descriptive text has changed a bit. Brief explanations follow.

✦ INTELLIGENCE shows the relative intelligence level of an awnshegh. Ratings approximate these Intelligence ability scores:

0	Nonintelligent or not ratable
1	Animal intelligence
2-4	Semi-intelligent
5-7	Low intelligence
8-10	Average (human) intelligence
11-12	Very intelligent
13-14	Highly intelligent
15-16	Exceptionally intelligent
17-18	Genius
19-20	Supragenius
21-25	Godlike intelligence

✦ ACTIVITY CYCLE is the time of day when the awnshegh is most active.

✦ DIET categorizes the abomination's food of choice. *Carnivores* eat meat, *herbivores* consume plants, and *omnivores* eat both plants and meat, to name some common diets. Less common are the *atmovores*, who gain sustenance from air, *synaptovores*, who eat thoughts, and others detailed in this book.

✦ ALIGNMENT defines the general behavior of an awnshegh. Its servants, followers, or offspring may be of the same alignment, though this is by no means the rule.

✦ MOVEMENT is an awnshegh's speed rating. Unusual movement types are noted as follows: Cl (climbing), Fl (flying), Ml (melding through solid objects), Sw (swimming), Te (teleportation), and Wb (moving across webs).

✦ SIZE reflects an awnshegh's height, length, or diameter. Size is abbreviated as follows:

Size	Explanation
T	Tiny (2′ or less)
S	Smaller than human (2′+ to 4′)
M	Man-sized (4′+ to 7′)
L	Large (7′+ to 12′)
H	Huge (12′+ to 25′)
G	Gargantuan (25′+)

✦ ARMOR CLASS measures an awnshegh's natural defense against damage before any magic, armor, or other protective bonuses are added. Such bonuses are noted in parentheses.

✦ HIT POINTS marks the total points of damage an awnshegh can withstand before death. This number is derived from Hit Dice (which are eight-sided), which are approximated under *Saves As*.

✦ SAVES AS tells the DM which table the creature uses to make a saving throw, and gives the relative power of an awnshegh using a comparable character class and level. This reference also estimates its Hit Dice. The following abbreviations are used for character classes: F (Fighter), P (Priest), T (Thief), and W (Wizard).

✦ THAC0 (abbreviated from "To-Hit-Armor-Class-0") is the attack roll the awnshegh needs to hit an AC of zero. THAC0 does not include any special bonuses noted in the descriptions of individual attack forms.

✦ NO. OF ATTACKS shows the basic attacks the awnshegh can make in a single melee round, excluding special attacks. This number can be modified by hits that sever limbs, spells such as *haste* and *slow*, and so forth. Multiple attacks indicate several combative limbs, raking paws, multiple heads, etc.

✦ DAMAGE/ATTACK shows the amount of damage a given attack causes, expressed as a number and type of dice. If the awnshegh uses weapons, the damage done by the weapon will be annotated by the parenthetical note "by weapon type" and explained in detail within the text. Strength bonuses to damage are listed following the damage range.

daznig's introduction

- ✦ **SPECIAL ATTACKS** lists unique attacks, such as breath weapons, spell use, poison, etc. These are detailed further in the text.

- ✦ **SPECIAL DEFENSES** are unusual resistances to harm and are further detailed in the text.

- ✦ **MAGIC RESISTANCE** is the percentage change that any magic cast at an awnshegh will fail, even if creatures nearby are affected. If the magic penetrates the resistance, the creature is still entitled to any saving throw allowed. Certain awnsheghlien are resistant to specific spells, but "magic resistance" as described here is effective against all spells and magical abilities.

- ✦ **MORALE** is the general rating for the abomination's resolve in combat and its willingness to continue a battle, even under dire circumstances. Morale ratings correspond with the following:

Morale	Explanation
2-4	Unreliable
5-7	Unsteady
8-10	Average
11-12	Steady
13-14	Elite
15-16	Champion
17-18	Fanatic
19-20	Fearless

- ✦ **BLOOD** lists the being's bloodline and its rank and strength.

- ✦ **BLOOD ABILITIES** are the powers granted by this bloodline, and they are cataloged here. The use of these powers is explained in the appendix and in the *Rulebook* of the BIRTHRIGHT Campaign Set.

- ✦ **XP VALUE** is the amount of experience points PCs can earn for defeating or slaying the awnshegh. DMs might want to provide smaller amounts of experience for simply surviving an encounter with one of the awnsheghlien.

"Good morrow, kind patron, and welcome to my humble attempt at gathering information on those terrors stalking our land who are called the Awnsheghlien. I intend to provide you with knowledge in the hopes that a bold knight (or, mayhap, our beloved ruler himself) might learn how to send an abomination onto its rightful death, just as Haelyn and his fellows smote down the Shadow at Deissmar. For, while I shall give all rulers their due respect, the awnsheghlien fill my heart not with loyalty but with fear and loathing. It is hoped that my tome will grant you the knowledge you need to find and destroy them.

"Interviews or autobiographies of those awnsheghlien who could communicate with us were done under great risk to my fellow sages and interviewers. Some awnsheghlien herein were unknown (save by reputation or by name alone) before we undertook this task. To make this tome invaluable to its readers, My associates and I felt that actual interviews would be ideal ways to delve into these beings' evil minds. Of course, knowing the source of their powers, one should assume that many awnsheghlien lied to us, for it is not in their nature (nor was it ever in Azrai's) to abandon deceit. Because of this, accept not their words but their characters, and hear what they do not say, for nothing can truly hide its mind when its mouth is open.

"The sage's notes, written by me, are culled from innumerable rumors and tales and from an assembly of manuscripts, tablets, scrolls, and diaries of those who have come into contact with an awnshegh. Moreso than the interviews, this legendary data could be in error, since much of it is more allegory and fable than fact, and folk seem unable to isolate facts from the telling of a good tale. While I expurgated most of such hyperbole, there are some instances (due to the power and excesses of the creatures) where it was impossible to discern between fact and exaggeration."

apocalypse

No interview or statement was possible with the creature (or whatever it is) known as the Apocalypse. Much of its entire existence is patterned on conjecture, rumor, and legends that this sage does not find particularly reliable.

Should it even exist, the so-called Apocalypse is an uncertain force of nature, and it is impossible to guess its motivations and its source of power. However, the Apocalypse has been mentioned in a number of different sources, which lead to its inclusion within our text as an abominable danger to Cerilia.

Occultic Phenomena is a unique and large tome of unknown authorship found only in the library of Ralath, an accomplished and revered sage in Talinie whose major fields of study are Rjurik and Anuirean folklore. In an entry dating 300 years after Deismaar, the tome states the following: "Strange weather was reported in Lipshaal shortly after dawn by a local farmer. He reported that an unusually warm wind blew in from the east, carrying with it a 'pekuliar odoure.' Soon thereafter, his neighbor's cattle dropped in mid-stride. The farmer's own dogs heaved and fell to whimpering instantly. Other strange effects were reported throughout that day by many folk in the village, all beginning with that strange wind. 'Surely the apocalypse itself is upon us,' cried the farmer, 'for the whole world crumbles all around us.'"

Sages studied accounts of the disaster as well as other local happenings and reached a logical conclusion. Earlier that week, a rat-infested town to the west of Lipshaal was burned to the ground to prevent a plague from spreading. The smoke from this inferno drifted with the local weather patterns, and the plague and other evil humors thus infested the next town.

the major awnsheghlien

Among Ralath's library are collections and transcripts of provincial poetry and folk songs, and an assortment of personal diaries sold to him for his research. One small, nondescript journal, written apparently by a young girl, contains one page of interest that pertains to the Apocalypse: "I saw a face in the gray clouds today. It looked like a huge, mustached man's face with pointed teeth like a starving beast. For a second, I thought it looked at me, but it didn't come at me, so it must not have. . . ." While Ralath himself wishes to believe this testimony, much of the girl's diary is filled with trite ramblings of lunacy and hallucinatory tales, discrediting her statements.

Another apocryphal text source within Ralath's library is the *Annals of the Divinely Disfigured*, a poorly constructed and badly researched text which nonetheless served as an authoritative text on awnsheghlien for the last two centuries; it exists in at least three languages and there are nearly 20 copies still in existence in Cerilia. In reference to the Apocalypse, a *speak with dead* spell was used on a fallen priestess of Anduiras after she succumbed to a mysterious rotting

disease, and her testimony adds more commentary on the nature of the Apocalypse: "A heinous wind plagues the land—the last dying breath of Azrai, the withering mist of the Shadowland, the waning scream of the dead gods. Azrai cannot enter this world as long as he is in want of his breath. Take heed; the putrid mist prowls the land in search of its master, hoping to once again be united with him. Do not allow the breath to enter Azrai's lungs, for the land is doomed if he should breathe once again. . . ."

The tome states that its researchers used a *detect lie* in conjunction with the *speak with dead* spell, but the results were inconclusive. It is unclear if the spirit of the dead priestess was telling the truth or if she was lying. Thesselon, an Anuirean sage learned of things awnshegh, conjectures that the spirit contacted was not even the priestess; instead, he surmises that some minion of evil was sent from the Shadow World to cause panic and disorder—something the god needs to feed upon in order to return.

INTELLIGENCE: Unknown
ACTIVITY CYCLE: Any
DIET: Atmovore and Hemovore (Blood)
ALIGNMENT: Neutral evil
MOVEMENT: Fl 6 (E)
SIZE: 5,000 cubic yards
ARMOR CLASS: Inapplicable
HIT POINTS: Inapplicable
SAVES AS: Unknown
THAC0: Unknown
NO. OF ATTACKS: Unknown
DAMAGE/ATTACK: Unknown
SPECIAL ATTACKS: Death touch (see below)
SPECIAL DEFENSES: None
MAGIC RESISTANCE: Unknown
MORALE: Unknown
BLOOD: Theorized—Great (Azrai) 34
BLOOD ABILITIES: Theorized—Death Touch (Minor), Detect Life (Great), Invulnerability (Great), Major Resistance—Magic, Nonmagical Weapons, Poison (Great).
XP VALUE: Unknown

The Apocalypse can move in any direction, despite wind and air currents. It usually travels with the wind to disguise itself, though even with a tail wind it never exceeds a movement rate of 6. If the Apocalypse discovers a large group of living beings (a village or settlement), it usually changes direction and heads directly for the largest concentration of people.

If this gray translucent cloud contacts an NPC or PC, he must save vs. death magic or contract a disease that causes 1d4 points of damage each day (starting immediately). This cannot be cured without casting both *remove curse* and *dispel magic* spells on the afflicted individual. Both spells must be administered within an hour of each other to be effective. *Cure wound* and *heal* spells negate the damage but do not terminate the condition, resulting in continued damage the next day.

The Apocalypse has no apparent pattern to its travels and no reason for its existence. It was first seen in Stjordvik where a small farming community, Lipshaal, was devastated, leaving it a ghost town. Since then, it was believed spotted in the Sielwode, Baruk-Azhik, and most recently in Rohrmarch.

banshegh

First, let me eradicate a popular and major misconception: I am *not* the Banshegh. I do not emerge from my den at night to scream at people, enter their dreams, and kill them in their sleep. I don't know how the rumor got started, but it is all baseless and untrue. I have, in fact, put a bounty of two thousand gold pieces out on the Banshegh, hoping that someone will destroy the creature and thus disprove the rumor. Despite the emptiness of this gossip, I am known across Cerilia as the Banshegh, and nearly everyone save my loyal subjects has forgotten my real name: Justina Heulough.

"I am a just and kind ruler. While I impose a tax on each of my subjects, it is a fair tax that all pay—paupers and nobles alike. I have little need of this money personally, but it is used well to protect my people from roving bandits and the threat of enemy incursion. When times are good, I use the additional funds to sponsor galas for my people's pleasure or have the money put to use in constructing granaries or other structures useful for all my people. I sleep well at night, knowing that my people have lived well under my rule. I suspect the rumors of my being the awnshegh known as the Banshegh were started by a grasping noble or another of the ruling class, jealous of the prosperity and benevolence of my rule.

"I use the essence I've inherited to ensure my people that my courts are just and right. All who come before the courts for any wrongdoing shall always, as long as I sit upon my throne, have a fair trial. To our knowledge, not one person innocent of a crime has been convicted. The guilty, though, bear the full responsibilities of their actions and the punishment of my laws.

"Thanks to those vicious allegations that I am the Banshegh, or that we simply inhabit the same form, my kind but simple people have need of a dusk-to-dawn curfew, and I am sealed in my chambers each night by my chamberlain to prevent my alleged nocturnal reign of terror. It is unsettling to see my people believe in such superstitions and falsehoods, but a ruler does what sufferance she must as a mild price for her people's happiness. I just wish that more sensible folk would rise to quench these wild theories about me."

Justina Heulough is a dangerous opponent, but she doesn't realize her own power. There are two versions of the Banshegh (well-documented out-side of her domain), and she is an awnsheph despite any personal protests.

The first Banshegh is Justina Heulough—the elven leader of a very small independent nation of humans nestled among the Mountains of the Silent Watch. She is a just leader who protects her people like a mother lioness does her cubs. She commonly visits the few hamlets in her domain so the people can talk to her and express their complaints and commendations. She truly listens to their ideas for a better country, though she is always careful before acting on any of them.

Justina is a handsome elven woman. She has never been an enchantress by any means, though her sweet disposition and kind wisdom have many seeing her through compassionate eyes. She is wid-owed, her human husband having died nearly 30 years ago, and she has three children who are grown and living with their spouses deep in her domain or in Rheulgard. Her half-elven children live under aliases, not letting anyone know who they truly are (though they have ways of proving their legitimacy and status as Justina's heirs, should the need arise).

The second Banshegh arises whenever Justina falls asleep. Almost like an *astral travel* spell, the Banshegh separates from Justina's corporeal body like a spirit and haunts the Mountains of the Silent Watch and nearby Treucht and Rheulgard. There is a connection between the two, which has been ascertained from the use of *locate person* spells on the sleeping Justina: they indicate that she is in two locations at once. Not even this evidence can sway Justina Heulough's mind to believe this, as she harshly dismisses anyone who even suggests that there is a connection between her and the hated name of the Banshegh.

Regardless of Justina's inclination to ignore the evidence, the Banshegh closely resembles her face and form, though it is made entirely of dark mists and some low, blue-glowing energy. The Banshegh is rarely seen directly, but is visible out of the corners of one's eyes; looking at her most often results in looking through her.

Sages who study the awnsheghlien have two the-ories on Justina and the Banshegh. Some believe that Justina and the Banshegh are one and the same, and her dual-form is simply a

unique way of manifesting her Azrai-born abilities. A second theory states that the Banshegh is some previously unknown form of divine essence, and it entered Justina some time after the destruction at Mount Deismaar; those who subscribe to this theory cannot offer any evidence that this essence inhabited other beings in the past 1,500 years. The Banshegh's activity in this area (or in Cerilia at all, by any accounts) did not begin until after the death of Justina's husband, and it has apparently lived within Justina for nearly 30 years.

Both theories are torn over how to dispose of the Banshegh, for all agree that the Banshegh is as malevolent and dangerous as Justina is kind and just. By killing Justina, the Banshegh will definitely be destroyed. However, sages can't decide if killing the Banshegh would kill Justina. If the Banshegh is actually a manifestation of the sleeping Justina's spirit, both would die if the Banshegh is slain. If the Banshegh is simply some malevolent invader linked to Justina, severing that link or destroying the Banshegh could either free Justina of her curse or set the Banshegh free to roam the land night and day, no longer held in check by Justina.

A set of scrolls rests in the Royal College of Sorcery's library at the Imperial City of Anuire, and it is collectively known as *The Scrolls of the Tainted.* These 20-year-old scrolls hold a different story on Justina. The scrolls' author used "unspeakable arcane methods" to locate the "true" relationship between Justina and the Banshegh. He allegedly found that she was cursed by Carat, a cousin of the provincial leader of Rheulgard and a priest of Azrai. Despite Azrai's destruction at Deismaar, Carat drew power from some source for spells, though this is not elaborated upon in the texts.

Carat evidently summoned a Shadow World wraith of sorts to haunt Justina. It is inactive during the day and can only come out at night, giving the impression that the Banshegh is only around when Justina sleeps. No spells have yet been used to check for such a curse.

Justina		Banshegh
16	INTELLIGENCE	16
Day	ACTIVITY CYCLE	Night
Omnivore	DIET	Synaptovore
Chaotic good	ALIGNMENT	Chaotic evil
12	MOVEMENT	15
M (6′ tall)	SIZE	M (6′ tall)
1	ARMOR CLASS	-1
56	HIT POINTS	79
F9	SAVES AS	F11
12	THAC0	10
1	NO. OF ATTACKS	1
By weapon	DAMAGE/ATTACK	1d8 (touch)
None	SPECIAL ATTACKS	Dreams, wail
None	SPECIAL DEFENSES	Spell Immun.
Nil	MAGIC RESISTANCE	50%
11	MORALE	13
Minor (Azrai) 33	BLOOD	Minor (Azrai) 33
2,000	XP VALUE	11,000

JUSTINA'S BLOOD ABILITIES: Invulnerability (Great), Persuasion (Major), Unreadable Thoughts (Minor)
BANSHEGH'S BLOOD ABILITIES: Bloodform (Major), Fear (Major), Invulnerability (Great), Major Resistance—Magic, Nonmagical Weapons (Major), Wither Touch (Minor)

The Banshegh and Justina do not share the same blood abilities and this, sages believe, tends to prove that the two are separate entities that share the same body during waking hours. In any event, the Banshegh is a very dangerous opponent in both forms.

In addition to her blood abilities, the Banshegh's nighttime incarnation has all the known powers of common banshees, including a *wail* that kills even the heartiest hero and an immunity to *charm*, *sleep*, and *hold* spells.

The Banshegh's unique ability allows her to enter the minds of sleeping victims and frighten them to death. The few who encountered her and

lived to tell of it aged 10 years in their sleep; Meson the Wolfman is an awnshegh whose dream-battle with her ended in a draw and forged a life-long enmity between the two. The dream-tales are wild and unbelievable, as the Banshegh can seemingly manipulate dream events and interact with the sleeper's mind, causing damage incurred to a dream-self to happen in the real world (25% of damage done in a dream is incurred by the character's real body). Of the few survivors of a dream-battle with the Banshegh, most report that she most often prefers to manipulate the landscape and setting of a dream rather than directly fight with a person's dream-self, putting "earthquakes" and deep crevasses underfoot to frighten and injure the dreamer.

DOMAIN NAME: The Banshegh's Domain
LOCATION: Mountains of the Silent Watch
ALIGNMENT: Neutral good
STATUS: Not available for PC use

PROVINCES/HOLDINGS: This domain consists of Pashact, a Level 2 province.

Law: Justina controls all law holdings in her domain.

Temples: There are currently no controlled temple holdings within this domain.

Guilds: Justina holds all the guild power in this domain as well as two guild (1) holdings in Müden and Treucht.

Sources: The source holdings within the domain are held by the vizier Gastus.

REGENCY GENERATED/ACCUMULATED: 8/20 RP
GOLD GENERATED/ACCUMULATED: 4/8 GB

ARMY: When a person reaches the age of 13, he or she is trained in fighting by members of the militia. For a year, members are taught to use the long sword, dagger, and either a crossbow or longbow (with sheaf arrows or bolts). Once this training is complete, each person owns a sword, a dagger, and a missile weapon.

The persons showing the best aptitude for combat or volunteering for further training are indentured as soldiers in the capital of Pashacht and are called The Patrol. These highly trained veterans are the elite fighting force for the Banshegh as well as the trainers of the militia. They are taught advanced weapon techniques for hand-to-hand and ranged weapons. They are also trained in survival methods needed to live indefinitely in the cold, the mountains, and the steppes. Due to their intense familiarity with the landscape of their country, they surprise their opponents most of the time (-1 on opponents' surprise rolls) and they can only be surprised 10% of the time (1 in d10).

Occasionally (10% of the time), trainers find a person with an aversion to fighting. Whether it's a religious or a philosophic view, these individuals are not forced into learning the techniques of war. Instead, those with the aptitude are trained in herbalism and the treatment of wounds. By training nearly every individual in her realm for either combat or healing, the Banshegh has created a loyal force that belies the size of her nation.

If there is a call-to-arms to repel an invasion, heralds are sent to each hamlet and village proclaiming the danger. All militia members grab their weapons and respond to the attack.

Militia (400): Int 11-12; AL N; AC 7; HD 1-1; hp 4; THAC0 20; #AT 1; Dmg 1d6; SA ranged weapons; Save F1; SZ M (6' tall); MV 12; ML 12; XP 15/ea.

Healers (50): Int 11-12; AL N; AC 7; HD 1; hp 5; THAC0 20; #AT 0; Dmg nil; SD animal lore, healing, herbalism, weather sense; Save F1; SZ M (6' tall); MV 12; ML 11; XP 15/ea.

The Patrol (50): Int 17-18; AL LN; AC 4; HD 2; hp 16; THAC0 19; #AT 1; Dmg 1d8; SA ranged weapon, -1 on foes' surprise rolls, proficient in most hand-to-hand weapons, animal lore, healing, herbalism, weather sense, survival in cold, mountains, steppes; SD surprised on 1 in d10; Save F2; SZ M (6' tall); MV 12; ML 17; XP 200/ea.

Constabulary (25): Int 13-14; AL LG; AC 7; HD 2; hp 10; THAC0 19; #AT 1; Dmg 1d6; Save F2; SZ M (6' tall); MV 12; ML 12; XP 35/ea.

REGENT: Justina Heulough/The Banshegh

LIEUTENANTS: Two men, Derf Greenfields and Trebor Terazzal, aid Justina in protecting her lands. Derf leads the militia as second-in-command of the Patrol, and he is responsible for training the citizens in warfare. Trebor, Master of the Patrol and the best friend of Justina's deceased husband, keeps the Patrol at battle-readiness at all times and maintains the weaponry with his battery of blacksmiths. Both Trebor and Derf are 10th-level warriors who will protect Justina with their lives.

Justina's vizier and court advisor is the elderly half-elven wizard Gastus Reigaart (W13). He is Justina's closest friend and confidant, and has spent years magically keeping those people close to Justina and the entire populace of Pashacht from falling into the deadly clutches of the Banshegh. This drives the Banshegh out into the rural areas, but Gastus' prime consideration is Justina and her welfare, not protecting the peasants.

IMPORTANT NPCs: Briel Threefingers is the domain's master smith, and he sets the standard by which all blacksmiths are rated in the surrounding three domains as well as his own. He is able to perform his tasks in half the speed normally required by lesser smiths, and he and his assistants report directly to Trebor when working on weaponry and other works for Justina or the Patrol.

DOMAIN DESCRIPTION:
The Banshegh controls a small semi-independent nation in a basin within the western Mountains of the Silent Watch. It consists of about 10 small villages and hamlets of farmers, woodsmen, herders, and a small population of miners. Mountainous crags frame the country to the north, south, and east, while soft, rolling hills border its western side. With mountains on three sides, the easiest access to the Banshegh's domain is from the west. Of course, the largest defensive fortifications for the domain are to the west. Since the nation is so small, it would normally be difficult to create a standard army to protect her land. However, the militia and army system established in this domain is highly effective and doesn't deplete the realm's resources by constantly maintaining a huge standing army.

The domain is surprisingly fertile for planting, with abundant sources of water and rich minerals washing down from the surrounding mountains each spring. However, the spring thaw also brings flooding into many areas of the country except the western hills. Due to the topography, the water drains off more slowly than normal, and there are a few weeks in the early spring where roads are next to impassable due to mud or standing water. A number of villages in the center of the domain

have their buildings' foundations built up a foot or more from the ground to prevent their homes from flooding in the spring.

Since nearly everyone in the nation is armed, the amount of crime—violent or otherwise—is lower here than in many other realms. Few individuals wish to rob a house when they know the homeowner is often as proficient in using weapons as they are. As a result, the constabulary is very small in relation to the number of people in the nation. Each hamlet has one constable and each village has five constables; the constables serve as peacekeepers and judges alike, and many are the higher ranked members of the militia.

DOMAIN CAPITAL: Pashacht
DOMAIN VILLAGES: Southbridge, Tabre Mountain
SPECIAL LOCATIONS: Mount Anglem, Mountains of the Silent Watch, Tabre Mountain
TRADE GOODS: The sole trade route into and out of the domain runs from Pashact to Müden at the city of Barrier. The people export surplus wool and grains, raw gems from Tabre Mountain, and carved woodcrafts from craftsmen in the southern forest. They import such items as clothing, literature, and raw materials and ore for weaponmaking.

ALLIES: The Banshegh has peaceful ties with the nation of Müden. The country covertly provides hers with raw ore for weapons to use against Rheulgard. This fight and this trade have continued for years. In return, Justina provides Müden with surplus weaponry and jewelry.

ENEMIES: The fight against Rheulgard began nearly 40 years ago, when Justina and her husband moved to rule this isolated province separate from Rheulgard. The war has fallen to minor skirmishes from the south, as the ruler of Rheulgard is afraid of the Banshegh's power.

OTHER NOTES ON THE BANSHEGH'S DOMAIN

Tabre Mountain: This medium-sized mountain is a source for high-quality emeralds.

The Banshegh's Castle: Justina's fortress lies nestled amid the slope of the mountains, overlooking the city of Pashact, where her former palace lies at the city's center; due to the danger of the Banshegh, her court has been moved here for protection (of Justina and her people). Thus, Pashact and the center of the domain is guarded by the castle (4).

basilisk

It is has been nearly a century since any reports of intelligence were attributed to the awnshegh called the Basilisk. Its depravities and corruption have apparently stripped it of its original intellectual faculties. This is not to say that the Basilisk is not cunning, malevolent, or dangerous; it simply no longer has the capacity for communication with intelligent beings nor its original capability of casting spells.

The normally poor reference known as the *Annals of the Divinely Disfigured* provides a clear view of the Basilisk as it existed between one and two centuries ago. Four complete copies of this reference exist in the Khinasi lands along with a number of other

incomplete copies. All of them have an interview with the Basilisk, which is reconstructed here. Notations have been added by this author to correct or corroborate any apparent elaborations on factual history by previous scribes or the Basilisk itself. The Basilisk may lack intellect now, but the awnshegh's savage cunning existed even at this stage.

"I Hate. I am Hate incarnate. Everything that is Hate is me and everything that is me is Hate. There's no way to separate me and Hate. Once the son of the Prince of Malik el-Badr, I was forced into this form from a curse—*The* Curse from Azrai, the creation that built Hate, and I Hate for that. My name, long forgotten in time, is now Hate.

"My father stood for everything loyal and beautiful. His gardens were always neatly trimmed; his wife, daughters, and son were beautiful to the eye: and his house was the finest in the land—bright and cheerful, even at night. His knowledge was infinite, and his use of that knowledge was wise. He knew what to say and when to say it. There was nothing he could not do. How could a child live up to such perfection every moment of his life?

"My father was so proud of his son. So proud was he, that he forced me into a mold my body and my mind were neither ready nor inclined to fit. He wanted a clone of his younger self, someone to fit into his shoes when he died. He wanted me to be him: proud, beautiful, loved, and a great leader. All I wanted was to be left alone to my studies, so I rebelled.

"Rebelled, I did, and I brought discord into the perfect gardens. I placed worry onto the noble features of my father and family. My wicked tongue spread malice and guile upon many targets, to justify my quest for isolation. My eyes could deter the kindness of others with a brutal look. And I rejoiced, for it left me to my own council and my own wants and desires.

"One day, it became apparent that I had fallen from my father's favor and the favor of the gods themselves. My voice became so caustic, I poisoned myself and everything I touched. Everything of beauty I gazed upon wilted and died. That was the moment I turned fully to Hate, for I had nowhere else to dwell. The Hate in me renounced everything my father stood for, and I now punish all that is not Hate and destroy all that is beautiful."

What motivates the loathsome creature called the Basilisk? Long ago, the answer was simpler, as is told by the monster's own tongue: It is angry for being born to a destiny it did not wish to bear, and its internal venom and hatred molded its body to the reptilian form it wears today. Now, it simply responds to primal drives of hunger and territory, though it is certainly more dangerous than any animal.

Originally the son of the Prince Malik el-Badr, a sorcerer and the last ruler of the lands now known only by their monstrous inhabitant, Bali rebelled at an early age. He preferred the security of the isolated study of magic, and he put his faith in shadows and intrigue, not the honor and trust of his father's way. The Prince wanted nothing but the best for his son and raised him to the best of his ability; his son's darker side, however, was too strong and too deeply rooted.

The Scrolls of the Tainted gives a brief history of the Basilisk, but it contradicts what the awnshegh says about itself. The scrolls state that the Prince conjured the Basilisk from a vat of venom, sulfur, and malignity, and cast his heinous incantations over the vile fluids. Out from this abominable ichor rose the Basilisk, who followed the Prince's every bidding.

It is certainly likely that neither source is perfectly accurate, and the Basilisk as it exists today can never tell us the truth of its existence. Its past and its path of becoming the heinous abomination it is now are lost deep within the recesses of a poisoned, corrupt mind. All anyone needs

know now of the Basilisk is that it is a shrewd, malignant brute that enjoys torturing its prey, not unlike a cat toying with a mouse. It has brought ruin upon this once spectacular plain, and its poisonous reek lingers on everything it has ever touched.

INTELLIGENCE: Semi- (3)
ACTIVITY CYCLE: Day
DIET: Omnivore
ALIGNMENT: Neutral evil
MOVEMENT: 15
SIZE: M (7′ long)
ARMOR CLASS: 5
HIT POINTS: 74
SAVES AS: W16
THAC0: 12
NO. OF ATTACKS: 6 (bite/tail lash/4 claws)
DAMAGE/ATTACK: 1d8/1d4/1d6 (×4)
SPECIAL ATTACKS: Stench, Poison gaze
SPECIAL DEFENSES: Stench
MAGIC RESISTANCE: Nil
MORALE: 12
BLOOD: Major (Azrai) 48
BLOOD ABILITIES: Bloodform (Great), Death Touch (Major), Invulnerability (Great), Major Resistance—Poison (Great), Poison Sense (Minor), Regeneration (Minor)
XP VALUE: 17,000

Once human, the Basilisk barely retains the appearance of such. The Basilisk is a man-sized creature that appears closer to a reptile than its formerly human nature. It is covered with rusty scales that ooze a clear, poisonous secretion. That same poison drips from its fangs and sharp claws in more concentrated forms. The Basilisk's eyes have no irises, its external ears have fallen away, and its spine has extended into a large, prehensile tail. The Basilisk has no body hair, and it has a crest running from head to the small of its back.

The Basilisk's standard attacks involve slashing with its claws and biting its primary foe. Both the claw and bite attacks deliver the awnshegh's *death touch* ability in addition to their normal damage. The Basilisk's tail is often used as a bludgeoning weapon, though it can wrap around one target and hold it with 18/00 Strength.

The slime covering the awnshegh's scaly skin has a caustic reek that can be detected miles away, and this stench can linger for weeks after the Basilisk's passing; in a calm breeze, the stink can even be detected upwind. Within 60 feet of the Basilisk, the stench has a ruinous effect on the creature's opponents (or any creatures). A saving throw vs. poison must immediately be rolled; if failed, the victim can do nothing but fall to the ground paralyzed by nausea that continues for 1d10 rounds or until the stench is gone. Those who make the saving throw suffer a -2 on all attack rolls and saving throws while in the stench. If any flesh touches the slime, it takes 1d3 points of damage.

With its gaze, the Basilisk can cause any fluid to change into deadly poison. Pools of water it glances at are instantly envenomed, bodies of water are temporarily polluted, and heavy fogs change into poisonous mists; all who drink or breathe the poisons must make a saving throw vs. poison or suffer 1d8 points of damage. If a living creature is looked at, the water contained in the eyes, tear ducts, and mouth are poisoned unless a saving throw vs. poison is successful. If the saving throw is failed, the victim loses 1d4 points of Strength and Constitution per round. If either statistic is reduced to 0 or four rounds elapse without aiding the poisoned character, the victim dies. If the toxins are neutralized in four rounds, all statistics and the Movement Rate return to normal in 1d6 hours.

REALM NAME: The Basilisk's Domain
LOCATION: East of the Tarvan Waste
ALIGNMENT: Neutral evil
STATUS: Not available for PC use
PROVINCES/HOLDINGS:

Law: There is nothing but lawlessness in this poisoned land, with brigands, giants, and an awnshegh imposing order by force. The giants control a holding (1) in Broken Hills.

Temples: The once-great temples were shattered over a century ago by one of the Basilisk's rampages.

Skeletal remains of the clerics litter the ruins of their temple in el-Besr.

Guilds: Guild holdings are restricted to the paltry collections of loot made by Kalilah Sun-eyes' Dark Blades or the giants' raiding parties (one point each in el-Besr and Broken Hills).

Sources: Up until the last century, the magic here was strictly and greedily controlled by the Basilisk. There are ley lines established to draw power to its seat of power at Brokendale, but it has been decades since any force has used the powers here. While most agree that the beast cannot control the power any longer, few are willing to venture into Brokendale to test their theories. They also believe the pollution of the lands by the Basilisk have destroyed much of the magical potential of the territory anyway.

REGENCY GENERATED/ACCUMULATED: 2/10 RP
GOLD GENERATED/ACCUMULATED: 0/12 GB

ARMY: None

REGENT: This lawless land is directly ruled by no one, but the Basilisk remains the only true controlling power within its blasted homeland.

LIEUTENANTS: The Basilisk has no followers or immediate support, since no one survives its venomous presence for long.

IMPORTANT NPCs: Outlaws called the Darkblades have recently established a lair in el-Besr. Unlike the other marauders scattered within the Basilisk's domain, the Darkblades consider themselves exiles from their native land of Aftane. Their leader, Kalilah Sun-Eyes, claims to be the daughter of the deposed sultan of Aftane, and heir to the throne usurped by the Red Kings. Kalilah is a striking woman, a skilled sorceress, and an accomplished leader. Her band has done well in the new hideout, and many Darkblades wonder if their leader's enchantments have charmed the Basilisk since it has not challenged their presence.

The Broken Hills are home to a hill giant clan that lives in a stock-ade overlooking

the Zhaïnge. The giants periodically trade with bold rivermen, exchanging their livestock for tools or baubles. More often, they raid the southern provinces of Kozlovnyy. The Basilisk has eaten the giants' cattle and sheep for years, and several giants have died trying to slay the beast. Now, they simply drive their herds into the stockade when they smell the Basilisk.

DOMAIN DESCRIPTION: Once this area was part of Djira and was known for its ideal grazing land. The Basilisk's arrival 400 years ago changed that. The awnshegh destroyed the towns and palaces of the Djirans, leaving a scarred and poisoned landscape littered with nothing but ruins and corpses in its wake. After dozens of attempts to kill the creature, the region was abandoned and inhabitants migrated elsewhere.

Now, the entire domain is an envenomed wasteland. Great tracts of land are permanently fouled by the beast's presence; trees and the soil are blackened and dead, all normal animals have fled, and even springs and aquifers are poisonous. Anyone entering this region should bring food and water to survive the passage through this domain.

Crumbling boroughs and castles dot the landscape. Looters have picked these ruins clean, although many perished as a result of their foolhardy ventures. Many treasure hunters believe that these ruins still hold much wealth, and insist that vaults still lie unspoiled beneath the ruins of the Golden Horn, the great castle now inhabited by the Basilisk.

DOMAIN CAPITAL: Golden Horn
DOMAIN VILLAGES: Broken Hills, el-Besr
SPECIAL LOCATIONS: Zhaïnge River
TRADE GOODS: No trade is conducted with surrounding domains due to lack of leadership.

boar

No interview was possible with the Boar, since it was and still is a dangerous beast with no discernible mind whatsoever. However, sages were able to peaceably contact the druids of Thuringode to gain their insights on the beast. The druids of Thuringode are a secretive group and they allowed this interview only on the grounds that the location of their stronghold never be revealed. The interviewed druid appeared to be a younger man of Anuirean descent, and his name was Samovel.

"So you would learn of the Bane of Thuringode, for that is how it is known within our sylvan home. Listen well and record my words for those who might read this long after my voice should fail to reach others' ears.

"Now, the outskirts and the outer rim of the forest are left wild and almost hostile to its inhabitants and invaders alike. Bandits, gnolls, and a few goblin tribes exist within that harsh territory, and we are careful to stay well-hidden from such distasteful people. That dense, dark thicket and its unsavory inhabitants should be enough to deter all but the most foolhardy explorers. Still, there are rare occasions that a person or group of inimical intentions enters the heart of the woods searching for treasures or some other wild fabled goal. It is in human nature to seek that which is hidden, and the shadowy boughs of Thuringode apparently hold enough mystery to drive greedy souls into its murky depths in search of answers.

"It was a number of seasons ago—thirty, more or less—that the heart of our forest was invaded by human despoilers. Someone dressed as a local noble—his heraldry was unknown to me and my comrades—led a hunting party into the forest and was wantonly destroying trees and wildlife. We and a few dryad allies descended upon the plunderers, giving them fair warning and

suggesting they remove themselves from the woods. They resisted with weapons and spells, slaying my mother and two dryads in anger. This brought the wrath of Thuringode's protectors down on the noble's party.

"In the battle that ensued, the noble escaped, ignobly abandoning his allies in panic, though he was sorely wounded. In my rage, I followed with my father, Aldran, both of us wanting this evil man to pay for his crimes. Staggering through the forest, the fool stumbled across a boar's den and disturbed a mother boar with her young. In his wounded state, he was hardly a match for an enraged boar, and it gored him to death.

"While I said a silent prayer to Erik in thanks for his servant's aid in the death of my enemy, my litany was interrupted by a loud crackling, the likes of which I had never heard. My father and I turned and witnessed a wild maelstrom of energy erupt from the corpse of the nobleman. Some of the energy leapt into the boar, turning its coat white and increasing its size by more than half! The rest of the energy vortex felled a number of trees all around and blasted the ground beneath the corpse to bare rock. We realized then that this corrupt, grasping nobleman was undeservedly filled with the power of the gods themselves—the dark blood of Azrai, most likely—and his death passed on this power to the boar, transforming it into an awnshegh. My father and I saw the birth of the abomination against Erik and nature itself, now known as the Boar of Thuringode. Not knowing what it would become, we let it live that day.

"In the intervening years, a number of folk have entered the Forest of Thuringode seeking to slay the beast. We fully support this, as the creature is an abomination against nature and we have little enough power to protect our sylvan glades at the forest's heart than to kill it ourselves. Unfortunately, many of the blooded heroes who seek to hang the Boar's white pelt as a trophy have fallen to its savage tusks. With each hunter's death, the Boar increases in size, till it is now the size of a house. My father also fell to its ravening tusks, and I pray daily to Erik to see us and our forest saved from this baneful monstrosity. Mayhaps your chronicle will bring someone of valor and strength enow to bring this beast low. Erik be praised, should it be so."

The Boar is an easily documented awnshegh because, unlike many other awnsheghlien, the stories, eyewitness accounts, and fables regarding the Boar do not contradict each other. This, of course, makes a sage's or historian's job very easy indeed.

About 35 years ago, tales of a large white boar of unusual ferocity and constitution in the forest of Thuringode circulated through the country of Massenmarch. The tales spoke of a white beast the size of a fortress with tusks as thick as 12-year-old oaks and a tempered spirit to match. Everyone (those possessing rational thought, at least) avoided the woods and prayed the terror would stay put.

Like every powerful legend, there's always someone who wishes to prove something or make himself legendary by killing or conquering it. Thus was Alfredo Stade—a man of impeccable features and skill. He heard the tales of the Beast of Thuringode and believed them to be fables concocted by the ale-drenched brains of witless illiterates. He wanted to see for himself what the legends held.

Alfredo searched throughout the country of Massenmarch for a guide who knew the Forest of Thuringode well but found no one to aid him. No one was willing to step into the forest prowled by the infamous albino awnshegh. After searching for nearly a year, he was ready to give up all hope of finding the magnificent beast when he heard of an old, contorted wizardess with silver hair who lived in a tree on the western outskirts of the forest.

His source was true, and he found the tree of the Silver Wizardess, as she is called in Stade's journals. But upon discovering her lair, he also found to his amazement that she was hardly the bent old crone he had been told about. Within moments of meeting, Alfredo was madly in love with a dryad of Thuringode. After four years of happily enspelled servitude on the outskirts of the woods, he regained his freedom and she taught him about the Boar and its destructive ways.

Alfredo Stade went on his way, closely following the wizardess's directions on where to find the gigantic beast. After traveling through the thick trees, pushing through thickets as dense as stone, and crossing over steep hills, he reached the forest's heart when he heard a tremendous noise ahead.

He climbed an ancient oak and peered ahead through the dense leaves. What he saw almost sent his panicked heart into his throat. The Boar of Thuringode stood before him. Its pelt was the purest white, and its huge eyes glittered darkly. The beast stood at least 32 hands tall at the shoulder. The sparse, coarse hair on the Boar hackled when it caught Alfredo's scent, but the beast, even at its great size, never looked up a nearby tree for the invader.

After the huge beast snorted, stomped, and left, Alfredo climbed down from his lofty seat and ran in the other direction until he returned to the safe lands of Massenmarch. He never returned to the interior of the forest, fearing the power of the Boar more than desiring the honor of killing such a creature.

The Boar still roams Thuringode, killing any and all that cross its path. Alfredo Stade, on the other hand, now graying and showing the signs of distinction and age, comes once a year to the tree near the outskirts of the forest, hoping to find the wizardess. His yearning and searching are of no avail.

INTELLIGENCE: Semi- (3)
ACTIVITY CYCLE: Day
DIET: Omnivore
ALIGNMENT: N
MOVEMENT: 15
SIZE: L (14′ tall)
ARMOR CLASS: 4
HIT POINTS: 82
SAVES AS: F11
THAC0: 10
NO. OF ATTACKS: 1
DAMAGE/ATTACK: 3d10 (Tusk)
SPECIAL ATTACKS: Trample
SPECIAL DEFENSES: Nil
MAGIC RESISTANCE: Nil
MORALE: Champion (16)
BLOOD: Tainted (Azrai) 16
BLOOD ABILITIES: Bloodform (Great),
    Invulnerability (Great), Regeneration (Minor)
XP VALUE: 6,000

Like any wild boar, the Boar of Thuringode prefers the forested areas that have always been its home. It eats omnivorously, and its former bad temper has simply increased with its size, appetite, and power. Of the circle of druids that lives in the forest, seven of them have met death under the hooves or by the tusks of the Boar simply for crossing its path.

The Boar's tusks are its most frequently used weapons, and these have grown to the size of small logs. Shattered remnants of its tusks have been found in various parts of the forest, and the pieces are often carved into daggers by and for the druids.

The Boar also has a tendency to charge its prey and trample it to death. If the Boar charges for 30 feet or more and contacts an opponent, it inflicts 3d12 points of damage to the trampled victim. There are a number of "lanes" within the western and northern sections of Thuringode Forest, areas of fallen trees and cleared brush resulting from the Boar's charges. The only good effect this has for the forest's inhabitants is to create deadfall, lumber and firewood without having to incur the druids' or dryads' collective wrath.

The Boar has been hunted by a number of scions of Anuirean and Brecht realms, but none have slain the beast. There were two isolated instances where the beast appeared to be killed, but its wounds disappeared and it savagely gored the surprised hunters quickly thereafter. It is in my opinion that it has an ability protecting it from death. At the least, separate its head from its body to slow its recovery and perhaps remove its tusks . . . ?

PROVINCE NAME: The Forest of Thuringode
LOCATION: Massenmarch
STATUS: Not available for PC ownership
ALIGNMENT: Neutral

The Forest of Thuringode is a province of Massenmarch, and all holdings and resources are considered property of the ruler of

Massenmarch. However, the druids do control the magical sources in the forest, despite some attempts from Massenmarch to gain them.

The Forest of Thuringode has no official standing army, nor does Massenmarch place troops there. Instead, a circle of 12 druids and 20 dryads try to keep the inner forest in pristine condition, safe from human exploitation and relatively safe from the Boar's ravaging. The outer third of the forest is inhabited by four small tribes of goblins, two gnoll tribes, and at least one bandit band, all of which raid and harrass Kiergard and Massenmarch.

IMPORTANT

NPCs: Elias Oakheart leads the druids' circle of Thuringode. He has collected around him a group of eleven other druids who serve and learn directly from him. Among them are Samovel, Artus, and Elias' second, the lovely Gerydda, a Rjurik woman with strong ties to the dryads of the forest as well.

Elias Oakheart (D11): Int 17, Wis 18; AL N; AC 6; HD 11; hp 47; THAC0 15; #AT 1; Dmg 1d8 (battleaxe); SA spells; SZ M (6′ tall); MV 12; ML 18; XP 1,420.

Other Druids (11): Int & Wis 14-16; AL N; AC 6; HD 1-6; hp 1d4+1/HD; THAC0 Var.; #AT 1; Dmg 1d6 (quarterstaff, axe, or spear); SA ranged weapons, spells; SZ M (6′ tall); MV 12; ML 16; XP 65 (2), 120 (2), 175 (2), 270 (2), 420 (2), 500 (1).

Dryads (20): Int 13-14; AL N; AC 9; HD 2; hp 16; THAC0 19; #AT 1; Dmg 1d4 (knife); SA charm; SD dimension door; Save M2; SZ M (5′ tall); MV 12; ML 12; XP 975/ea.

DOMAIN DESCRIPTION: The forest of Thuringode was once a beautifully natural location throughout, but it is now primarily seen as a dark, unsettling place with the scent of menace all around. The outer rim of the woods has been reduced to a dark, tangled thicket with an evil reputation. Many bandits, goblins, and gnolls lurk in its trackless mazes. Due to this murky and dangerous perimeter as well as the horrific and powerful beast that lurks within its depths, the Forest of Thuringode is one of few in Cerilia that is free of human logging.

The Boar lives a relatively solitary life unlike normal boars who prefer to live in small groups, since there are no others of its size.

Recently, a rumor has circulated in the capital of Massenmarch stating that the druids are trying to give the Boar a lifemate. This is a truly frightening concept to many. This rumor has spawned many a quest into the forest to destroy the Boar and slay any and all druids in order to shatter the chances of that occurring. Sages, on the other hand, do not put stock into this rumor at all; knowing the druids' hatred of the twisted and corrupt creature, they fear this constant incursion into Thuringode is only going to fuel the druids' hostility against outsiders even more.

On occasion, loggers or hunters will enter the area to hunt game or saw down trees. If not discovered immediately by the Boar, dryads, or druids, they will fell trees while the opportunity presents itself. This never lasts more than a few days before the incursion is discovered. Soon thereafter, the dryads charm the loggers, the druids weave their natural magic, and the Boar charges, scattering the loggers to the wind.

Druids, wherever they may live, are very strong allies of the inhabitants of the Forest of Thuringode. Everyone else throughout the land is either scared of the forest or wants the Boar, the druids, and the dryads all slain in order to exploit the land fully. The lumber available from this area is considered some of the best on the continent, second only to the quality wood that can be found in the domain of another awnshegh, the Spider's wooded domain of Spiderfell in central Anuire.

chimaera

Immortality. Though few have the temerity to admit it, immortality is the ultimate quest in life; for taking your life in your hands and seeking to postpone its end makes life worth living.

"Of course, many a soul has tried to achieve this goal, but most have failed. Correction—all have failed before me. Yes, there are those corrupt beings known as awnsheghlien who have slowed time's effects on them, but that is a godly gift. I, on the other hand, chose to seek immortality and grant it to myself. Immortality *given* to you is not a prize; to *win* immortality through your own efforts, skills, and creations is the true test and a true reward.

"Now am I known as the Chimaera, and this name suits me. There are those who believe that my other, more . . . bestial form belies a lack of sanity or purity. How droll. How . . . jealous. I chose my own path to immortality—who am I to curse the gods for the forms I wear in that immortality? I am satisfied in my goals—I shall live forever, and I have power. True power. Power over the beasts, power over the rabble who laughed and scorned me, and power over the destiny of our land of Cerilia.

"I, Danita Kusor, spent my life learning the ways of elves and the ways of humanity. I studied the living and the dead. I learned from the animals, mundane and monstrous alike. That knowledge gained for me a glimpse into life itself and how to postpone the coming of death. Am I mad for having done this? I say nay, a thousand nays! Immortality is worth far more than the tortures one endures when sharing the form of a beast. And power, as many can attest who bear Azrai's tainted blood or the purest of Anduiras' blood, is worth nearly any price. Should these powers make me mad, then I shall suffer the burden of being called mad by lesser, weaker minds. Only those who share my gift can know the majesty and magnificence of true power and life everlasting."

Danita Kusor was a wizardess with a penchant for necromancy, and an alchemical specialist by trade. With skills learned from her parents (a Vos midwife and an elf herbalist), she specialized in creating potions and herbal remedies for common ailments like boils, warts, heartburn, rashes, and hair loss. She used the profits of her alchemical trade to finance her studies of death and her quest for immortality.

She studied with unequalled vigor, trying to determine the reasons for death and aging. Her greatest desire was to discover the secrets of immortality and eternal youth.

Danita's first step toward her twisted form of immortality was to study death, corpses, and the effects of decay on the human condition. Once she understood what happened after death, she needed to find out if life could be restored to a dead body without the intervention of the gods. It was at this time that some close friends noticed a change in her thinking, an obsession in her goal barring all else, which they blamed on overexposure to her elixirs.

After years of trial and error, Kusor created a glowing, azure elixir that would theoretically saturate a corpse with life once again. Her experiments with this elixir led her to believe that no one race or species alone could regenerate fully, but a combination of factors in dwarven, elven, and human physiology could allow her potion to work and reanimate the dead tissues. Danita's murders of a number of people in Sendoure and the Coulladaraight resulted in her being driven away from civilization and into the Harrowmarsh. Many of her potions drew their power from the rare and exotic animals that dwell within the swamp. Eventually, she ended up in the Iron Peaks. There, more than a century ago, she completed her horrific creation which is now called the Binman (see page 115).

For nearly a year, Danita Kusor attempted to put life into her creation using potions, elixirs, and other magics, but none animated the constructed corpse-being. After brewing yet another potent elixir, Kusor made her latest attempt to resuscitate her creature. During the Binman's immersion in a vat of alchemical brew, a minor awnsheghlien (a menace then called the Iron Troll by miners of the Iron Peaks) invaded Kusor's laboratory, searching for food and treasure. She slew it with an array of deadly spells, but

she
suffered grievous
wounds in the process.

With the Iron Troll's death, his birthright was released in an explosive display of energy drawn to both the wounded Danita and her inert creation in its alchemical bath, inundating them with cascading energy. After absorbing the blood taint of Azrai from the deceased awnshegh, the Binman quickened to life without being fully alive at the same time. It smashed its way out of its bonds and alchemical tank, soaking its wounded creator in the magically charged chemicals.

Danita noticed some physical changes in her body immediately, but did not gain a chance to act on them or study them. The mute Binman quickly gained control over its powerful body and attacked, using sharp shards of its life-giving tank as weapons. Having retained some basic warrior's abilities, it attempted to kill its creator, but succeeded only in forcing her to flee for her life. Soon after its reanimation, the Binman left the now-ruined tower behind and headed out of the Iron Peaks to Binsada. Danita Kusor, reluctant to abandon all her equipment and her still-unique library of knowledge, soon returned to her tower to finish her quest for immortality.

After her battles with the Iron Troll and the Binman, Danita knew she had gained some power but its exact nature remained unknown to her. She believed the energy affected every potion within her laboratory, and she needed more of that power to gain immortality. She combined a number of older potions in a reconstructed vat with new ingredients such as dried dragon's blood (for ties to a nearly immortal creature—a truly rare find!) and the saliva of a displacer beast (a connection to the Shadow World, where death is near but always far). She cast various spells into the magical mixture, charging it with energy she believed would revive the power left by the Iron Troll's death throes. When she immersed herself in her magical, energy-laden vat of liquids, she was a highly focused and powerful half-elven wizardess; what exited the vat in an eruption of power and pain was a partially human form with dragon's wings and four arms that soon became known as the Chimaera.

Over the past century, Danita's form has advanced further into an awnshegh state, though due to the odd circumstances of her power acquisition, she can revert to her original form for short periods of time. Neither her Chimaera form nor her true half-elven form are fully sane, but she is a bit more lucid in female form; her beast-form is feral and dangerous. Since her initial transformation, she allegedly can wear her normal form only when calm or under a full moon, though this may be little more than a false tale. Danita Kusor has been seen in a

23

number of forms over the past few decades, and there seems to be little rhyme or reason to her shapechanging other than her own will. With her newly assumed power, Danita used her burgeoning might to exert her will over the areas surrounding her tower, and the land now bears her name as the Chimaeron.

What was once the greatest library in Anuire devoted to the studies of life, death, and states in-between has lain in shambles for over 50 years.

While Danita can still talk in either form with intelligent beings, her reasons for destroying her research are hidden. Does she wish for no one else to learn her secrets, or is it just a sign of madness? None are so curious as to ask her directly and risk almost certain death, and she offers no clues to her motives.

In recent decades, many blooded daredevils from Rohrmarch, Coeranys, and Osoerde have tried to kill the Chimaera, to no avail. With the death of these empowered heroes, she has grown even stronger still, but at an apparent cost. Her usual contacts with the governing body of Chimaeron report that she is less clearheaded and far more brutal now than ever before. Some goat herders who live close to the ruined tower of Danita Kusor, now known as the Chimaeron Refuge, say the creature has been changing, altering her appearance, and increasing her appetite. She is never seen wandering the hills in her female form, a habit she had for nearly three decades. These uneducated herders are incapable of fully vocalizing what horrors they may have seen, but their fear and their anger at the losses in crops and animals are real enough.

Danita		Chimaera
19	INTELLIGENCE	6
Any	ACTIVITY CYCLE	Any
Omnivore	DIET	Omnivore
Chaotic evil	ALIGNMENT	Chaotic evil
12	MOVEMENT	15, Fl 18 (C)
M (5′ tall)	SIZE	L (11′ long)
10	ARMOR CLASS	1
87	HIT POINTS	87
W13	SAVES AS	W13
9	THAC0	5
1	NO. OF ATTACKS	5 (bite/claws)
By weapon	DAMAGE/ATTACK	3d4/2d4 (×4)
Spells	SPECIAL ATTACKS	Nil
Nil	SPECIAL DEFENSES	-2 on foe's THAC0
Nil	MAGIC RESISTANCE	Nil
Elite (14)	MORALE	Elite (14)
11,000	XP VALUE	13,000

BLOOD: Minor (Azrai) 38
BLOOD ABILITIES: Bloodform (Special; Great), Divine Aura (Major Aura), Enhanced Senses (Minor), Long Life (Major), Regeneration—Standard and Major (Great)

The Chimaera prefers to begin combat with a surprise attack; usually, she swoops down on her opponents from the air. Aerial tactics are her standard, as she often hovers low over targets and claws at them with four or more of her bestial claws. Her second set of arms always stays in humanoid form, and she can wield wands or daggers in them.

The Chimaera can be bargained with, and she is willing to discuss terms with any she considers her prey. This, of course, depends on a variety of factors, including her hunger, patience, and the moon's presence—Danita's intense personality stabilizes as the moon grows fuller. While still intelligent, she lacks Wisdom (Wis 8); if she is angered by insults, attacks, or mere whim, make a Wisdom check to keep her from immediately attacking in beast form.

REALM NAME: Chimaeron
LOCATION: North of the Gulf of Coeranys, near the Iron Peaks
ALIGNMENT: Chaotic evil
STATUS: Not available for PC use.

PROVINCES/HOLDINGS:
While the Chimaera is the official regent of her namesake domain, she is most often a ruler in absentia, allowing the Council of Leaders relatively free reign in controlling the land. On infrequent occasions, she will emerge from Chimaeron Refuge and make demands of the Council of Leaders, though she has not done so in over 10 years.

The Chimaera does, however, keep incredibly tight control over the magic sources within the Chimaeron, and anyone attempting to tap into any of this power is subject to her immediate attack; she has played a game of cat-and-mouse with a group of mages known only as Three Brothers, allowing them to find and control some sources and biding her time before removing them from her domain.

There allegedly are temples to Nesirie and Cuiraécen hidden high up in the peaks of the mountains, but no one knows what lone priests might maintain them.

Province	Law	Temples	Guilds	Sources
Barniere (1/4)	CoL (1)	—	CoL (2)	Ch (4)
Careine (2/6)	CoL (1)	TF (1)	CoL (1)	Ch (5)
Hamein (1/5)	CoL (1)	WB (1)	CoL (1)	TBM (4)
Lyssan (2/7)	CoL (2)	WB (1) TF (1)	CoL (2)	Ch (7)
Mhowe (2/4)	CoL (2)	—	Col (2)	TBM (4)
Ruorkhe (1/6)	CoL (1)	—	Col (1)	Ch (6)
Salviene (1/5)	CoL (1)	—	—	Ch (5)

Abbreviations: CoL=Council of Leaders; Ch=the Chimaera; TF=The Fortress (Tugaere Issimane); WB=Water's Blessing (Phisaid Uriene); TBM=Three Brother Mages.

REGENCY GENERATED/ACCUMULATED: 26 RP/35 RP (Chimaera); 2 RP/4 RP (Council Leader/ea.)

GOLD GENERATED/ACCUMULATED: 0 GB/8 GB (Chimaera); 1 GB/2 GB (Council Leader/ea.)

The leaders of the Council, as the Chimaera's vassals, donate 1 RP/turn and 1 GB/turn to her.

ARMY: The Chimaeron does not have a standing army, relying instead upon a militia-like constabulary. Summoned from each village or small city, the total forces that can be rallied in the Chimaeron count 100 members. These 100 policing officials are effective as local sheriffs and peacekeepers, but they are not trained to work as an army. However, they are very good at small-group skirmishes and ambush attacks.

Constabulary (100) Int 8-12; AL N; AC 10; HD 1-1; hp 3; THAC0 20; #AT 1; Dmg 1d4; Save F0; SZ M (6' tall); MV 12; ML 8; XP 15/ea.

REGENT: Chimaera, with the Council of Leaders

LIEUTENANTS: The Council of Leaders consists of nine members, one from each town and village. They make laws, collect taxes, and pay for the salaries of the constabulary. All of the leaders are charismatic and powerful local bosses, though their power bases vary in nature; only two of them are natives, while all others are fugitives from the justice of outlying domains. The Council's leaders are as follows:

Barniere: This poor village is occupied by farmers, expatriate Khinasi, and fugitives from other domains' justice. Living on the outskirts of the Chimaera's shadow, this village has more Khinasi influences than Anuirean, reinforced by its mayor, Hakim el-Qadr.

Careine: This town is one of the most developed in the Chimaeron and is ruled by Lord Mayor Cowell, an exiled Anuirean wanted for murder in three provinces in Medoere and Avanil. While he is a known extortionist, he manages to maintain a few small trade routes with Coeranys and Baruk-Azhik.

Hamein: This inner port controls the mouth of the river leading into Rohrmarch, and thus holds a large bargaining chip with that country. The town's mayor, Lord Myonos, often is heard promising visitors "anything is possible here in Lagos for a price." The town is named after the natives' original name for the lake to the north.

Luandar: Ruled by an unscrupulous paranoid Rjurik named Otslof, Luandar is a poor, dirty port on the border with Coeranys. About the only reason for folk to visit this port in the province of Lyssan is to seek a pirate crew or an assassin.

Lyssan: The domain capital solely by its central location, this town is a small collection of stone and wood buildings built onto a mountain plateau. A large tower rises against the eastern cliff, and this is the meeting place of the Council of Leaders. This town's money is garnered from mining and smithwork (both in weapons and jewelry). Lord Mayor Yuri Khavlor was once a Vos druid who lost his faith in Erik and gained a love for gold.

Mhowe: This is the richest town and port of Chimaeron, hands down, and it is the best kept town simply because of its distance from the attentions of its monstrous overlord. The self-proclaimed "Prince" Denerik is a fugitive from Brecht justice and has been branded a "pirate and thief of the lowest order." Denerik controls much business and trade from his tower at the town's center, including some minor smuggling through the brigands in Harrowmarsh. He, foremost among all his compatriots in the Council of Leaders, wants to take control of the country, and hoards poisons of a most virulent sort in planning the removal of his fellow Council members.

Ruorkhe: Directly under the gaze of the Chimaera, Ruorkhe is a blasted, ruined village of poorly kept hovels and storehouses. However, Ruorkhe is also one of the Chimaeron's richer towns. Much of Ruorkhe's life takes place underground, as it affords better protection from the Chimaera's rages. The person responsible for this deceptive place and its lower tunnels and chambers is the town's leader, an exiled dwarf named Charrek Ironfist.

Salviene: Farther out in the Gulf of Coeranys, Salviene is prosperous due to its gambling and excesses not found in ports within Coeranys. Its ruler Chandol, a self-proclaimed duke, is a native of the Chimaeron.

Tulear: This small port in the province of Mhowe stays alive because of its industrious shipbuilding. It is the only settlement within the Chimaeron not dominated by criminals and fugitives, and its leader, Mayor Shanol, seems woefully out of place as an honest, hard worker among his fellow leaders.

DOMAIN DESCRIPTION: Thirty years ago, the isolated and self-sufficient settlements within the Chimaeron attempted to rid themselves of the Chimaera. It was the first time they worked together, and this brought them under one flag and under one

TRADE GOODS: Filled mostly with herders and hunters, the Chimaeron exports beef and lamb, as well as hides and wool for clothing and rope. Several businesses in Tulear utilize these raw materials to make sails, leather armor, and clothing, selling them to nearby countries and at the docks. The Chimaeron also has a few farms, but the produce is for internal consumption.

ALLIES: The Chimaeron has good relations with Rohrmarch. Open trade exists between these countries. A single trade route runs through the Chimaeron and passes through Careine, Ruorkhe, and Barniere, allowing Rohrmarch to trade freely with minimal fees for routing through the Chimaeron.

SPECIAL CONDITIONS: A blooded hero—well on his way to becoming an Ehrshegh—is rumored to exist within the Chimaeron, and will destroy the Chimaera; a few of the Council and many natives cling to this hope. A few guides for our sages identified a lonely cave within the Iron Peaks as the home of this rumored savior. If rumors are held to be true, this hero is a blooded warrior dedicated to Vorynn, and he is slowly taking a huge bear's form. Called the Bruin, this rumored savior keeps his true name secret.

leadership. When this new country was formed, Lyssan was chosen as its capital due to its centralized location, size, and revenue. The Council of Leaders was stationed there the following week.

When the Council of Leaders at Lyssan were unsuccessful at destroying the Chimaera, she met with them and threatened each of them with the utter destruction of their towns and their power bases, while sparing their lives. She would withhold such destruction if she were granted titular rule and granted concessions at her whims. Having little or no bargaining positions to work from, the Council of Leaders acceded regency rule to the Chimaera.

To placate her (and the populace), dangerous criminals who are caught are "allowed the chance to work for society and slay the fearsome creature that holds us in her grasp." Serious disruptors of the status quo are ushered to the Chimaeron Refuge under the pretense of slaying the Chimaera; these criminals are quickly killed by the Chimaera. The Council enjoys this easy method of disposing of overly troublesome elements.

This new realm, called the Chimaeron, is not a force in the political arena of either Anuire or Khinasi. It has trade agreements with nearby domains, but it carries no political weight whatsoever. Militarily, they are even weaker—the only thing that prevents an invasion is the awnshegh and the outsiders' fear of her leading the troops.

DOMAIN CAPITAL: Lyssan
DOMAIN TOWNS: Careine Town, Salviene, Hamein, Mhowe, Tulear
DOMAIN VILLAGES: Barniere, Ruorkhe, Luandar
SPECIAL LOCATIONS: Broken Hill, Chimaeron Refuge, Iron Peaks, Table Mountain

gorgon

I was the firstborn of the Lord of the First House of Andu, but since I was a bastard birth, I did not enjoy the prestige and glory my two younger legitimate brothers were given. I never let this disappointment show, and that might have been my downfall. I think our father loved me more, but found it impossible, due to cultural restraints, to show it properly. But then again, that was also his downfall.

"In spite of the restraints placed on me because of my lack of proper station, I was able to associate with my half-brothers; my father was kind enough to let me live in the same house as he, his wife, and his two legitimate sons. I taught my brothers much of my skill at swordplay and horsemanship, and my tutoring gave both Haelyn and Roele an excellent grasp of the fundamentals of warfare. After several years as their teacher, I started yearning to see the world, so when I turned 16 years of age, I left to explore Cerilia. I felt my brothers were the only ones who cared about my leaving.

"I traveled about, grappling with monsters and bandits, slowly increasing my abilities as a warrior. I felt that I was on the way to help shape the course of the world. Everywhere I went, I was seen as the charismatic leader and heroic warrior of great promise that I truly was. For once in my life, I was seen as someone other than an illegitimate heir, and my confidence grew with my popularity among the people.

"I eventually fell in with a woman and her band of warriors in southern Anuire. She hoped to lead us against a tribe of gnoll raiders and take back the wealth the jackal-men had spent years stealing from passing caravans. After two months of constant fighting, we succeeded in capturing their den and securing their horde. Unfortunately, my companions all died in that last battle or shortly thereafter from wounds. Despite the victory, there was no one to share it and the wealth. I was overwhelmed with grief that day, for that woman, the fair Syllandara, was to bear me a son. I lost both that day.

"When I returned home, battle-weary and scarred, my father gave me the title Black Prince, as my armor had turned a sooty color during my adventures. Despite my many victories

and the accolades from our people, one thing changed about my relationship with my sire: He never told me anything in confidence after my return, as if he no longer trusted me. I felt that my newly-acquired experience and popularity should never have gained me such treatment—it should have granted me rightful recognition with my far-less-deserving brethren. I never forgave him for that, and over many months, my anger grew.

"After a particularly exceptional night of indulgence soon after my father's death, I had a remarkable dream which set my feet on the path to power undreamt by mortal man before. Fog enshrouded our entire empire, and out of that fog came a clear vision of a handsome male face. He spoke to me, consoled me in my discontent, and made me see things the way I should have seen them years before. He told me he understood the anguish I felt because I, being my father's eldest son, received no birthright when he passed away and held nothing now except pitiable indulgences. He told me he held the legacy that was rightfully mine, and all I needed to do was ask for it. I did, and he made me his son and heir. I knelt to this powerful vision that filled me with power and might and rage. I now was the offspring of Azrai, and no longer would I hold ties with my more worthy brothers.

"I quietly garnered supporters from across the Andu lands, for my new sire recommended guile and patience in building our power, not wielding the brute rage I had held in check for so long. With my best artfulness, I went to the tribes of the Andu to seek allies and was not disappointed at the backing I received. Many people, especially the warriors and magicians, were ready for change and itching for power. The complacency they upheld was wearing thin and not suited to their restless spirits. When our time came, my allies and I made our true power and desires known at Deismaar; I had the chance to show my upstart brothers Roele and Haelyn who should truly rule.

29

"When the gods destroyed themselves to kill my patron and the only one of them who understood power, I gained much as Azrai's third Champion, though not as much as Azrai's other favorites. My anger against my brothers kept me on Cerilia, rather than rising to godhood like Kriesha and Belinik. I absorbed much of Azrai's dwindling essence, and the battle I fought with my brothers over the empire was over for the moment. The earth-splitting force of the gods' destruction shattered both Mount Deismaar and the empire, scattering all the armies and their principals far and wide.

In the years of wandering that followed, I showed the many lessers who crossed my path what made me the sole remaining Champion of Azrai and rightful ruler of Cerilia. And with each victory, my might grew. And my power changed me, shaped me into a fearsome creature that men called Gorgon. It matters little—I am still Raesene, no matter what tag they give me, and I shall rule.

"When the time came for Michael Roele and me to meet on the field of battle, I was victorious. From his faintly beating heart, I tore the power and the birthright that was due me all those years before. Anuire's power was crushed and fear and confusion blew society apart like the house of cards that it was. For the House of Roele knew nothing of power nor how to wield it. Look at it today—the landscape dotted with idiots pompously perched on little thrones, hardly conceiving of what they do, let alone how they do it. Should they ever learn to act in concert and wield their might, I could be interested in hearing what they say. As it is, they are little more than crowned lambs awaiting slaughter."

While it is not my place to correct or argue truth or its nature with one so versed with power as the Black Prince, Raesene, much of his diatribe is peppered with subjective half-truths, to say the least. If one reads the historical records of Cerilia (all cultures, not just Anuirean), the truth always falls somewhere in between, and the Gorgon's story does not in many cases. According to the personal diary of a known tutor of

Roele's at the Anuirean court, Raesene returned from his adventures across Cerilia a changed man. His mind was corrupt and power-mad, and his anger rotted him away from inside, leaving nothing but contempt and feelings of vengeance. The king sensed this and confided his dread in the tutor with this dread fully in mind, Raesene's father granted him the title of the Black Prince, a title which still follows him today. Normally, this version of events might be ascribed as hearsay, but Roele's memoirs also recount this scene and both accounts are identical in all ways. Raesene's fall and Azrai's ultimate plans for the Anuirean traitor are not recorded for history, leading many into conjecture about exactly what drove both the Shadow Lord and his Champion to their fates. It can be assumed that Azrai wanted to have an ultimate champion in Cerilia, and he wanted that champion to lead the destruction of Anuire, the gem of Cerilia. He accomplished that havoc when Raesene chose his power and thus split the ruling family. With Azrai's destruction at

Mount Deismaar, any of his plans for Cerilia through Raesene ended, and the Gorgon's own plans and intrigues began.

Raesene's motivations began as rather straightforward and simple things, though they have grown hydralike over the passing centuries. A thirst for power and influence drove him first from his father's favor and finally from the favor of any save the most evil of the gods. Raesene, blind with years of anger and jealousy, once wanted nothing more than to destroy his privileged half-brothers. Now, his original goal either accomplished or out of his reach, he seeks to undo any of their works and garner more power for himself.

A number of hidden sources within Kal-Saitharak and outlying provinces within the Gorgon's Crown say that the Gorgon's final battle with the House of Roele was not as great a victory as often painted. When they fought at Battlewaite, Raesene underestimated his young foe's determination to save his people from the Gorgon. He gained huge amounts of power, but that drove the last remnants of humanity out of him. While he still believes himself to be Raesene, all that truly remains is the Gorgon.

The greatest rumor of this battle involves Michael Roele's final sacrifice for his people. With his dying breath, he apparently was able to somehow tap into his reservoirs of strength and ground much of his escaping power as he died. If this is true, the Gorgon ultimately lost more power than he gained with the murder and bloodtheft; some who believe in this tale also believe the Gorgon's own power is tied to his castle, and he may be diminished if he should he leave the walls of Battlewaite. There is little evidence, beyond hope, to support this idea, but anyone who visits the castle can feel the walls hum with confined power.

INTELLIGENCE: 19 (Supragenius)
ACTIVITY CYCLE: Any
DIET: Carnivore
ALIGNMENT: Lawful evil
MOVEMENT: 9
SIZE: L (8′ tall)
ARMOR CLASS: 0 (base); -10 (with armor)
HIT POINTS: 170

SAVES AS: F25
THAC0: -4 (base); 8 (Strength plus spec.)
NO. OF ATTACKS: 2 (fists) or 5/2 (specialized weapon) or 2/1 (ordinary weapon)
DAMAGE/ATTACK: 1d8 (fist or by weapon)
SPECIAL ATTACKS: Kick, gaze attack, weapon specialization.
SPECIAL DEFENSES: +2 or better weapon to hit, immune to gaze attacks
MAGIC RESISTANCE: 40%
MORALE: 20 (fearless)
BLOOD: True (Azrai) 100+
BLOOD ABILITIES: Alertness (Minor), Bloodform (Great), Divine Aura (Great), Heightened Ability (Great), Long Life (Great), Poison Sense (Minor), Regeneration—Standard and Major (Great)
XP VALUE: 32,000

S: 20 (+3/+8)   D: 15 (0, 0, –1)   C: 21 (+6 hp/level)
I: 19   W: 18   Ch: 18

The once-human Raesene the Black Prince has been the Gorgon for centuries now, and he is the most feared awnshegh in all Cerilia. He is a massive, giant, stony-skinned humanoid with a bull-like head complete with horns, and powerful goatlike legs with diamond-hard hooves. Everything about the Gorgon suggests that he is power and terror personified.

When human, Raesene was one of Anuire's premier swordsmen. He was skilled in many weapons, and even specialized in a few, making him a truly dangerous foe. Now, with more than a thousand years of weapons practice and warfare, he wields nearly every weapon found in Cerilia as if he were a specialist with it (only a 5% chance that the Gorgon does not gain specialization bonuses).

As if his physical skills are not complete, the Gorgon has two potent gaze attacks that he can use once every other round. After a full round of concentrating on one foe (no more than parrying attacks), he can turn his target to stone or cause it to fall dead on the spot. The stone gaze attack requires a saving throw vs. petrification with a -2 penalty. The second demands a save vs. death magic.

Finally, the Gorgon can but rarely uses his goatlike legs to deliver a powerful kick (2d6 points of damage). He can kick even while making an ordinary attack, but he takes a +2 AC penalty for the entire round to do so.

The Gorgon's defenses are formidable as well. First, his stony skin gives him an AC of 0. His *bloodform* also grants him a 40% magic resistance and immunity to weapons of less than +2 enchantments.

His magical armor and weaponry includes: *Kingstopper*, a giant-sized suit of *plate mail +5*; *A Gentle Word*, a *shield +5*; and *Lifender*, a great sword made of tighmaevril and the Gorgon's primary weapon of choice.

REALM NAME: The Gorgon's Crown
LOCATION: North of Kiergard and southeast of the Giantdowns
ALIGNMENT: Lawful evil
STATUS: Unavailable for PC use

PROVINCES/HOLDINGS: While the Gorgon controls everything within his domains, he does parcel out some small amount of responsibility to his vassals, both to test their loyalties and to free him from the drudgery of overseeing all such operations directly.

Province	Law	Temples	Guilds	Sources
Abattoir (3/6)	Go (3)	—	—	Go (6)
Anathar (1/6)	Go (1)	HOA (1)	—	Go (4)
Elfseyes (2/7)	Go (2)	—	—	Go (7)
Jogh Warren (3/3)	Go (3)	—	—	Go (2)
Kal-Saitharak (4/5)	Go (4)	HOA (4)	—	Go (5)
Mettle (2/4)	Go (2)	—	—	Go (3)
Motile (2/3)	Go (2)	—	—	Go (3)
Mutian's Point (1/6)	Go (1)	HOA (1)	—	Go (4)
Orog's Head (2/5)	Go (2)	—	—	Go (4)
Pelt (1/6)	Go (1)	—	—	Go (4)
Plumbago (2/5)	Go (2)	—	—	Go (5)
Sage's Fen (2/5)	Go (2)	HOA (2)	—	Go (5)
Sere's Hold (2/4)	Go (2)	—	—	Go (4)
Sideath (2/7)	Go (2)	HOA (2)	—	Go (5)
Stone's End (1/6)	Go (1)	HOA (1)	—	Go (4)
Sunder Falls (1/4)	Go (1)	HOA (1)	—	Go (3)
Zaptig (2/5)	Go (2)	—	—	Go (4)

Abbreviations: Go=the Gorgon; HOA=Hand of Azrai.

◆

REGENCY GENERATED/ACCUMULATED: 90+ (additional RP from vassal rulers of Kiergard, Markazor and Mur-Kilad) /200 RP.
GOLD GENERATED/ACCUMULATED: 60+ GB/150+ GB

ARMY: The Gorgon's army is a collection of the dregs of Cerilia. He controls captive goblin forces from the Stone Gaze campaigns, gnolls expelled from the Giantdowns, orogs from the south, a number of troll mercenary troops out of the Hoarfell Mountains, and evil dwarves and Anuirean humans whose ancestors believed Raesene to be a true power of unstoppable proportions. Kiras Earthcore, the Gorgon's immediate lieutenant, spends much time keeping the racial factions in the army from killing each other. Aside from harsh discipline or keeping them on the march, he has yet to find a way to keep the differences from causing skirmishes and brawls.

Because of the dangerous nature of the Gorgon's Crown and hearsay, it is rarely possible to get exact counts on the size of the Gorgon's armies. The last confirmed report was made almost 20 years ago, but his troops were also mixed with those of his vassals, fouling a completely accurate account. At that time, the troops under the Gorgon consisted of 10 units of goblin infantry, five units of human archers, eight units of human infantry, six units of human light cavalry, three units of human heavy cavalry, six units of gnoll infantry, and five units of orog infantry. The state of his current army is unknown, though it is no doubt the largest and most powerful army in Anuire with the widest racial mix of malevolent beings.

REGENT: The Gorgon

LIEUTENANTS: Kiras Earthcore, titular "Hand of the Gorgon," is the subcommander of the Gorgon's military forces. He also controls the production of weapons and armor for the troops.

Tollan manages the money in the Gorgon's Crown and the income from the vassal states. Tollan also supervises the network of spies and assassins used by the Gorgon across Cerilia. Kiras and Tollan are detailed further in the "Lesser Awnsheghlien and other NPCs" section.

The Gorgon's other lieutenants are the puppet rulers and important personages within Kiergard, Mur-Kilad and Markazor. These latter two are noted within the *Ruins of Empire* book from the BIRTHRIGHT Campaign boxed set.

DOMAIN CAPITAL:
Kal-Saitharak
DOMAIN CITIES: Abattoir, Mettle,
Mutian's Point, Plumbago
DOMAIN VILLAGES: Anathar, Chalybrate,
Elfseyes, Motile, Orog's Head, Pelt, Sage's
Fen, Sere's Hold, Sideath, Sunder Falls, Zaptig
SPECIAL LOCATIONS: Stone Gaze Mountains

IMPORTANT NPCs: The Hand of Azrai is one of the most powerful and influential people within the Gorgon's Crown, and she is the only figure in power that is not blooded. She is a mysterious woman from the lands to the far east, and her reasons for arriving and staying in the Crown are unknown. Some speculate that she is in love with the Gorgon, though her reticence and the Gorgon's impassive glare tell of nothing that might pass between them. While she is unblooded, she is a high-level priestess to Azrai, Kriesha, and Belinik, and maintains their temples in states far better than most other buildings outside of Kal-Saitharak.

The other most important NPCs are the chiefs and respective leaders of the Gorgon's armies, for they are a loose assembly of tribal factions held together only by Kiras' cruel discipline and the fear of retribution from the Gorgon. The gnolls are led by Courrak Lone Hunter, an old but powerful gnoll chieftain. The Goblin King Charqek Talnos unifies the goblins under his banner, and the humans and dwarves are immediately led by the awnshegh Kiras.

DOMAIN DESCRIPTION: The Gorgon rules the Gorgon's Crown, a huge expanse northeast of Anuire. Under his indirect rule are a few neighboring domains. The Crown is a mountainous wasteland filled with small volcanoes, barren terrain, and valleys and sheer cliffs rife with avalanches. At the center of the Gorgon's land is a forest of pines that stay firmly rooted in the harsh soil in spite of the mild earthquakes that occasionally rock the region.

At the center of the forest sits Kal-Saitharak, the Gorgon's castle; this citadel is better known as Battlewaite throughout Anuirean lands. The Gorgon commands and controls his hordes from this mammoth structure. Beneath Battlewaite, dungeons extend deep into the heart of the earth; thus far, no one, save perhaps the Gorgon, knows the extent and the true awesome size of these earthen formations.

The Gorgon's throne room is well adorned with weapons in easy reach of the throne. Among these are the *Sword of the Anuirean Empire*, a tighmaevril weapon once believed destroyed in battle with the Gorgon, a morning star known as *Thunderclap*, a spear called *The Spear of Destiny*, and his own great sword *Lifender*.

TRADE GOODS: Wood used for fuel and building supplies is the Gorgon's greatest import. The Gorgon exports ores, metals, and weapons to his vassals, his only trading partners.

ALLIES: The Gorgon doesn't invite allies, though he accepts vassals. There are several domains that he now controls (Kiergard, Markazor, Mur-Kilad), and their peoples are considered little more than slaves. Rumors talk of a pact among Raesene, the Raven, and the Magian to destroy all other regents in Cerilia, though few believe this rumor.

ENEMIES: Any who are not slaves or underlings of the Gorgon are ranked among his enemies.

SPECIAL CONDITIONS: The Gorgon has ordered his mercenaries to kidnap miners and smelters to smelt the iron of the Crown into weapons. All the domains bordering the Gorgon's Crown have suffered a number of blacksmith disappearances, and the Gorgon is most likely responsible for most, if not all, of them.

the hag

Well, my pretty . . . heh. Pretty. I used to be pretty. I used to be *beautiful*. Men from across Cerilia knew of my beauty, and sought my favors. Heh, heh. Would they like my kisses now, do you think?

"It's nice to have someone to talk to, I suppose, after all these years. Oh, yes, the men stopped coming when I began to exert my . . . abilities. It cost me, yes, it cost me everything I had, but look at what I have now! My own land, my powers, and eternal life. That's right, I'll live forever, forever! And you, pretty? Why, your warm skin is already starting to cool.

"But don't worry pretty, you'll . . . be around a little longer. Pretty-pretty, so beautiful, so arrogant, so foolish. Thought you could tempt power and not pay the price? No, there is a price for everything—everyone pays a price. My price for power was my looks, my loves, my men. What is your price, pretty-pretty? What did you have to give up? Was it worth it? Do you even *know* what you had to give up, what you lost? Do *you* seek to avenge yourself on those who've never paid a price for power?

"Well, that's not my concern, pretty. I've talked enough, and I'm . . . hungry. Oh, you don't shudder at that, you don't even move! Are you brave, pretty, or foolish? Well, you needn't worry . . . I don't eat cold meat, pretty, and your skin has grown quite cold indeed."

The Hag has been an exiled ruler in her own domain for generations. Some legends say that the Hag is actually just the current incarnation of a terrible awnsheghlien bloodline. Whichever legend you believe, they all start with the story of a young Brecht woman of noble birth named Fulda Geissen.

Fulda was a first cousin to the then-ruler of Grabentod, the regent Mordan Furgal. She was active at court, and those chronicles that still speak of her (mainly those from Drachenward) say that she was both beautiful and intelligent, if somewhat haughty.

Growing up in the court of Grabentod, Fulda learned to use her looks and her intelligence to her advantage. She made many allies among the nobles, many of whom resented their regent, Mordan, because of his youth and untried valor.

But Mordan was not blind. He saw Fulda's growing influence and he found a solution. There was a small, unsettled province to Grabentod's east, claimed by both Grabentod and Drachenward, but neither pushed the matter. Peasants from both domains hunted and fished in the mountains, and shipwrights took lumber from the region.

Mordan was eager to expand his holdings, but Drachenward was a strong neighbor with a friendly regent—and Kordan (as the region was called) was hardly worth a war. But Mordan saw a way to gain the area without a fight . . . and to solve another problem.

He sent heralds to Erach of Drachenward and his son, Kurrel. He proposed a marriage between Fulda and Kurrel "as a bond between our two friendly realms." Mordan hinted that Kordan would be an excellent bride-price, and he would send two of his best ships as a dowry.

Erach and Kurrel agreed, for Erach was old and ready to resign his regency and Kurrel was unmarried. Fulda, apparently, was pleased with this solution as well. Even though she would be giving up influence in Grabentod, she would be a consort of a larger domain. She had no doubt she could work her wiles in this new land.

So the marriage took place. The bride and groom took a honeymoon aboard ship, touring the coastlines of Grabentod and Drachenward. They returned to Drachenward, apparently content . . . though not for long.

Mysteriously, Kurrel took ill and died. It happened so quickly that the court priests and physickers could do nothing. Rumors of foul play would come later, but the court of Drachenward was in shock. Erach, who had planned to abdicate in his son's favor, was heart-broken. His only other heir was his daughter, a mere six years old. He would have to rule for at least another decade before taking his well-deserved rest. But there was Fulda.

Fulda was out of her grave-clothes, Drachenwardians say, almost before her husband's grave was filled. While that is undoubtedly inaccurate (both Drachenward and Grabentod had proscribed periods of mourning for their royalty), there is no question that Fulda hardly grieved for her dead husband. Instead, she saw a tremendous opportunity.

In both domains, it was not uncommon for an aging ruler to appoint a guardian regent for a youthful heir. That guardian would rule until the heir was old enough to assume the bloodline and rulership of the domain, and then the guardian would usually become a chief advisor. In most good or lawful kingdoms, this was an accepted practice. Had Fulda waited and bided her time, she might have won her suit for guardianship. But, judging wrongly that Erach was on the verge of death, she asked too soon. Proposing such things so quickly after her husband's death caused only hard feelings and even harder talk. The aged ruler chastised her for her rudeness and asked if she might be more happy in her home domain. Ashamed and enraged, Fulda made preparations to leave.

Mordan was incensed at both Fulda and Erach. He was less wise than in later days, and instead of sending an appeal to Drachenward asking that Fulda be allowed to make amends, he sent a scathing reprisal filled with insults and accusations.

Had Erach been younger, he would have answered the insult directly. Instead, he sent an army into Kordan to evict Grabentod's settlers and claim the province. This grew in responses until a border war erupted. At its end, Grabentod had the worst of it, but Drachenward fared little better. Hatreds seethed on all sides, but neither could act without ruining both domains.

Fulda, with the help of a few loyal retainers and some Drachenward nobles, kidnapped the heir and fled to Kordan. There, she planned to rendezvous with her cousin's forces and bargain with her father-in-law for the area. Fulda wanted revenge on Erach and a return to a prominent position back at Grabentod's court.

The move backfired. When he heard his cousin's boastful report, Mordan was horrified. A duel was his way of avenging insult—and if not a duel, war was acceptable—kidnapping innocent children was not. He commanded Fulda to return Drachenward's heir unharmed and to present herself for punishment. He sent apologies to Erach, assuring him that he would do everything to get the child back unharmed.

When Fulda heard she was to return to court in disgrace, she panicked and fled with the child into the mountains. What happened to the young heir of Drachenward is unknown to this day. Fulda herself escaped pursuit and hid herself away. During this time, her heart twisted with paranoia and hatred and evil, she became the awnshegh known as the Hag.

Since that time, Drachenward and Grabentod have not seen peace. While no wars have been fought, skirmishes and disputes occur with regular frequency. Treaties have been signed over the years only to establish efforts to destroy the Hag. Distrust and old enmities have unfortunately always arisen to break the peace.

The Hag herself enjoys goading the two sides against one another. She uses her powers to throw up nets in her mountains to trap the unwary scouts and messengers, and her illusions assault both Drachenward and Grabentod. Occasionally, she will capture folk from either domain, and send them home mad with fear, sick with poison, and telling tales of horror and depravity. Any children that come into the Hag's clutches are never seen again.

INTELLIGENCE: Genius (18)
ACTIVITY CYCLE: Day
DIET: Omnivore
ALIGNMENT: Chaotic evil
MOVEMENT: 9
SIZE: L (10' long)
ARMOR CLASS: -2
HIT POINTS: 90
SAVES AS: W15
THAC0: 5 (base)
NO. OF ATTACKS: 2 (weapons) or 6 (claw/claw/bite/bite/bite/bite)
DAMAGE/ATTACK: By weapon type or 1d6 (×2)/2d4 (×4) (+8 for strength on claws)
SPECIAL ATTACKS: Poison, spells
SPECIAL DEFENSES: Nil

MAGIC RESISTANCE: Nil
MORALE: Champion (15)
BLOOD: Minor (Azrai) 39
BLOOD ABILITIES: Alertness (Minor), Animal Affinity (Great), Bloodform (Great), Enhanced Sense (Major), Fear (Major), Long Life (Great), Major Regeneration (Great), Regeneration (Great)
XP VALUE: 25,000

S: 20 (+3, +8)　　D: 19 (+3, -4)　　C: 22 (+6)
I: 18　　　　　　W: 12　　　　　　Ch: 11

SPELLS MEMORIZED: The Hag casts spells as a 15th-level wizard. Memorized spells are:

1st Level: *Alarm, charm person, grease, magic missile, sleep.*

2nd Level: *Darkness, 15' radius, ESP, flaming sphere, stinking cloud, web.*

3rd Level: *Blink, dispel magic, hold person, lightning bolt, non-detection.*

4th Level: *Charm monster, Evard's black tentacles, hallucinatory terrain, shadow monsters, wizard eye.*

5th Level: *Cone of cold, hold monster, shadow door, summon shadow, transmute rock to mud* (or its reverse).

6th Level: *Programmed illusion, shades.*

7th Level: *Shadow walk*

Realm Spells: The Hag can cast realm spells. The only spells she knows or can tap are *Dispel Realm Magic, Scry,* and *Subversion.*

Once a beautiful woman, Fulda Geissen became a monster in a few short years. The blood of Azrai runs deep, and her heinous acts against the most innocent creatures awakened her bloodline's evil potential and exposed Fulda's inner evil in the ugliness of the Hag.

Because of the Hag's horrific appearance, all who see her must save versus petrification or flee in horror from her for 2d6 rounds. Hirelings and henchmen must make morale checks immediately at a -4 penalty (even if they do save). This check or saving throw occurs only upon the first viewing of the Hag, not later confrontations.

The Hag can wield weapons, often those taken from fallen foes. A report had her using a two-handed sword in one hand, while another said she wielded a long sword and dagger like a ranger. She always has at least a dagger.

The Hag is not without her own natural weapons. Her lower body no longer has legs, but consists of a mass of very dangerous snakes. These can make up to four attacks per round (while the Hag uses her clawed hands or weapons) on one or more opponents. A bite from these snakes does normal damage, but bitten characters must save vs. poison at -2 or fall into a deep, nightmare-ridden coma. A character sleeps for a number of hours equal to 24 minus his Constitution score. At that time, a successful system shock roll allows him to wake; unsuccessful rolls result in death. A survivor of the Hag's poisons wakes up feeling tired and looking pale. For one week (unless a *neutralize poison* and a *remove curse* are used on him), he performs all actions at a -2 modifier from lack of energy and focus. Poisoned victims are usually taken back to the Hag's lair and tormented until they die or are inexplicably let go to wander back to known lands in a daze, to recover or die soon after.

REALM NAME: Kordan (The Hag's Domain)
LOCATION: South of Drachenward, East of Grabentod
STATUS: Not available for PC use
ALIGNMENT: CE
PROVINCES/HOLDINGS: The Hag's domain is a single province. She has set up access to a Level 5 magical source in the domain, but its location is entirely unknown. There are no other holdings controlled by the Hag, since there is nothing in trade or law to control.

REGENCY GENERATED/ACCUMULATED: 6/18 RP
GOLD GENERATED: 0 GB/2 GB; The Hag gets gold from fools or adventurers who venture into her domain. As she spends none of it, it has accrued over the centuries to an impressive hoard, which is kept in many caches.

ARMY: The Hag has no army in the conventional sense, though there are many serpents in the domain that respond to her will. She uses her magical powers to entrap, bewilder, and charm adventurers, and she may have servitors from the Shadow World, though it is uncertain how she maintains them in Cerilia.

REGENT: The Hag
LIEUTENANTS: Recent reports state that the Hag somehow managed to enslave a nobleman of Drachenward, named Orin Hawk, and his entourage, and they now guard the northern border of her domain. Orin is, or was, a ranger of some ability, and now he uses his skills in her service. There have been, and still are, others over the years who serve the Hag willingly or unwillingly.

DOMAIN DESCRIPTION: The Hag's domain is little more than forest-blanketed mountains. Several known hunters' camps or long-abandoned settlements are shown on the map. Sometimes, they are used by brave folk who dare to venture into the Hag's domain; at other times, they are used by the Hag herself as temporary lairs. The Hag has many lairs in her domain, and she hides treasures throughout the province to tempt treasure-hunters into her clutches. Where her central lair lies is unknown; the Hag is wily and evil, and does not reveal secrets easily.

the harpy

So few folk of the mainland have the courage to come out to the Harpy's island, and seeking only knowledge rather than power—your bravery is greater indeed for that. Such boldness deserves reward, and your reward is the information you seek and your lives.

"Memories of our life before we came to rule this island are unclear, as we have little need to dwell on those days and that was also before our life truly began. Still, for your tome to provide a true and accurate account of ourselves and our reign, one must push aside the fog of the past and look upon it again.

"We were not always the Harpy—in fact, we were once two separate beings. Part of us was the queen of the harpies and much of us was an acknowledged worker of magic and music. Khabarah Habban, our mortal self, learned her magics in the form of music and song, and she sang her spells to life beautifully. Her only trouble in life was keeping in check a dark blood taint her great-grandfather left to his offspring, and she led an upstanding life of goodness to counter its corrupt nature.

"She adventured along the Zikalan coast of the Baïr el-Mehare with a number of comrades, seeking to gain fame and strike down injustice. She sang of the mighty warrior Garik Olafssen when our other self first met her. The wanderers were set upon by a group of harpies and their mates, the warbirds, led by ourself, their queen. They fought bravely, both the heroes and the harpies, and we claimed lives on both sides. Still, the heroes were outnumbered and weary, and victory fell to the harpy queen.

"Only Khabarah and one other—a wounded fellow close to death—still lived and she faced the harpy queen alone. Her only thought was flight, and she began a song to change her shape to a bird's to escape. The harpy queen was armed with a sword that she received from a gray man in her dreams the night before.

She struck as the magician's form began to shift toward falcon form. Whether it was some property of the sword, the disruption of the song spell, or perhaps the woman's blood taint, we know not, but the magic went awry and both Khabarah and the harpy queen converged into us, the regal being you see before you as the Harpy.

"Since that time, we have lived as one on the Harpy's island, fully in command of our magic and the flocks of harpies and warbirds that populate these isles. We lead our fellow harpies and warbirds on minor raids against nearby lands and passing ships, seeking plunder that is rightfully ours by force of arms and wings. We do not lead our flocks wantonly or without purpose—everything we do is for the good of the flock.

"There are those that call us awnshegh, and we suppose there is merit in that title, but that is inaccurate in assessing who we are and why we rule. We are not defined by such 'blood of darkness.' We continue to live our life in a true and honorable fashion, fulfilling our purpose with zeal. The blood taint of Azrai may mark us, but it does not rule us. Make sure we have made ourself clear on that, chroniclers. We, the Harpy, are not held to lies. Believe that."

Khabarah Habban, as stated in the interview, was united mysteriously with one of the harpies from the Island off the coast of Binsada during an attack over a century ago. History recorded her use of songs in spells, and spell failure was rare for Khabarah. A sage versed in the knowledge of gods old and new (especially Azrai, Belinik, and Kriesha), believes the song was tampered with by one of Azrai's successors to achieve some greater end. That end is still merely conjecture, but the inhabitants of the Isle of the Harpy are now more controlled and organized than they ever have been. Luckily for mainlanders, some of Khabarah's morality remains in the Harpy. Raids on Binsada or Zikala are rare, and passing ships are raided only slightly more frequently. However, when the Harpy and her forces strike, their precision and deadliness are devastating.

The mysterious short sword wielded by the harpy queen was dropped and forgotten in the initial pain and

agony of her merging with Khabarah. Soon after, the warbirds collected their wounded queen, now an amalgam of the lovely half-elven bard and the harpy, and flew off with much of the fallen heroes' treasure. The only survivor was the wounded priest of Avani, Iman Tenek, and he healed his wounds and recovered the sword after the harpies had fled.

After surviving and returning to Andujar, Iman discovered through research that the mysterious dull gray short sword was once called *The Heartsword* and it was wielded by an ancient assassin known to have been banished to the Shadow World. The sword's original enchantments, which still seem to be in place, allowed a wielder to assume the form and shape of a person or creature killed by the sword. Few humans even know of this sword's existence, though it is well-known among the halflings, who shudder at its mention. The sword was recently stolen from the son of Iman and its whereabouts are unknown.

INTELLIGENCE: 16
ACTIVITY CYCLE: Day
DIET: Carnivore
ALIGNMENT: Lawful evil
MOVEMENT: 9, Fl 18 (C)
SIZE: M (6′ tall)
ARMOR CLASS: 4
HIT POINTS: 62
SAVES AS: M12
THAC0: 14
NO. OF ATTACKS: 3
DAMAGE/ATTACK: 1d4/1d4/1d4 (claw/claw/dagger)
SPECIAL ATTACKS: Songs (see below)
SPECIAL DEFENSES: Songs (see below)
MAGIC RESISTANCE: Nil
MORALE: 16
BLOOD: Tainted (Azrai) 18
BLOOD ABILITIES: Enhanced Senses (Minor), Long Life (Minor), Major Resistance—Charm (Major)
XP VALUE: 10,000

SONGS

1st-level: *Comprehend languages, featherfall, gaze reflection, hypnotize, spider climb.*
2nd-level: *Alter self, darkness 15′ radius, ray of enfeeblement, strength, whispering wind.*
3rd-level: *Blink, fly, haste, hold person, wraithform.*
4th-level: *Polymorph other, polymorph self, solid fog, stoneskin, wizard eye.*
5th-level: *Avoidance, fabricate, stone shape, teleport, transmute rock to mud (rev).*
6th-level: *Death fog, disintegrate, move earth.*

What remains of Khabarah Habban in her new amalgamated form is her intellect and her basic beautiful shape, though she now has wings, blue hair, and the claws of a harpy. She also retains her ability to sing spells, though she cannot sing a spell and attack with her claws or dagger simultaneously. When she casts a spell song, it has the same initiative modifier as the spell when cast normally, and all have the same effect as though cast by a 12th-level spellcaster.

REALM

NAME: Isle of the Harpy
LOCATION: South of Binsada
STATUS: Not available for PC use
ALIGNMENT: Lawful evil

PROVINCES/HOLDINGS:

The Isle of the Harpy and surrounding islands are considered her domain, though it is hardly a controlled realm. The islands are populated only by harpies, warbirds, and a few other indigenous wild creatures.

Law: Aside from the pattern of food gathering and a few organized raids, there is no law within this domain.

Temples: There are no temples or any organized religion on these islands.

Guilds:
There is little trade and commerce with the Islands of the Harpy, aside from what the birds bring back from raids, and money from a

trader in Binsada who buys a rare herb that grows only on the Harpy's main island. This small amount of money is held by the Harpy.

Sources: The Harpy controls the magical sources of the islands, though she cannot establish ley lines between islands and tap all their power from her main home island. On the main isle, she can tap a Level 4 source.

REGENCY GENERATED/ACCUMULATED: 5/10 RP
GOLD GENERATED/ACCUMULATED: 1/2 GB

ARMY: The Harpy doesn't have a standing army by any means. She does, however, have close to 1,000 bird and harpy followers that live on the island chain. All the males, about 200 in strength, help guard the island from attack as well as reinforce a raiding party.

Harpies (200) Int 5-7; AL CE; AC 7; HD 7; hp 42; THAC0 13; #AT 3; Dmg 1d3/1d3/1d6 or 1d3/1d3/weapon; SA charm touch, singing; SD nil; Save F7; SZ M (6′ tall); MV 6, Fl 15 (C); ML 13-14; XP 1,400/ea.

War Bird (200) Int 3-5; AL NE; AC 7; HD 5; hp 28; THAC0 15; #AT 3; Dmg 1d6/1d6/2d6; SA diving attack (2xDamage); SD nil; Save F5; SZ M (6′ tall); MV 3, Fl 48 (D); ML 13; XP 420/ea.

REGENT: The Harpy
LIEUTENANTS: None
IMPORTANT NPCs: None
DOMAIN DESCRIPTION: The domain of the Harpy consists of a cluster of eight islands off the southern coast of Binsada. The main island is long and thin with a large bay on the northern shores; the second largest island lies to the southeast. To the northeast are the remaining islands. Five of these are uninhabited while the largest of these northern six is populated by a few small clutches of independent birds and other animals.

The interiors of these islands are mostly plains, but the coastlines are often high cliffs with only a few beaches on which to land. The interior of the largest island sports several rocky crags that house the birds and their leader, the Harpy. The Harpy's domicile is on the highest peak at the center of the island. The aerie (the harpy and bird equivalent of a town) and the Harpy's domain capital is called Wingedbutte. Here, the birds living on the island and its neighboring two tiny islets pay homage (with spoils taken from their victims) to their leader.

Many of the place names used to mark certain locations are simply old references from a map of the islands made years ago by a sage and traveler; the Harpy simply uses these same place names as familiar location names for various aeries and clutches of warbirds and harpies under her rule.

DOMAIN CAPITAL: Wingedbutte
DOMAIN TOWNS: The Alp, Salt Crag
DOMAIN VILLAGES: Aerocourt, The Boroughs, Driftwood, Flit Hill, Windsail

TRADE GOODS: The fishing in the Bay of Aerocourt is controlled by the Harpy. She allows Binsadan fishermen to fish these fertile waters for a small (5%) portion of the take. The fish are distributed to all the birds and harpies living on the large island.

ALLIES: While a number of rulers believe there to be some official alliance among Binsada, Zikala, and the Harpy, their only ties are in information. The island serves no real political purpose in the greater scheme of diplomacy of the countries along the Suidemiere, but Binsada and Zikala

use the island and its inhabitants as a source of sailing information. Whenever ships pass within 30 miles of the island, the Harpy's servants inspect the ship's banners, cargo, passengers, and crew, and relay all this information to the Harpy. She, in turn, gives this information to the leaders of Binsada and Zikala in exchange for news from the mainland. Rumors talk of a loose agreement between the Harpy and Zikala that would have the Harpy and a token force of warbirds act as mercenary forces if the Sphinx should attack Zikala; few believe this rumor, though the Harpy is one of a few wizards who might be able to slow down the Sphinx.

SPECIAL CONDITIONS: The Harpy, while very lucid and in control, has adopted a number of paranoid tendencies unconsciously. She has broken and destroyed all her musical instruments, and little survives of her original equipment except her songbooks of spells. The spellbooks and about 30% of her total treasure are stored at her main home in Wingedbutte, while the rest of her treasures are kept in caves all about the islands, guarded by servant harpies and warbirds.

hydra

Our team of sages, eager to discern information firsthand about the deadly Harrowmarsh and its awnshegh inhabitant, had secured passage on a barge that traveled the Asarwe River, and the barge captain gave them the following testimony before delivering them to the outer edge of Harrowmarsh.

"Ok, friend—you asked and I'll tell you what I know of the Hydra and its home. Many a fugitive from Binsadan justice hides out within the twisted, dark trees of that swamp, and that alone makes it dangerous enough to traverse. Add to those small outposts of renegades a huge variety of creatures—the hydra's hideous offspring—that fly, hop, and slither throughout the Harrowmarsh that are not as powerful as a normal awnshegh but are still dangerous. Lastly, you've got the Hydra itself to worry about. Some say that the Hydra's got eight heads, and all of 'em are of different races; whenever the Hydra eats some noble folk with the bloodright of rulership, they become part of it and it gains some of their power. If tales are true, it's defeated and consumed at least seven or eight blooded folks in the past thousand years. All I know is that no money is enough to make me enter that swamp and meet it!"

Sages theorized about the Hydra's existence and power and appearance for centuries, and few had any proof to back up their theories until now. Careful study of all travelers' accounts of the Harrowmarsh and its monstrous inhabitants (there are over a dozen texts that mention legends and tales of the Hydra and the swamp it lives in) led to these conclusions:

The Hydra is, in truth, a monstrous reptilian creature with multiple heads and a voracious appetite. It was once a large crocodile that was infected with the taint of Azrai at some point after the fall at Deismaar. It grew to larger proportions and consumed nearly everything it encountered. Each time it consumed a blooded scion who came to slay it, that scion's head sprouted out of its gargantuan body, now linked with the Hydra's brain. The various blooded heroes

who fell victim to the Hydra and are now evident as part of the creature's collection of heads are: Astrid, a famous and mighty wizardess and psionicist from Müden who specialized in telepathic skills and necromantic spellcraft;

Garik Blackhand, a warrior (some say a paladin!) of incalculable bravery who was dedicated to the service of Anduiras;

Charboth Ruhrfoot, a male halfling of Anuire who bore the title of the Quickfoot, whose head now screams incessantly, and whose birthright granted the Hydra its speed today;

Bhaervas Whyrven III, the human grandson of the ehrshegh called the Golden Unicorn and a priest of Haelyn in his own right;

Illyram, a powerful elf warrior and alleged son of Rhuobhe Manslayer himself, who may have kept more of his original mind than any other victim in the Hydra;

An unknown male human with gold eyes; and

An equally unknown female half-elf whose head cries pitifully and continuously.

INTELLIGENCE: 8
ACTIVITY CYCLE: Any
DIET: Omnivore
ALIGNMENT: Chaotic neutral
MOVEMENT: 16
SIZE: L (21' tall)
ARMOR CLASS: 2
HIT POINTS: 113
SAVES AS: F18
THAC0: 12
NO. OF ATTACKS: 4 or 6
DAMAGE/ATTACK: 1d4/1d4/2d8/2d10 (bite/bite/bite/tail)
SPECIAL ATTACKS: Grapple
SPECIAL DEFENSES: Nil
MAGIC RESISTANCE: Nil
MORALE: 18
BLOOD: Minor (Azrai) 47
BLOOD ABILITIES: Detect Life (Major), Fear (Major), Invulnerability (Great), Long Life (Great), Unreadable Thoughts (Minor)
XP VALUE: 18,000

Finding the Hydra is almost as difficult as surviving a meeting with it. It has absorbed some intelligence and cunning from its own prey, and it uses the swamp to avoid being seen until it can get an easy attack on its foes.

The Hydra's primary attacks are bites from its collection of heads on one prey. Usually, only two smaller heads (with the faces of heroes that died fighting the Hydra) and the large, central crocodile head can bite one target and the Hydra lashes its tail at another. If the Hydra foregoes any bite attacks in one round, it can attempt to grapple a foe with its stunted but strong limbs; with a successful hit, the Hydra holds a foe with 18/00 Strength and then can hold onto that foe so up to five heads can bite it automatically in the next round.

When in combat, all the Hydra's heads make noise, some of them even using their original languages. Attempts to communicate with any but the central crocodile head will be met with an attack by adjacent heads.

DOMAIN DESCRIPTION: While not a domain, the Hydra's swampy habitat is large enough that someone could conquer it and claim it as a domain; few, however, wish to fight for a swamp infested with insects, criminals, and awnsheghlien. Originally named Sodden Falls by Binsadan cartographers, this area has simply reverted to "The Hydra's Domain" or its widely used name of Harrowmarsh. It consists of water-logged land with hundreds of small islands of solid, damp earth. The salty sea water mixes with the fresh

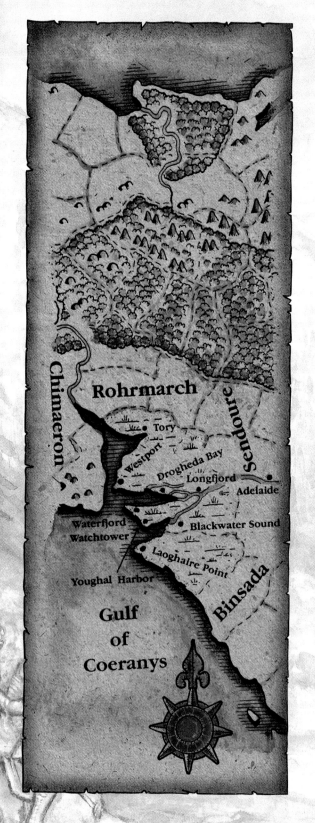

watershed in the southern half of the domain, creating an unusual ecological system. Tall trees with wide, bell-shaped trunks that feed off the saltwater silt dominate the southern half of the domain, while a highly fragrant tree similar to eucalyptus struggles for precious fresh water rooting soil.

The rest of the world views Harrowmarsh as a wet, swampy, insect-infested area that has no attraction other than that it confines the Hydra and a number of fugitive criminals. Rumors of the Hydra's beastly habits and the wild, feral creatures that populate the lands keep outsiders from invading Harrowmarsh. Some of these rumors about the Hydra are started by those in Harrowmarsh to keep people out.

The people of Harrowmarsh are all fugitives from the justice of other outlying domains. Life in the swamp is tranquil, simply because there are hardly any sizable collections of people to breed trouble. Among human settlers within the swamp, no one has ever laid eyes on the Hydra itself, and some of the inhabitants now believe it is nothing more than a concocted fable. Others who have encountered some of the hydrakin monstrosities that infest the central and southern parts of Harrowmarsh are less swift in writing off the Hydra as only a nightmare to scare children.

The Hydra, however, keeps to itself in an old, abandoned watch tower called Waterfjord Tower, in the fjords near the gulf. No one who lives in Harrowmarsh has the backbone to pay the awnshegh a visit. Anyone who visits the tower will most likely find it empty. Soon after, he will be ambushed by the ever-hungry Hydra—its ability to sense the location of prey does not allow folk to approach its lair safely unless it's asleep.

OTHER DENIZENS OF HARROWMARSH: Harrowmarsh supports all the standard wildlife of a swamp, from crocodiles and frogs to insects. In addition, the Hydra and its offspring infest the swamp; the caracdir are now a viable species that breeds true, and the creatures known as hydrakin cover nearly every part of the swamp in various frequencies.

The Hydrakin: Scattered all over the swamp, the Hydra's young—the hydrakin—glean what food they can from fish, crawfish, ground-nesting birds, and unwary hunters or fishermen. The hydrakin are not a species, but simply random results of the Hydra's asexual reproduction; what it eats is sometimes reproduced as a composite with traits of the Hydra and other prey. Whenever prey is eaten, there is a 2% chance per hit point that it will be disgorged in 1d8 days as hydrakin.

humans and the Hydra. Caracdir scavenge Hydra attack sites for any armor or weapons they can find.

Caracdir (3-30; total of 900 within swamp): Int 10-12; AL N; AC 5; HD 3+3; THAC0 18; #AT 3; Dmg 1d3/1d3/1d8 (claw/claw/bite); SA poison bite; SD immune to poison and disease; B Minor (Az); BA *Death Touch*; Save F3; SZ M (5′ tall); MV 9, Sw 12; ML 12; XP 65/ea.

DOMAIN VILLAGES: Althlone Island, Blackwater Sound, Chalky Inlet, Drogheda Bay, Dundalk, Gweebarra, Laoghaire Point, Longfjord, Nenagh Birr, Tory, Westport, Youghal Harbor.

TRADE GOODS: Harrowmarsh natives export exotic pets like birds, lizards, and other unusual animals to the rich of surrounding countries or traders from ships that stop at the marsh ports on the Gulf of Coeranys.

An alchemist who lives in Westport, Dwynaa the Böse, collects virulent poisons secreted by frogs found in the swamp. He sells the ceramic vials of poison to the highest bidder. They are highly effective and fast acting poisons; a saving throw vs. poison at a -4 penalty is required to survive such a poison.

As the Hydra is a very old awnshegh, there have been hundreds or even thousands of different hydrakin. Types recorded by sages included a human head with crocodile jaws on tarantula legs, a tiny human torso on a dragonfly, and a water snake with a female's torso, eyes, and hair. No one can predict what bizarre blooded creatures might be found within Harrowmarsh.

Hydrakin : Int 1-10; AL CN; AC 5-9; HD 1d6; hp 8+4/HD; THAC0 21-HD; #AT 1d4; Dmg 1d4 (bite), 1d8/1d8 (claws); SA poison in claws or mouth; SD immune to poison and disease; B Minor (Az); BA *Bloodform, Death Touch*; Save F10; SZ S-M (3-6′ tall); MV 9-18; ML 3-12; XP 35-175/ea.

The Caracdir: Soon after the Hydra was invested with Azrai's power, it was possessed of a hunger that drove it to eat many crocodiles and salamanders as well as a few humans living in the swamp. Among the first hydrakin, these creatures were a blend of crocodile, human, and salamander that bred true and are now a race known as the aracdir. These "lizard men" live in primitive tribal camps throughout the swamp, and they avoid

kraken

If you want to hear about my 'near-death experience' with the Kraken, you're cinching up the wrong brace-hook, lad. There aren't 'near-death' brushes with it—there's only death and there's life. All you'll hear about the Kraken is from sailors who saw an attack from afar.

"The Kraken was swimmin' the waters of Krakennauricht and the Black Ice Bay before there was ships. I heard once it was one'a those monsters from the wreckage of Deismaar. Maybe. But, then again, maybe not. Maybe the Kraken's been here *longer*.

"They say there's natives on the Krakenstaur who worship the Kraken as a god. I don't know about that, since I've never been there. Tales I hear about ships sunk by the Kraken all say it happened within a few miles o' that island's shore. Sailors steer clear o' those waters and hug the Zweilunds tight when they go north.

"My experience with the Kraken? Well, we were making the switch around the Zweilunds and going south, not north, when the lookout starts screaming. Not 'land ho!' or 'ship ahoy'—no, he just starts *screaming*!

"I get sent up to calm him down, but halfway to the nest, I see what he's screamin' about. Don't ask me to describe it, 'cuz I can't. It was wrapped around some poor ship that looked like a toy splintering in the beast's grasp. Little figures—I guess they were men—were falling into the sea, and a moment later, everything went beneath the waves. Everything was gone.

"When we made landfall, I heard *Todden's Pride* had been sent out of Grabentod to look for pirates in the Krakennauricht. No other ships were in the area at that time, and the *Pride*, with her armored sides and hold full of weapons and marines, never made port again."

The Kraken is not a typical awnshegh—it is far larger than any landbound awnshegh, and it has no confirmed origin. It haunts the Krakennauricht, the former 'Great Bay,' and attacks ships that come too close to its island. Why the Kraken chose the bay as its territory, none can say.

The oldest theory about the Kraken involves Azrai in the years before the battle at Deismaar. They say he came to Cerilia by water with corrupted, monstrous sea creatures, and one of these creatures was the Kraken. With the passing of Azrai, the Kraken moved its territory north into the bay, where it remains today.

Recently, certain Brecht priests have begun to preach another, less dogmatic idea that the Kraken is from another plane entirely—perhaps the Elemental Plane of Water. They think the Kraken is some sort of monster brought to this world by the cataclysm at Mount Deismaar. They also say it is bound here by a blood tie to Azrai until its purpose on this plane is fulfilled.

INTELLIGENCE: Genius (19)
ACTIVITY CYCLE: Any
DIET: Carnivore
MOVEMENT: Sw 9, Jet 24
ALIGNMENT: Chaotic evil
SIZE: G (110' long)
ARMOR CLASS: 0 (tentacle) / -5 (body)
HIT POINTS: 220
SAVES AS: F24
THAC0: 2 (base)
NO. OF ATTACKS: 9
DAMAGE/ATTACK: 1d10+10(x2)/2d8(x6)/10d4
SPECIAL ATTACKS: Constriction, ink cloud
SPECIAL DEFENSES: See below
MAGIC RESISTANCE: 30%
MORALE: Fearless (20)
BLOOD: Major (Azrai) 47
BLOOD ABILITIES: Death Touch (Major), Long Life (Great), Major Regeneration (Great), Regeneration (Great)
XP VALUE: 29,000

The largest monster in Cerilia, the Kraken acts like nothing more than an animal, though some say it has exceptional intelligence.

Two of the beast's tentacles are barbed, and it uses them to latch onto the sides of ships, whales or giant squid when it hunts. These tentacles do 1d10+10 points of damage per hit, and can be used with all the creature's other attacks. The smaller tentacles are used for constricting and crushing targets; Six can be used each round, though only two can attack a single man-sized creature. A character hit by a smaller tentacle takes 2d8 points of damage and must save versus paralyzation or be wrapped up, immobilized in the tentacle (automatic damage each round) until the Kraken lets go or someone severs it with 20 points of damage (the larger tentacles take 30 points before severing). All tentacles are AC -5 because of their extreme toughness.

The Kraken's bite is used only on a ship itself or on food; its beak does 10d4 points of damage to anything it bites.

Unlike other kraken, the Kraken does not retreat once it attacks a vessel. The creature heals quickly, so it can lose a few tentacles or even an eye, to gain a goal. Should the Kraken wish to retreat, however, it shoots a jet of black ink 80 feet high and 120 feet long toward its opponents. The ink is poisonous—this is the Kraken's *death touch*, as described under "Blood Abilities" in this book—but dissipates in 2-5 rounds, while the Kraken uses its jets to flee.

Some say the Kraken devours the crews of ships and hauls the shattered vessels to a cavern beneath the Krakenstaur. No wreckage or survivors are ever found after a Kraken attack, but its treasure hoard must be monstrous, if this theory is to be believed.

DOMAIN DESCRIPTION: The Krakennauricht is a large bay in a cool climate. While it never completely freezes over, icebergs and whitecaps are not unusual sights throughout much of the year.

The Krakenstaur is a small island with two tall peaks. Some years, only the mountains themselves are above the water. Contrary to popular belief, expeditions have reached the island and returned unharmed. There were reports in the past of men, or some humanoids, dwelling on the island and worshiping the Kraken as some deity. Evidence of sacrifices had been found on the island, though no one was ever able to question the natives.

About 170 years ago, a Brecht explorer named Morik von Luftar swore to find the secret of the Kraken. Morak landed on Krakenstaur four times in two years, and on his fourth trip, he was determined to question a native. When Morak searched the island, he couldn't find one humanoid—they had all disappeared.

the lamia

I am insulted that you must journey this far to compel me to answer your questions. I thought my accomplishments would have preceded me. I guess the destitute, the witless, and the illiterate would not know me, for how could they? My intellect, my beauty, and my magnificence far exceed the paltry awarenesses of the plebeian.

"Five centuries ago, my parents were born poor in eastern Mhoried, and they spent their lives selling trinkets, small totems, and fetishes to survive. They made the items in their tenement above the store, but they told the customers that the items were authentic, ancient items of jewelry. This scheme continued until my fifteenth year when they made the mistake of inviting a customer for an early-evening dinner. When he saw the workshop, he told other customers. In their rage, they broke in and stole everything of value. My parents tried to stop them, but one of the men rewarded my father and mother both with a knife in their stomachs. They burned my home and my parents' bodies, and I was left a destitute urchin, destined for a hard life in the streets. At that moment, I vowed vengeance.

"Later that year, after locating all the murderers, I set out late one night and took a torch to the homes of the people responsible for my parents' horrid deaths. Only one person escaped from those fires. He was badly burned, but I remembered his face well: He was the one who put the knife into my father's belly and struck down my mother. I made sure I returned the favor that night.

"I joined a traveling carnival and spent my time as a vulgar side show attraction. Many believed that I was as vulgar as my act, but I sought to improve my lot. Every coin that job gave me was spent on learning. An old magician taught me to read, write, manage money, and wield a dagger.

I left the carnival a few years later after a quick-profit scheme soured and the authorities tried to imprison us all for swindling a bunch of greedy fools. We ended up as criminals with a two thousand gold piece bounty on our heads. Loren, my paramour, and I left Mhoried and headed east through the Iron Peaks. "Shortly after we left the mountains, we came across the scene of a great battle. Cadavers littered the ground and the stench of blood attracted carrion feeders. Loren and I searched the bodies for any coin they would no longer need, but I found a corpse that still lived, though barely so. In his delirium, he attacked me and almost buried his blade in me. I fought and killed him with my dagger.

"As the last breath left his mouth, I felt an incredible charge of energy fly from him and invade my mouth and nostrils. His blood burned my skin and the energy washed over me, sending horrible sensations all through my body. I think I passed out, but I awakened later, cared for by Loren. As we kept moving across the Khinasi lands, heading east, I began to notice changes in my body. I was becoming swifter than Loren by far, and my feet had become padded like lion's feet.

"When we were later beset by a trio of gnolls, a rage in me fueled my savage counterattack. During the battle, my leathers stretched and burst as my lower body became that of a mighty lioness. With my new claws, I shredded two of the gnolls as Loren claimed the third. After the battle, I saw that I maintained my beautiful self only from the waist up. Loren, horrified by the changes, fled from me, and I have not seen the boy in more than five hundred years.

"I accepted my fate and kept moving onward. I finally came to Besaïam, a principality south of Cwmb Bheinn. Seeking naught but solitude, I settled in an isolated forest, but my troubles were not quite over. When the ruler discovered my existence, his sentinels arrested me and took me to him. He wished to prove his power to his courtiers, and challenged me—'a mortal divinely maimed by the evil blood of Azrai!'—to battle. As I am here with you, I was obviously triumphant. I absorbed more strange energy from the foolish king's death, but this was different—I felt now that I belonged here. The land was a part of me, and with his death, I slid neatly into the vacant throne. The name of the country soon changed to my newly received alias: The Lamia. I've ruled my domain for over five hundred years and none can say that I have not done well."

The Lamia once was a proud and beautiful human woman named Keta Pechaya, an exotic dancer who used her wiles and beauty to rob male customers charmed by her sensuality. Keta's greed and lust for power grew stronger with each suitor; soon she was under suspicion of fraud, along with her accomplice, Loran. They fled east, encountering a dying man on a field of battle whose blood taint was transferred to his murderer—Keta. Her abilities quickly manifested, and she later slew the last ruler of Besaïam, absorbing his birthright and regency, claiming the land itself as her prize. She now uses her domain to fund vainglorious monuments and trappings of her rule, for no one is more important to the Lamia than herself.

INTELLIGENCE: 14
ACTIVITY CYCLE: Day
DIET: Omnivore
ALIGNMENT: Lawful evil
MOVEMENT: 24
SIZE: M (4½′ tall, 7′ long)
ARMOR CLASS: 3
HIT POINTS: 63
SAVES AS: F9
THAC0: 11
NO. OF ATTACKS: 1 or 2
DAMAGE/ATTACK: 1d6 (hand talons) or by weapon; 1d4 (x2) (front foot claws)
SPECIAL ATTACKS: Charm gaze, Wisdom drain
SPECIAL DEFENSES: Nil
MAGIC RESISTANCE: 30%
MORALE: 14
BLOOD: Minor (Azrai) 38
BLOOD ABILITIES: Bloodform (Great), Charm Aura (Great), Divine Aura (Major), Long Life (Great), Persuasion (Major).
XP VALUE: 8,000

When the Lamia is first encountered, all male viewers must roll a saving throw vs. spells (females automatically save). If successful, the victim is horrified by the Lamia's appearance; the victim is *charmed* as per the spell if the save fails. While *charmed*, victims have total devotion to the Lamia and see her as a perfect woman, and they will protect her from enemies to the best of their abilities.

The Lamia can use her *charm* ability with a glance whenever she chooses. To reinforce this ability, the Lamia's touch permanently drains Wisdom from a victim with each touch; when a victim's Wisdom drops below 6 that person obeys the Lamia's orders indefinitely and never sees her as anything other than a beautiful mistress. This is how she keeps her lieutenants under her control.

The only limitation to the Lamia's immediate powers is her inability to *charm* women; while her other blood abilities can affect females in her presence, those abilities are not nearly as reliable as her enthralling powers. In fact, the Lamia can't abide the sight of another pretty woman within her castle at Cravengate, as it reminds her of her lost human beauty.

The Lamia's left hand is slightly different from her right—her left fingernails have become black talons that extend when she is angry, like a cat's claws. Stronger than bronze, the Lamia's hand talons can score a metal shield and can certainly shred weaker armor, dealing 1-6 points of damage to her target.

REALM NAME: Besaïam (The Lamia's Domain)
LOCATION: South of Cwmb Bheinn
STATUS: Not available for PC use
ALIGNMENT: Chaotic evil
PROVINCES/HOLDINGS: The majority of the holdings within the domain fall under the control of the Lamia, as her charmed puppets are in positions of power and control. While she takes a direct interest in trade with the Gradny Coster of Kozlovnyy, she leaves much of the other governing to her underlings.

Province	Law	Temples	Guilds	Sources
Binessin (3/4)	La (3)	Med (2)	Bes (3)	Das (4)
Coromandel (1/6)	La (1)	Med (1)	Bes (1)	Das (6)
Cravengate (3/4)	La (3)	—	Grd (3)	Das (3)
Kaniera (1/6)	La (1)	Med (1)	Bes (1)	Das (3)
Motere (2/5)	La (2)	Med (2)	Bes (2)	—
North Marten (2/5)	La (2)	Med (1)	Grd (3)	Das (4)
South Marten (2/5)	La (2)	Med (2)	Grd (2)	—

Abbreviations: La=Lamia; Med=Medecian Way of Avani (Iocas Narvadae); Bes=Besaïm Guild (a group of local traders); Das=Dashid the Astronomer; Grd=Gradny Coster of Kozlovnyy.

REGENCY GENERATED/ACCUMULATED: 36/60 RP
GOLD GENERATED/ACCUMULATED: 24/12 GB

ARMY: The Lamia's army consists of hundreds of charmed and fanatic warriors, led by her chief lieutenant, the gigantic Vos warrior Pyotr Borochevsky. However, most enthralled forces are used strictly in the defense of Cravengate. Most invasion forces of the Lamia are mercenary troops from the Iron Hand Tribes.

P.B. '95

REGENT: The Lamia

LIEUTENANTS: The most important lieutenant is a Vos warrior, Pyotr Borochevsky, who serves as the captain of her personal guard. A withered old Khinasi man named Jamal el-Numir acts as the Lamia's majordomo and watches over the day-to-day business of the government. The Lamia also has the wizard and stargazer Dashid the Astronomer ready to use his potent arsenal of spells as she commands.

DOMAIN DESCRIPTION: Settled 600 years ago by Khinasi pioneers from Medeci, Besaïam soon fell under the control of the Lamia. The Lamia's domain consists of deep, twisted forests and rugged mountains. The eastern quarter opens to hilly pasture that is often roamed by bands of the Iron Hand Tribes. The two adjoining domains do not fight over this land; it absolutely belongs to the Lamia, but its use allows the Iron Hand tribes access to attack the frontier of Rhuannach freely—and the Lamia likes Rhuannach to stay busy and away from her domain borders.

The Lamia is more concerned with personal wealth and power than with the kingdom she rules. Her taxes are ruinous, and she often resorts to extortion and terrorism in her quest for money to create her latest personal vanities, whether they are public buildings or murals of her or new trappings of unimaginable expense.

The common people of Besaïam have known the Lamia only by way of rumors and stories. The *charmed* nobles and leaders insist that the rumors are lies and that nothing's wrong. At least the Lamia doesn't ravage the countryside, and this is a major factor in the people's willingness to live under her rule.

DOMAIN CAPITAL: Cravengate
DOMAIN CITIES: Motere, North Marton
DOMAIN VILLAGES: Coromandel, Kaniera, Ruapuke, South Marton
TRADE GOODS: The Lamia exports lumber to a few of the Iron Hand Tribes, but she's competing with Min Dhousai and Cwmb Bheinn and losing heavily. She also sells the powdered horns of a near-extinct breed of deer to alchemists and spellcasters, who use the powder for divination potions and spells. This breed of deer was once found throughout the forest, but she sent hunters into nearby domains to exterminate their numbers in order to make them rare and under her control. Also exported is iron ore and gold from the hills south of North Marten. The domain imports grain, weapons, and mining equipment.

ALLIES: The Lamia maintains a close alliance with the Iron Hand Tribes, allowing them free access to her eastern highlands as long as her citizens are not plundered. This access assures continued raids from the Iron Hand against Rhuannach. While Rhuannach forces are busy fending off the plundering Iron Hand Tribes, they're not harassing the Lamia's lands.

The Lamia has a mysterious ally in the Raven. They have met regularly over the past few years, and a rumor the two are romantically involved has crept up in the Raven's Domain. The two have a vocal nonaggression pact and share a common hatred of Cwmb Bheinn. It's believed they will soon move against the country that separates the two with the desire to divide the land between them.

SPECIAL CONDITIONS: In the forest of the domain, there is a clearing with a low hill. From that hill grow shards of crystal and metal. None know why, but they are highly magical, and they are tightly guarded by tribes of brownies and centaurs.

the leviathan

Like other entries, there was no way to interview the Leviathan, as it has not been seen in almost a century and it is most likely incapable of communication. There are also few recorded survivors of Leviathan attacks. Mikhail Kaninskiy, former Vos captain of the Brecht ship *Unquenchable Pride*, heard our plight and offered this interview. The meeting took place in the Imperial City of Anuire, where he lives out his remaining years.

"'Twere near seventy years ago. I was master of the trading vessel, and I'd agreed to take a load of spices from Khinasi to Grevesmühl. We were hugging the shore since there'd been reports of pirate activity in the area. Winter 'uz drawing near, and the ices were forming over the northern waters.

"I thought we could make it through the Leviathan's Reach before the ice froze that over, too, but no such luck. We were stuck in the middle of the Reach in one of the coldest winters in remembered history. We knew the Leviathan was rumored to be active after its last 80-year sleep, but we'd heard that before and weren't really expecting to see much.

"When the ice froze us in, I sent some of the swabbies to walk south and see how far the ice sheet extended. I suppose their steps must've hit a particularly echoing patch of ice, 'cause they didn't make it more than 50 yards more.

"A great spray of ice and freezing water erupted from below 'em, sending most of 'em flying. We never saw the bodies of a couple sailors; figured it meant that the Leviathan'd taken 'em right away. Those who'd been knocked around lay on the ice in all directions, scattered by the blow. Even as we readied a party to go out and get 'em, the Leviathan started picking 'em off one by one. Anything that cast a shadow through the ice was fair game, and I lost a quarter of my crew out on that shattered ice. The only good that came of the whole episode 'uz that the Leviathan had shattered enough of the ice that we were able to get ourselves out of that Nesirie-forsaken place.

"Unfortunately, it wasn't far enough. We traveled near 40 miles back east through the slush-filled waters, trying to steer clear of the Leviathan. While the ship was at anchor for the night, we heard the sound of ice creaking back to the west; like a fool, I assumed that it was just the booming of ice forming. I found out different about ten minutes later.

"I was hurled from my bunk and landed in a rapidly growing pool of water. It seems the ship'd been bitten in half, and we were sinking to a watery grave. I managed to squirm through a porthole, and I struck out for shore. I knew I wouldn't last for long in the icy water, and it was only through pure luck that I managed to reach an ice floe that was close to a stable ice sheet. It was even more luck that the Leviathan didn't take me. It certainly got most of my friends. I heard their screams through the night.

"After making my way through the wilds of Vosgaard and the Hag's domain, I finally made it to Grevesmuhl. 'Course, they didn't believe my story any more than I would've, but I was still insulted when they suggested it was my incompetence that lost the ship.

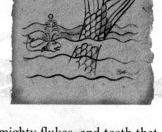

"I never got a clear look at the monster. All I saw was a tail that'd put a whale to shame—though it DID look like a whale's tail—a pair of mighty flukes, and teeth that were longer than I am tall, shining like metal under the winter sky.

"I still have nightmares about the Leviathan. Even though it was seventy years ago, the thought of that thing keeps me awake nights. They say that you can't get the call of the sea from your blood; I'm living proof that you can. I haven't set foot on even the smallest boat since that day."

There is no actual depiction of the Leviathan in any records. All accounts recall the flashing teeth and the mighty flukes, but some call it a large whale and others a gigantic serpent.

Perhaps it is a strange mix between the two.

The history of the creature is unclear as well. By all reports, it was one of the few awnsheghlien that began its career as a monster, mutating further as the blood of Azrai twisted it. Ancient Masetian records found near the Khinasi lands tell of a creature that bedeviled their ships as they sailed off to fight the War of Shadow; this may well be that beast.

Whatever the case, the monster has become less intelligent over the passage of centuries. Once able to demand tribute from ships in the Reach, the past five hundred years have seen it degenerate into simple savagery. Now it attacks anything that sails, swims, or flies nearby.

INTELLIGENCE: Semi- (4)
ACTIVITY CYCLE: Any
DIET: Omnivore
ALIGNMENT: Neutral (evil)
MOVEMENT: Sw 36
SIZE: G (200+′ long)
ARMOR CLASS: -2
HIT POINTS: 150
SAVES AS: F20
THAC0: 1
NO. OF ATTACKS: 1 or 2
DAMAGE/ATTACK: 3d10 (bite) or 2d10(×2) (flukes)
SPECIAL ATTACKS: Swallow, tail smash
SPECIAL DEFENSES: Nil
MAGIC RESISTANCE: 30%
MORALE: Champion (16)
BLOOD: True (Azrai) 85
BLOOD ABILITIES: Long Life (Great), Regeneration (Great)
XP VALUE: 22,000

The Leviathan attacks with a powerful bite from its shining metalic teeth, which are able to pierce armor and crush mighty ships with a single motion of its jaws. The Leviathan also strikes with its flukes to drive waves over the vessel, usually swamping ships that managed to stay afloat after its first strike. The flukes are also excellent for scattering bodies, longboats, or killer whale pods to the four winds.

If there is a particularly troublesome vessel or opponent, the Leviathan attempts to destroy it with a pass of its great tail. One smash of the tail causes 4-40

points of damage, and raises a wave over 20′ high. Anyone who can weather these two is truly a sailor of some ability.

The Leviathan can swallow elephant-sized prey whole. If it rolls a natural 16 or better on its attack, the victim is swallowed alive. Those so ingested take 1d8 points of damage per turn while inside the great belly of the beast. The Leviathan takes only ½ damage from any weapon inside, and only weapons of size M or smaller can be wielded in the belly of the beast. If a victim inflicts over 20 points of damage, the Leviathan spits its last 24 hours of prey back into the sea, leaving them behind.

NOTES: The Leviathan swims alone in the Leviathan's Reach. It's unknown exactly how the Leviathan chooses its victims. Are they simply those who sail near, or do certain types of travelers draw its ire more than others? As the interview shows, the Leviathan pursues its prey doggedly, attacking until either its hunger is sated or that which offends it is gone.

Though all the animals of the reach allow the Leviathan swimming room, great white sharks follow behind it, as do killer whales, hoping to feed off food left behind by the Leviathan.

Some say that the Leviathan has a huge treasure trove under the waves. Anyone brave enough to venture into the reach can find shattered ships decorating the ocean floor. Some are treasure or trading galleons, while others are simply pleasure ships or something equally useless. All told, the combined treasure of these hulks is well over 100 GB.

The Leviathan is known to hibernate frequently. It has not been seen for over eighty years, and it is well known that the creature lies dormant for decades at a time. Unfortunately, when it awakens, it does so with a ravenous hunger that isn't easily slaked.

maalvar the minotaur

I hardly know why I'm talking to you. I don't know why I haven't ripped you limb from limb yet. I suppose you should feel honored I've granted your request for an audience. I know not why you should or why I did. That's just the way things are.

" 'The way things are.' I've heard that often enough. It's a major tenet of Itave philosophy. They're a small people, easily frightened, and they use that philosophy to explain why they're grubbing around in a dirty little land while those around them have castles and cities and finery. I think they're pathetic, but they've survived. There are a lot more who haven't.

"Not too maudlin for you, am I? Not that I care, but if I thought you weren't listening, I might just grab you by the ears and shake some sense into you. Heard that, didn't you? I should hope so.

"I suppose I 'rule' the Itave in your limited way of understanding life and society. They live in my Maze and they do what I say. They don't do anything stupid like try to kill me or take what's mine. If that's rulership, I guess I have it. I haven't seen any of 'my people' in weeks, and I've hardly noticed.

"Vede? No, he's not an Itave. He's a . . . no. You want to know about Vede, you ask him. You said you wanted to know about me.

"Where did I come from? What am I doing here? My plans? Well, I came from somewhere else, a long, long time ago. My plans are my own—I keep to myself and I expect others to do me the same courtesy. Anyone who doesn't finds that I can defend my territory better than he might suspect. . . .

"What's my true name? What was I before? This interview is at an end. Get out."

There are few awnshegh more cryptic than the Minotaur. In all the years of his existence, few scholars have found out more than a tiny part of his history. In recent years, bards and loremasters have linked the Minotaur by name with a legendary adventurer named Maalvar. Not all historians (this sage included) believe this is a true link, but the theory hinges on it.

Maalvar was an adventurer—a blooded mercenary in the pay of any regent or general who would have him. To his credit, no chronicle tells of Maalvar ever fighting on the side of evil, and there are several tales in his history that tell of his heroics on the side of good. Still, Maalvar may have been cast in such a light because he was almost always on the victor's side of any fight. Victory ensures that history and battle-songs will report events as the victors wish them to be viewed.

Early in his career, Maalvar was recognized as a gifted leader and, some say, a military genius. He was respected by his employers and enemies alike. He fought well, and with honor, despite which side of the battle he fought on. But Maalvar grew bored with the military. Too often he went to war for trivialities and saw good men die for no purpose. Maalvar decided to strike out on his own.

Some say this is when Maalvar first felt the pull of his Azrai bloodline. Maalvar's victories became more and more costly and vicious. Due to his reputation, Maalvar often fought forces three to four times the size of his army, and his battles were all hard-fought. Some say Azrai was trying to corrupt him and force him to butcher, rather than kill honorably.

Maalvar gave up his considerable influence and power to become a nameless adventurer, and he disappeared for a time. Mention of a masterful warrior-for-hire, who always gained victory for himself and his friends, popped up across Cerilia every so often.

The last mention of Maalvar in the histories of Cerilia comes from a 300-year-old Khinasi tale. He went into the desert after his companions were all brutally murdered by the Sandpiper, an awnshegh of ample power in the Tarvan Wastes. The tale makes no mention of success or failure, but the Sandpiper's remains were found later, surrounded by blasted ground and shattered trees—but no sign of Maalvar.

A few years later, a power rose in the Maze, driving out those Khourane forces who secured it and leaving only the Itave, an ancient race of native Cerilians.The Itave and the Minotaur are the only inhabitants to this day. The Minotaur has been seen on the edges of the Maze many times. Sometimes he is attended by a few Itave, but more often, he is alone.

The power now known as the Minotaur was once a large, hirsute human whose torso is now mounted on a

bull's lower body, and a large pair of curling horns glowing with carved runes sprouts from the sides of his head. The Minotaur's link to Maalvar is clear, however: Maalvar wore an ancient suit of blackened scale mail similar to that worn by Prince Raesene millennia ago—some believe it may even be the actual suit!—and the Minotaur wears the chest armor on his human torso when patrolling his boundaries. These circumstances lead to curious questions. Is the Minotaur actually Maalvar, the hero of the south, or did the awnshegh slay Maalvar centuries ago? Why did Maalvar have this particular suit of armor? Is there a connection between the Gorgon and the Minotaur? These questions can only be answered by the Minotaur, and he is not willing to talk much.

INTELLIGENCE: 16
ACTIVITY CYCLE: Day
DIET: Omnivore
ALIGNMENT: Chaotic neutral
MOVEMENT: 18
SIZE: L (10′ long and 8′ tall)
ARMOR CLASS: 0 (base)
HIT POINTS: 152
SAVES AS: F18
THAC0: 3 (base)
NO. OF ATTACKS: 2 (weapons or fists)
DAMAGE/ATTACK: By weapons or 2d8 (+12 Strength bonus for both)
SPECIAL ATTACKS: Trample
SPECIAL DEFENSES: Nondetection
MAGIC RESISTANCE: 50%
MORALE: Fearless (20)
BLOOD: Minor (Azrai) 36
BLOOD ABILITIES: Alertness (Minor), Battlewise (Major), Detect Illusion (Minor), Enhanced Sense (Major), Iron Will (Minor), Long Life (Great), Major Resistance—Magic (Major), Resistance (Great) XP VALUE: 22,000

S: 24 (+6, +12)   D: 18 (+2, +2, -4)   C: 23 (+6)
I: 16   W: 15 (+1)   Ch: 16 (+4, +5)

The Minotaur looks more like a bull-centaur than a classical minotaur. His bull-body is muscular and remarkably agile, while his ruddy, powerful human torso is developed in proportion to his size and weight. The horns that protrude from his head are more ram-like than bull-like; they are carved with glowing runes that protect the Minotaur just like an *amulet of proof against detection and location*, but the real nature of the runes is unknown.

The Minotaur retains the fighting skills and knowledge of battle he learned while still human, and he has shown on several occasions that he is more than willing to defend his isolated domain from all intruders, whether they are good or evil.

The Minotaur's *trample* attack is a frightening show of savagery and strength. Maalvar can trample an opponent standing, sitting, or lying on open ground with a normal attack roll. If he hits, he does 2-16 points of damage from the weight of the impact. The victim must save versus paralyzation to roll out of the way. Otherwise, he takes an added 4-40 points of damage from the trampling hooves, and the victim is *stunned* during the next round.

In battle, Maalvar will try to use strategy and his instincts to overcome any opponent. Maalvar grew up fighting and winning against forces and opponents many times his own size. Now, with his blood abilities and his awnshegh form, he is nearly unstoppable.

The only "advantage" a would-be opponent has over the Minotaur is his berserker fury. When in battle, Maalvar will sometimes, for no apparent reason, go mad with bloodlust (1-5 on 1d20 after any damage taken). He will attack and try to kill anyone within reach. During these rages, Maalvar will not use any blood abilities he has to concentrate on, but simply his hands or weapons. When enraged, he gains 50 temporary hit points and a +3 bonus to his damage bonuses, but he cannot plan, retreat, or yield. If reduced to zero hit points in this state, Maalvar merely falls unconscious—it takes another twenty hit points to kill him.

The Minotaur can come out of these rages as easily as he enters them. Once every turn, the gamemaster should roll a d20. On a five or less, Maalvar returns to normal. Otherwise, he keeps raging.

As powerful an opponent as Maalvar is, however, he would rather avoid contact with other people—especially the Itave, whom he protects from outsiders lest he fall inexplicably into a berserker rage and attack them without reason or honor.

REALM NAME:
The Maze of Maalvar the Minotaur
LOCATION: South of the Magian's Domain
STATUS: Not available for PC use
ALIGNMENT: Chaotic neutral
PROVINCES/HOLDINGS: Beïd is the only permanent habitation in the Labyrinth, where

Maalvar lives. The other provinces are merely temporary seasonal dwellings of the Itave.

Vede maintains one-point temple holdings in el-Saroume, Itave, and Beïd provinces. Maalvar himself holds all sources within el-Saroume (1/3), Ras Nabíil (0/3), Itave (1/2), Cape Aswír (0/4), and Beïd (1/5).

REGENCY GENERATED/ACCUMULATED: 20/10 RP
GOLD GENERATED: 1 GB/3 GB; The Itave "sacrifice" gold and animals to the Minotaur. While the Minotaur has no use for the gold, he keeps it in his fortress with other treasures.

ARMY: The Itave are mainly warrior barbarians and rangers. The Minotaur keeps no obvious standing army, but there are rumors that Maalvar trains selected Itave champions to serve him from time to time and sends them back among their people to teach the ways of warfare. Anyone who invades the Maze of Maalvar and gets through the Labyrinth and its dangers may find a few unpleasant surprises waiting among the Itave.

REGENT: Maalvar the Minotaur

LIEUTENANTS: The Itave are led by chieftains and elders in the tribal unit. Sometimes, the Minotaur will summon champions from different tribes to the Labyrinth and command them to perform some service for him. At any time, there could be two to twenty of these Itave rangers or warriors (usually with the barbarian kit) in attendance somewhere in the Labyrinth. The only permanent lieutenant is a druid of unknown origin named Vede, whom the Minotaur often uses as a go-between when he wants to talk to the Itave or trespassers in his domain.

DOMAIN DESCRIPTION: The Maze was constructed before men came to Cerilia by forces or peoples unknown to present day men, elves, or dwarves. There are some who say halflings made it, but most scoff at such a suggestion. The Labyrinth is a darksome maze of blank stone. In the center is Beïd, where the Minotaur has his residence. The Minotaur has been using his own skill at masonry, and the strong backs of the Itave, to add to the

Labyrinth for years now. Some say the Minotaur now worries about invasion by the Magian or other forces, but most believe it is a safeguard against his own irrational impulses to protect the Itave.

The Labyrinth is so convoluted and extensive that even exhaustive mapping and spells are unlikely to provide an accurate picture. Some magic is embedded in the stone, too strong for anyone to dispel. Only the Minotaur (when calm), Vede, and a few Itave can navigate the Labyrinth without becoming lost for days.

Finally, the Labyrinth and the Minotaur's domain outside the Labyrinth are home to fearsome and unusual creatures. Animals and monsters that appear nowhere else on the continent exist inside its walls. Some hypothesize that portals to the Shadow World also exist within the Labyrinth, explaining some of its odd, magical effects and monsters.

the magian

Too much chaos. Absolutely too much chaos. Caravans pay duty to a hundred border taxes and again to bandits, though the differences between them are scarcely noticed. The world is full of strife over this or that piece of territory, and all that does is remove the base from which taxes are acquired—the people. All this leads to one thing: commerce, the distribution and acquisition of wealth, is affected.

"If this world is to prosper and see economic, technological, and magological growth, things must change. The land must become one with itself, and the peoples of all races and creeds must become unified. This land has very few leaders with the vision and tenacity to achieve this. Only one visionary in the past might have reached this goal: Roele. He was Cerilia's great leader, but his vision was undermined from within by his own corrupt, chaotic brother.

"If this lack of order and law continues, the land will fall into another dark age. Another visionary is needed to pull the lands together into one unified body and mind, and this leader is needed at any price. I am that visionary. The price is my tainted blood and my body's decline with my rising power. While I am fed by this power of chaos in my blood, it rules me not—I rule it, unlike these awnsheghlien who seem only fit to provide sport for noble hunters.

"Since my arrival in the lands I now inhabit there has been no rebellion. The people are fed and happy, and only one tax is paid by any one individual or business. I've constructed an unstoppable army with an ingenious battle plan to crush any incursions into our lands. This same force is designed to unite the world under one leader, and that leader is called Magian.

"I plan to unite the land under one banner, with one law, one court, one allied people, one coin and one tax. In this world, no longer will merchants be forced to pay border fees at realm boundaries or grease the palms of crooked constables, and no longer will their customers be charged these extra fees. The price of goods will drop and the overall wealth of every citizen on the land will increase, as will the quality of life. And they shall gratefully thank me, their liege lord that brought them together into this new Golden Age for the continent, the Magian."

The Magian's origins are obscure, and his name was unheard of in Cerilia until six years ago. The Magian was a spellcaster from across the Sea of Dragons, and he landed on the shores of Pipryet (that which is now known simply as the Magian's Domain) with his band of loyal followers. The Magian quickly dispatched the domain's leader and his family. With the birthright powers absorbed from the rulers and his own sorcery, the Magian proclaimed himself sovereign with little difficulty. His tyranny, since his emergence as a ruler, is legendary outside his own domain; within the domain, he is revered. He and the followers crush whole armies with magical and military might.

Once the Magian empowered himself as ruler of this domain, he completely changed the way the country treated its citizens. Despite his ruthlessness during the coup, he's apparently been a just and fair monarch. Quality of life has increased, and people live more comfortably than ever. Prosperity has its price—the country has gone to war more times in the last 6 years than in the previous 60 years. Tacticians believe his sights are set to the west and north, and if his army proves as potent as it has in the past, the Magian will crush Min Dhousai and Khourane in short order. He denies that he has any plans to annex these two domains.

The Magian's exact appearance is unknown to his people, as he cloaks his form in magical darkness whenever he appears. Few inside the realm know exactly what he looks like, and that is all part of the plan. The figure most see and understand to be "the Magian" is a figurehead placed there by the true ruler to draw attention (and any potential assassins). The puppet is the Magian's protege, Ahazarus, and he is a mage of some power and blood ability, though not nearly enough to challenge his master.

The Magian is a powerful being, but he has not been alive for nearly 200 years. Sheer willpower and magic sustained it for much of that time. Now, he is immortal, as the blood of Azrai removed the frailties of his undead state.

INTELLIGENCE: 22
ACTIVITY CYCLE: Any
DIET: None
ALIGNMENT: Lawful evil
MOVEMENT: 6
SIZE: M (6¼' tall)
ARMOR CLASS: 0
HIT POINTS: 160
SAVES AS: W20
THAC0: 9
NO. OF ATTACKS: 1
DAMAGE/ATTACK: By weapon or *death touch*
SPECIAL ATTACKS: Blood abilities, spells
SPECIAL DEFENSES: Spell immunities
MAGIC RESISTANCE: 25%
MORALE: 19
BLOOD: Minor (Azrai) 44
BLOOD ABILITIES: Death Touch (Great), Divine Aura (Major), Fear (Great), Invulnerability (Great), Major Resistance—Magic, Nonmagical Attack (Great), Wither Touch (Great)
XP VALUE: 27,000

S: 12   D: 18 (+2, +2, -4)   C: 17
I: 22   W: 18   Ch: 15

As a 20th-level spellcaster, the Magian regularly memorizes the following spells:

1st Level: *Burning hands, hypnotism, shield, spook, wall of fog.*

2nd Level: *Alter self, ESP, hypnotic pattern, scare, summon swarm.*

3rd Level: *Blink, clairaudience, clairvoyance, fireball, phantom steed.*

4th Level: *Confusion, enervation, ice storm, phantasmal killer, polymorph other.*

5th Level: *Animal growth, animate dead, cone of cold, domination, feeblemind.*

6th Level: *Chain lightning, disintegrate, eyebite, veil.*

7th Level: *Control undead, mass invisibility, prismatic spray.*

8th Level: *Mass charm, maze, sink.*

9th Level: *Imprisonment, blood line corruption (see p. 65).*

Realm: All.

The Magian's *divine aura* and *fear* are linked in an aura of power that surrounds him at all times. Anything of less than 7

59

Hit Dice or levels that comes within 50 feet of him must save vs. spell or flee in terror for 5d4 rounds; the Magian cannot deactivate this power. If he touches a living being, he automatically invokes his *death touch*, but the *wither touch* is under his control.

The Magian is totally immune to all *charm, sleep, enfeeblement, polymorph, cold, fire,* or *death* spells, or any spells that affect living tissue or the mind. Also, the Magian is immune to the turning effects of clerics and paladins.

REALM NAME: The Magian's Realm
LOCATION: Esenshal Peninsula
STATUS: Not available for PC use
ALIGNMENT: Lawful evil
PROVINCES/HOLDINGS:

◆

Province	Law	Temples	Guilds	Sources
Aktarsk (3/3)	Mg (3)	Bnk (3)	DrC (3)	Mg (3)
Boloshy (2/5)	Mg (1)	EtS (1)	MCS (1)	Mg (4)
Donskoy (3/6)	Mg (3)	Bnk (3)	DrC (2)	Mg (4)
Kiyegov (3/5)	Mg (3)	Bnk (2)	—	Mg (5)
Melekes (2/6)	Mg (2)	EtS (1)	MCS (1)	Mg (5)
Pipryet (2/3)	Mg (2)	Bnk (3)	DrC (2)	Mg (3)
Ry'Peski (2/7)	Mg (2)	EtS (2)	MCS (1)	Mg (6)

Abbreviations: Mg=the magian; DrC= Huseti Trosane (Dragonsea Coster); BnK=Almighty Temple of Belinik (Gabrend Sontrene); EtS=Church of the Eternal Seas (Cedriane Alghasne); MCS= Sarand Fasir (Merchant Consortium of Suiriene).

◆

REGENCY GENERATED/ACCUMULATED: 48/25 RP
GOLD GENERATED/ACCUMULATED: 30/10 GB

ARMY: The Magian is a shrewd individual. He has gathered together a very potent army. Totalling over 12 units, his army is divided into three distinct groups.

The Riders, a group of 12 undead warriors and wizards are the Magian's generals and oversee all aspects of his rule throughout his domain. The Riders came across the Sea of Dragons with the Magian, so their true identities and aspects are unknown. They wear burnished armor painted in cryptic runes, and helmets cover their faces, though sharp-eyed individuals can spot pale white bone and red, glowing eyes behind the visors.

They coordinate closely with the Magian himself whenever they're out in the field. Most likely responsible for the sheer brilliance in the Magian's armies' tactics, the Riders are usually found in the forefront of any attack formation. The Riders collectively are considered one unit of infantry.

The Riders (12) Int 17-18; AL LE; AC 1; HD 10; hp 90 (at 0 hit points, a rider is dispelled for 2d4 days unless *holy word* is cast as it reaches 0 hit points); THAC0 11; #AT 1; Dmg 2d4 (+6) (broad sword); SA *fear* (5' radius), *detect invisibility*, *detect magic* at will, *dispel magic* and *fear* twice/day, 12 HD *fireball* once/day; SD cannot be turned except by *holy word*, power over undead as evil P6; Save F10; SZ M (7'

tall); MV 12; ML 19; MR 75% (10 or less on d100 roll reflects spell back at caster); XP 8,000/ea.

The Battle Division is the backbone of the Magian's army. Two units are on horseback and considered medium cavalry; there is one unit each of lightly-armored archers and scouts; and three units of standard infantry round out the group. They are strong and well trained, and quickly gaining a name for themselves. Simply called the Magian's Battle Division, they are well known throughout nearby lands.

Battle Division: Int 10-12; AL LN or LE; AC 5-8; HD 1; hp 6; THAC0 20; #AT 1; Dmg 1d6; SA Ranged weapons (1d6); Save F1; SZ M (6' tall); MV 12 or 15; ML 14; XP 35/ea.

The Construction Brigade is a group of five units of hard-working individuals who construct bridges, build siege weapons, and raise army defenses. They can build, destroy, or dig twice as fast as any other team throughout the land. In a fight, they are considered light infantry.

Construction Brigade: Int 12-14; AL LN; AC 8; HD 1; hp 5; THAC0 20; #AT 1; Dmg 1d4 (tools); Save F1; SZ M (6' tall); MV 9; ML 12; XP 15/ea.

REGENT: The Magian
LIEUTENANTS: Ahazarus (MAw/W10/Az13/LE) is the figure most often seen ruling in Aktarsk. He is a 10th-level mage with some small blood abilities gained during the culling of the old bloodline; as a result, he has a *bloodmark* that has altered his coloration to ashen hues. He knows who is in charge, but he relishes the opportunity to be of service to his master. Only the Magian and the Riders know of this deceit; all others see Ahazarus as the Magian, ignoring their true ruler as "that cloaked advisor." IMPORTANT NPCs: The Riders are the other most powerful individuals in the realm. Three of them in particular could be considered the Magian's closest companions. Perdue the Shadow-borne, Breadthe the Deathknight, and Kevel the Lichlord are the leaders of the Riders and the liaison between the Magian and the Riders whenever they're on a mission (via magical communication through their *amulets*).

DOMAIN DESCRIPTION:
The Magian's Domain rests on the eastern coast, bordering the Sea of Dragons. Once called Pipryet, this domain was conquered within a matter of months by the Magian and his forces (including the citizens of the Pipyet province who joined his ranks to fight for a better future). Since then, the Magian has entrenched himself in the capital city, and has earned the respect and love of the citizens, despite his merciless tactics in battle and "governmental restructuring." He will soon set his sights beyond his own borders.

DOMAIN CAPITAL: Aktarsk
DOMAIN CITIES: Melekes, Pipryet
DOMAIN VILLAGES: Donskoy, Gur'yev, Kiyegov, Ry'Peski
SPECIAL LOCATIONS: Boloshoy Kavkaz, Essenshaal Penninsula, Sea of Dragons

TRADE GOODS: The Magian's Domain exports fish and crustaceans to the interior domains of Rhuannach, interior Khourane, and the Lamia. The Magian imports ores from the Iron Peaks for forging into weapons for the Magian's army.

ALLIES: Officially, the Magian has no allies. He views every leader and every blooded individual as a hindrance to his long-term plans of continental conquest. He knows, however, that publicizing his contempt would unite the realms against him, so he keeps this personal view in check. Instead, the Magian has made peace pacts with nearby countries, including Mbasa, Yeninskiy, and Rhuannach in particular. He feeds them lies about the two domains he wants to overthrow immediately (Min Dhousai and Karusha) in order to justify his intentions of amassing troops and constantly keeping his troops in battle-readiness.

manticore

No, I am sorry, learned ones. The Manticore is not one to be disturbed lightly. While we advisors and folk of knowledge understand the importance of proper historical records, I am afraid our liege deems them of little import to him. If you should need an account of the Manticore's arrival in our lands, then I, his faithful Y'urre, can accommodate you in that.

"Soon after the Magian began his conquest of the Esenshal Peninsula and the domain therein, news of the atrocities committed there spread. Just-minded folk for domains around were outraged and set out to stop this interloper. Qandar the Right-eous, a paladin of Avani and relation to the ruling bloodline of Djafra, joined the many heroes seeking to stop the Magian.

"Nothing was heard for months, though news often moves slowly through enemy lines. After a year, most folk assumed the heroes were either captured or dead, and that was correct. Of thirty crusading heroes that set out to stop the Magian, only seven returned home, scarred and broken. Nine of the thirty heroes had blooded abilities, and of these, only Qandar escaped after nearly a year of captivity.

"Qandar came north, avoiding his normal haunts, and arrived in our fair land four years ago a broken, tormented soul. He was a friend of my cousin, the crowned prince of this realm, and the royal family took him in. He told of unspeakable tortures and some strange magical ceremony forced upon him by the Magian itself; while he did not elaborate, he said that since that time, his demeanor had turned dark, his temper raged to break his control, and he could not use his paladin's abilities. Soon after his arrival, the entire royal family was found slaughtered in its banquet hall, victims of Qandar's rage. With the assumption of their blooded abilities, Qandar's corruption was revealed: He was becoming an awnshegh! He now had a massive tail and claws that ripped right through his own skin, and Qandar became known as the Manticore.

"I, and all of us here, serve him out of fear, though I must admit he tries to fight his now-corrupt nature.

Rather than return to lands of his own people, he remains here, his power tied to the land where he will not bring harm upon his own family and comrades in Djafra. Would that he thought so kindly of our people."

INTELLIGENCE: 12
ACTIVITY CYCLE: Any (night preferred)
DIET: Omnivore
ALIGNMENT: Lawful evil
MOVEMENT: 9
SIZE: L (8′ tall)
ARMOR CLASS: 5 (base), -2 (with armor)
HIT POINTS: 120
SAVES AS: F14
THAC0: 7
NO. OF ATTACKS: 2
DAMAGE/ATTACK: 2d8/2d8 or by weapon
SPECIAL ATTACKS: Weapon specialization
SPECIAL DEFENSES: Nil
MAGIC RESISTANCE: Nil
MORALE: 16
BLOOD: Minor (Azrai) 31
BLOOD ABILITIES: Alertness (Minor), Bloodform (Great), Divine Wrath (Major), Regeneration (Minor), Travel—Azrai or Basaia (Great)
XP VALUE: 12,000

S: 19 (+3, +7) **D:** 16 (+1, +1, -2) **C:** 18 (+4)
I: 16 **W:** 14 **Ch:** 12

Qandar's corruption into an awnshegh is happening slowly, but already he has sprouted a monstrous tail, and his finger bones burst through his skin and formed into claws. His left arm is longer than his right, and his eyes are changing to be more catlike and reflect light. While his skin currently looks normal, it is as hard to the touch as chain mail, and grants him a natural armor class of 5; some predict that when the Manticore is wounded and heals, his skin will start to take on a more metallic look.

Qandar was once a paladin of Avani, but all that remains of that noble figure is his armor and weapons, and they are swiftly falling to disrepair. As the Manticore, he still retains his fighting skills, including weapon specialization with his bastard sword, a *vorpal blade +3*.

The Manticore can attack with both claws for 2d4 points of damage with each claw attack. Qandar is still ashamed of his appearance, but if suitably enraged, he will abandon use of weapons and slash at foes with his claws.

The Manticore can use his tail as a bludgeon, inflicting 1d4 points of damage and knocking foes over, if they fail a Dexterity check.

REALM NAME: The Manticore's Domain
LOCATION: North of the Raven
STATUS: Not available for PC use
ALIGNMENT: Neutral evil
PROVINCES/HOLDINGS: The Manticore's domain contains four provinces: Arrowsmith, a province (2); Madrik and Morrins, two provinces (4); and a province (1) called Okati. While Y'urre acts as the Manticore's servant, he truly controls many holdings within the domain.

Law: Y'urre "passes all military commands to the army from the Manticore himself," thus controlling the law of the land. Local leaders are restless, and resistance has begun to form, though none can yet challenge the awnshegh.

Temples: Temple holdings are controlled by local priests of Kriesha. Y'urre plans on goading the Manticore into destroying their main temple at Morrins, as religion gives people the hope and respite to resist the tyranny of their rule.

Guilds: Y'urre's manipulation of trade with Velenoye, Melyy, and Zoloskaya has given him the bulk of control over the domain guilds. He also has a rare spell-components trade with other awnsheghlien, particularly with the Magian and the White Witch.

Sources: All magical sources are currently uncontrolled, though sharp eyes keep watch over them should anyone attempt to use the power against the Manticore. Many wizards capable of tapping that power have been methodically killed by Y'urre and the Manticore.

Province	Law	Temples	Guilds	Sources
Arrowsmith (3/4)	Y (1)	TCV (1)	Y1	—
Madrik (4/1)	Or (3)	TCV (3)	Or (3)	—
Morrins (4/1)	Y (3)	TCV (3)	Y (3)	—
Okati (3/5)	—	TCV (3)	—	—

Abbreviations: Or=Order of the Moon (Darec Guinsky); Y=Y'urre; TCV=One True Church of Vosgaard (Petrov Dlinskar).

REGENCY GENERATED/ACCUMULATED: 18/6 (Y'urre)
GOLD GENERATED/ ACCUMULATED: 10/4 GB (Y'urre); 6 GB per turn go to the Manticore

ARMY: Y'urre has a small army compared to the size of the domain; many of its more honorable commanders and soldiers met death in attempts to rid the domain of the Manticore. Currently, there are three units of light infantry within the standing army.

Vos Infantry (300): Int 13-14; AL LG; AC 6; HD 1-1; hp 6; THAC0 20; #AT 1; Dmg 1d6; Save F1; SZ M (6' tall); MV 12; ML 12; XP 15/ea.

REGENT: Y'urre (pronounced ee-OOR-ee; MVos/W7/Az14/NE) is the true domain ruler, though the rest of the world believes that the Manticore controls the land. Y'urre is behind all the political dealings, though he has everyone believing he is only a go-between or messenger. He's the man who taxes and builds armies, deals with foreign powers, and decides what laws govern the people. This closely guarded secret is only known to the Manticore, Y'urre, and Y'urre's wife N'chel. He does not enjoy playing the cowardly sycophant, but it does afford him a way to ferret out rivals and keeps him safer than most rulers, "sitting on their thrones, making themselves targets."

Y'urre, in fact, is responsible for the domain's current situation. He eavesdropped on the prince's audience with his friend Qandar upon his arrival, hoping to overhear something to use as blackmail. He discovered the paladin's loss of faith, his corruption by the Magian, and his hopes that he could keep this blood-taint under control. The prince agreed and swore a vow of secrecy to his friend. Y'urre built a bond of trust with Qandar over a few months, and then he let loose Qandar's secret to gossips and blamed the prince for the impropriety. Qandar, enraged over being exposed and betrayed, lost control. In a fury, he slaughtered the entire royal family at the banquet where the gossip exposed his shame. That day, he grew his claws and tail and began his status as the Manticore. Y'urre, once ninth in line for the throne, was now the heir, but he "was forced into a life of servitude under my family's destroyer to save my life."

For years, Y'urre has managed the Manticore, working with him as a friend and allowing no one else to see him. It is a partnership that still works for Y'urre, and the brooding Qandar would rather be left alone in his misery. Invaders, including the Raven, stay outside of his borders for fear of the awnshegh "ruler."

Y'urre's method of ridding himself of troublesome warriors and nobles is unique. He clandestinely recruits them to "kill the nasty beast that is despoiling our fair land," but to no avail. Dozens of his finest, most honorable warriors and spellcasters have been dispatched throughout the years in hopes of sending the beast to its final resting place, but the brave men and women never return. Y'urre has yet to have anyone suspect his duplicity, and those that have, met the Manticore soon after. To maintain appearances that the government wants to be rid of the Manticore, Y'urre currently has a 5,000 gp reward for the Manticore's proven death, though he certainly does not wish anyone to claim it soon.

LIEUTENANTS: Y'urre has no lieutenants, aside from his wife, simply because he is paranoid and trusts no one. To public eyes, Y'urre is the much-beleaguered servant, advisor, and mouthpiece of the Manticore, kept at his side for fear that the awnshegh will slay his wife.

IMPORTANT NPCs: A famous herbalist named Morita Greenfingers lives in the sparsely populated province of Arrowsmith. She is best known for the ability to grow any plant in any condition or environment. The plants she works with are excellent components for potions and spells, making her services much in demand.

DOMAIN DESCRIPTION: The domain borders the Raven's northern perimeter and is hemmed on the east by the Sea of Dragons. A mountain range, lacking in quality ores, helps stabilize the western border with Rovninodensk. Arrowsmith, the domain's southernmost province, is populated by a small bandit group called the Order of the Horn that makes its living by blocking trade routes and demanding a toll. If the toll is not paid, the bandits take everything—including lives if necessary.

Madrik, a province with ley lines to all other provinces in the domain, is the Manticore's home. Several army units reside here, trying to keep the Manticore at bay. Y'urre, the domain's true regent, has lost more troops to the Manticore's voracious appetite than to any outside influences.

DOMAIN CAPITAL: Morrins; The capital is relatively small, but it is set up as two separate cities: one main city and port on the bay, and one fortified small city set a mile south of it. Both are referred to as Morrins, though one is officially "the port of Morrins," and the other is colloquially known as "the Manticore's Lair." The southern Lair used to be the major seat of the ruling family, but is now a relatively empty castle inhabited only by Y'urre, his family, the Manticore, and a number of press-ganged servants from surrounding areas.

DOMAIN CITIES:
Okati
DOMAIN VILLAGES: Arrowsmith, Madrik.
SPECIAL LOCATIONS: The Manticore's Lair

TRADE GOODS:
The domain
exports plants used for magical concoctions and enchantments to every area in the world. Most of the plants are grown in the province around Arrowsmith under the intense scrutiny of Morita Greenfingers. Ores and weapons are a great import, since the northern mountains lack quality ore.

ALLIES: The province's only allies are those who depend the most on the domain's imports of rare herbs and plants. The Magian and the White Witch depend greatly on the components from this area, and they are always ready to back the Manticore's domain in any political strife. The Manticore himself knows nothing of this alliance, set up by Y'urre.

ENEMIES: The Raven is a quiet, respectful enemy, and he bides his time against the Manticore's rulership. The Raven's spies found out the secrets of how this domain is run, and the former Warlord Tusilov simply waits for the delicate house of cards to fall in on the greedy "servant" of the Manticore. Once that occurs, he can easily enter and conquer the domain, including its remorseful awnshegh "ruler."

SPECIAL CONDITIONS: The Manticore is an awnshegh brought into being by the Magian. When Qandar was captured by the Riders, he had shown his blooded powers. The Magian wanted to

learn more, especially since he still needed to understand his own new blooded abilities.

Qandar was held in a dungeon for months while the Magian studied him and other blooded captives. He was the only survivor when the Magian perfected his new spell. During a three-day ceremony, the Magian added the corruptive taint of Azrai's blood into Qandar; while Qandar still kept his old blood abilities, he gained *bloodform* and other abilities and became the corrupt awnshegh he is today.

BLOODLINE CORRUPTION **(Alteration)**
9th-Level Wizard Spell
Range: 50 feet
Components: V, S, M
Duration: Permanent
Casting Time: 60 hours
Area of Effect: 2 creatures
Saving Throw: None

This spell changes the bloodline of a creature from its original source to that of Azrai, forcing the creature to become an awnshegh. *Bloodline corruption* forms a link between the caster (or another creature) and the recipient; for every three points of bloodline strength in the target creature, the spell drains one point of bloodline strength either from the caster or a character set to donate its strength. The recipient maintains his current bloodline strength and abilities, but his blood becomes the blood of Azrai and he gains the curse of *bloodform* and 1d4 abilities available to Azrai bloodlines.

The Manticore is the only known recipient of this spell, and the Magian is the only wizard with knowledge of this spell on Cerilia. To foment chaos to exploit later, the Magian set up four scrolls with this spell on them to be "stolen" and scattered about Cerilia.

raven

According to the people, there are only three true powers in this world: The Magian, the Gorgon, and me, the Raven. They say that few have the ability to stop us, and thoughts of the ruin we will bring fills the air of this world with panic. It is rare when rabble are correct.

"I have watched for centuries from across the Evanescence—the barrier between here and what the masses call the Shadow World. I know everyone's weaknesses, and I know their strong points. I enjoy turning weaknesses against foes unexpectedly to cripple their strength. Fret not—'twill be your turn soon enough.

"Why has the Raven returned to Cerilia? A fool inherited this throne, he gave it to me, and I granted it to another for its own salvation. My plans, chroniclers, you shall write upon their fruition in days to come. You shall write that the Son of Azrai led the Vos to glory unheard of in a millennia. For that shall be the truth.

"The Gorgon, Azrai's grandest mortal champion, has survived since Deismaar; impressive, though his guile and artifice are child's play compared to mine. The Magian is new to this continent; like all those with power, the corruption runs deep, and even an immortal may fall from rot within. I have but recently returned to claim a throne and a rightful place of power. Even so, we are a triumverate and we shall unite to bring all lessers down before us. The Gorgon is our juggernaut, a primal engine of destruction. The Magian is our wizard, the twin forces of blood and magic fully attuned for chaos to bring about order. I, the Raven, am the general, a practiced leader and strategist beyond compare. I could exercise the strengths of both my comrades and none of their weaknesses, but my time of ascension is yet to come, and then I shall soon not need them. When the time is right, with the will of Azrai and Belinik behind me, all shall see me vanquish my partners and finally become my father's son in truth as in title." The Raven speaks strangely, as if he existed long ago on this continent. While there was once a wizard known as Raven before the Deismaar, he disappeared 2,000 years ago. Still, Warlord Tusilov has changed since taking the throne, and not all for the good.

By all accounts, Tsar Lenski of the Ust Atka domain was a weak leader. He couldn't get the noble families to work together, and territorial and commercial conflicts disrupted Ust Atka for decades. The five leading Vos families were always at odds over one issue or another. Tsar Lenski started looking for any sources to help unify his country. He looked toward his loyal army, and raised a Vos warrior named Pyotr Tusilov to his side as a military advisor. With Tusilov's aid, Lenski hoped to bring his people together—by force, if necessary. For a short time, this solidified the tsar's power, but civil war broke out soon enough, each noble family backing an army in the conflict. Tusilov made it clear that his support was temporary, and when he had quelled the unrest, he would return to claim the tsar's throne by force.

Tsar Lenski, in desperation, turned to magic to aid him. He bought help from Clemedh, an obscure wizard from Meraset, who promised a solution with a price. After much deliberation, the Tsar accepted. Closely following Clemedh's directions, Tsar Lenski traced an elaborate pattern of movements around his estate, unaware that he was being stalked by Warlord Tusilov. Both men were led by Clemedh's directions unwittingly into the Shadow World and to the edge of a large pool of blood.

Lenski, still oblivious to Tusilov's presence, spotted a large raven along the shore and approached it. The raven asked, "What is it you seek?" Lenski replied, "I search for a way to unite my shattered people, and I fear this lack of unity will be our eventual downfall. I want the power to coalesce my people, and I'm willing to pay any fair price." The raven cawed in joy and shook its feathers. "Very well, I can help you, and the price is quite fair. Pay him, warlord."

As Lenski spun around in horror, he met the blade of a broad sword ending his life. As the tsar's birthright

P.B.
'95

escaped, the raven absorbed every iota of energy from the dead ruler, much to the surprise of Warlord a Tusilov. "Worry not, my friend. You too have your purpose here, and your body shall wield more power than you ever dreamed!" croaked the raven. It flew toward the warlord and entered his body through his screaming mouth, evicting his own spirit and stranding it in the Shadow World.

When the warlord returned to Cerilia with the body of Lenski, changes started occurring. Warlord Tusilov took the throne and executed the heads of the noble families, absorbing power from their minor bloodlines as well. Soon, the once-handsome warlord began wearing a hood or helm to cover his face. In almost 75 years, no one has gazed on the face of Warlord Tusilov, now known as the most ruthless general of Vosgaard, the Raven. Given the harshness by which he conquered the realm, many believe he has started to change into an awnshegh, though none can prove it.

Despite the Raven's brutalities, he has managed to unite the country under one ruler and one banner (a red field with a raven with a single white eye stretching its wings across the banner). The Raven has even gained land to the east and southeast, conquering six provinces owned by Zoloskaya and Yeninskiy. They were easy acquisitions and the Raven plans on continuing east till he reaches the sea.

At times, the Raven refers to himself as the Son of Azrai, an affectation that disturbs many. Many say that the Raven wields power with an ease that terrifies even the hardest of hearts. Whether "Son of Azrai" is just an assumed title by a proud warrior or it has some shred of truth to it is unknown. The sheer hubris of this title (and the incumbent dangers it involves) is enough to impress even the mighty Gorgon.

Many rumors swirl about the Raven in terms of evils or powers he has "but keeps secret." If any are to be believed, the Raven can fly by night on wings of darkness, steal bloodline strength from a ruler with a glance, and attack a foe with at least seven sword blows in a second! Tales of its appearance claim its skin is covered by black feathers and his face has grown a beak; his armor is empty, filled only by his power; or the Raven is actually two people—a warrior and a mage—that appear in public covered with the same illusions!

BLOOD ABILITIES: Alertness (Minor), Blood-form (Major), Heightened Ability (Minor), Invulnerability (Great), Regeneration (Major), Shadowform (Great), Travel (Great).

XP VALUE: 21,000

S: 19 (+3, +7)   **D:** 21 (+4, +4, -5)   **C:** 23 (+6)
I: 22   **W:** 22   **Ch:** 17

The Raven is a formidable enemy in battles of arms or spells. His usual weapons include two long swords (a *frostbrand +2* and a *flametongue +3*, wielded simultaneously) and he keeps two *daggers +1* tucked in his belt. He also keeps a *scimitar of speed* and a magical bardiche in his chambers. Finally, he has a dagger that hums with latent power, but its magic cannot be tapped. It lacks a gem in the haft of the pommel, and this may be the key to its power. Only the Raven knows of this.

The Raven also casts wizard spells at 14th level of ability. His most common spells are:

1st Level: *Change self, color spray, enlarge, magic missile (×2)*

2nd Level: *Blur, ESP, fog cloud, scare, web.*

3rd Level: *Dispel magic, fireball, fly, haste, slow*

4th Level: *Charm monster, confusion, dig, mass-morph*

5th Level: *Chaos, demi-shadow monsters, shadow magic (×2)*

6th Level: *Demi-shadow magic, mislead.*

7th Level: *Shadow walk*

Realm: All

Finally, a recent rumor implies that the Raven is one of The Lost, the original human sorcerors taught true magic by Azrai. This, however, is in serious doubt since it is a well-known fact that all of the Lost were killed at Deismaar.

INTELLIGENCE: 22
ACTIVITY CYCLE: Day
DIET: Omnivore
ALIGNMENT: Lawful evil
MOVEMENT: 12
SIZE: M (6½)' tall)
ARMOR CLASS: 4, (-2 with armor)
HIT POINTS: 166
SAVES AS: F17 or W14
THAC0: 4
NO. OF ATTACKS: 2
DMG/ATTACK: By weapon type
SPECIAL ATTACKS: Spells
SPECIAL DEFENSES: Nil
MAGIC RESISTANCE: Nil
MORALE: 20 (fearless)
BLOOD: True (Azrai) 77

REGENCY GENERATED/ACCU-
MULATED: 82/100 RP
GOLD GENERATED/ACCUMULATED:
35/15 GB

ARMY: The Raven has a lethal and devastating army. Each province along the domain's northern, southern, and western borders possesses one unit of infantry. The eastern border provinces are occupied by eight units of cavalry and infantry in various concentrations along the border. Imminent plans for the overthrow of Zoloskaya and Yeninskiy have caused these severe movements. At this point, the plan is for one force to move into Zoloskaya, not stopping until the easternmost sections are reached. The second force will create a blocking file to protect the main force's southern flank from retaliation by Yeninskiy. Once the sea is reached, much of the force will be placed along the Yeninskiyan northern border. The blocking file then moves south into Yeninskiy, and the protective forces along the Raven's eastern border move in from the east. The only things in question are when the Raven plans to initiate the attack and how long his opponents will be able to hold his forces back.

REGENT: The Raven. He dresses all in black, and even his sword, armor, and helmet are coated in a black matte finish. The steel mesh mask he wears under his helmet completely covers the face, allowing only one glaring eye to be seen. In the decade since its appearance, no one has ever seen the Raven's face. It should be similar to the image of Warlord Tusilov, but this is doubtful, given the nature of the awnsheghlien.

LIEUTENANTS: The Raven has seven lieutenants that control his border patrols and armies. Three are in control of the western, northern, and southern border patrols (one per border), while the other four help conduct the eastern aggressions (two per front).

REALM NAME: The Raven's Domain (Ust Atka).
LOCATION: East of Kal Kalathor.
STATUS: Not available for PC use.
ALIGNMENT: Lawful evil
PROVINCES/HOLDINGS: Through agents, the Raven controls nearly all the law, source, and temple holdings in his domain. The Wing, a guild network, manages both his trade holdings and espionage activities for the domain.

◆

Province	Law	Temples	Guilds	Sources
Akar Bluffs (3/3)	—	TCV (1)	Na1	Rv (3)
Angar (3/2)	Rv (3)	Bnk (2)	W (3)	Rv (2)
Ayon (3/3)	Gr (2)	TCV (1)	Gr (1)	Rv (3)
Dmitriya (2/3)	Rv (2)	—	—	Rv (2)
Irtysk (2/3)	Rv (2)	Bnk (2)	W (2)	Rv (1)
Kolyma (1/4)	—	—	W (1)	Rv (4)
Laptevykh (2/3)	Rv (2)	—	—	—
Nikolai (3/4)	Rv (1)	TCV (2)	—	—
Patea (4/2)	Rv (1)	Bnk (1)	W (2)	—
Proliv (3/3)	Rv (2)	TCV (2)	W (3)	Rv (2)
Tommot (1/4)	—	—	—	Rv (4)
Ust Atka (3/4)	Rv (3)	Bnk (2)	—	—
Yanskia (5/2)	Rv (5)	Bnk (4)	W (4)	—
Zaliv (0/8)	—	—	—	Rv (5)

Abbreviations: Rv=the Raven; Bnk=Almighty Temple of Belinik (controlled by the Raven through Vlad Gruskaya, a lackey priest); Gr=Gregori Handl (Pietro's Men); TCV=One True Church of Vosgaard (uncontrolled); Na=Natalia Geriver (the Hunters); W=the Wing (trade/thieves'/assassins' guild).

◆

IMPORTANT NPCs: There are two main dissidents toward the Raven's actions. The first is a woman named Natalia Geriver from Akar Bluffs. Her people are a small group of hunters who don't take kindly to being forced into the roving armies of an insane leader. Natalia has killed about seven members of the army when they stray too far from their own numbers and are alone. The Raven is very well aware of her presence, but doesn't seem too interested. The army has standing orders to kill dissidents in the area, but they are not to actively search for them. Outside her small community, Natalia has little influence since the Raven has been responsible for increasing the spending capital of each citizen. Most are very content with their lives and see the recruitment of the army as a necessary side effect.

The second dissident is a Vos city guard from Ayon named Gregori Handl. This man goes by a wide number of aliases (Pietro is his most common pseudonym) whenever he's disguised and trying to rally people to his side. He's surprised at how few people are willing to fight for their beliefs. Most people, he's discovered, are content to wait and see what happens, or to allow their government to do what it will. Thus far, Gregori (disguised as Pietro) has rallied only seven core members, and together the eight are trying to increase their numbers.

The Raven has caught wind of a dissident called Pietro and has decided to try to stop him. Even though Pietro is not as powerful as Natalia, he happens to be close enough to the Yeninskiy front that the Raven fears the agitator may become effective—or worse yet, a martyr. Mouths can be silenced—martyrs cannot.

DOMAIN DESCRIPTION: The Raven has been the ruler of Ust Atka for only about 10 years. Before that time Tsar Lenski was the country's leader and the Raven was shackled in the Shadowland, never able to get out without an invitation from someone outside.

In the 10 years since his arrival, the Raven was able to coalesce the factions that threatened to split the country apart and to increase their land holdings by about 30%. His greedy needs are not yet kindled, and his aggressive posturing along his eastern border is evident of this. The only problem facing his successful conquest is the mountain ranges that border Zoloskaya and Yeninskiy. Luckily, these are soft mountains of great age which will make their ascension relatively simple.

DOMAIN CAPITAL: Yanskia
DOMAIN CITIES: Angar, Laptevykh, Proliv, Ust Atka
DOMAIN VILLAGES: Akar Bluffs, Ayon, Dmitriya, Irtysk, Kolyma, Nikolai, Patea, Tommot, Zaliv
SPECIAL LOCATIONS: The mountains along the Raven's eastern border, the Calumb Range, are rich in metal and bandits.

TRADE GOODS: The Raven exports huge quantities of food. Grains, breads, and meats are the domain's greatest exports. This is also what helps fuel the war machine. Without this necessary money, the Raven would be unable to properly feed and supply his forces.

The Raven imports ore, even though the mountain ranges in his domain supply a great deal of his metallic needs. He wants to make sure that his forces are well supplied—preferably over supplied.

ALLIES: There are unsubstantiated rumors that the Raven and the Gorgon have a silent pact of nonaggression. This rumor was given a bit more substance when a group of assassins from Alamie passed through Kiergard heading for the Raven's capitol city of Yanskia to assassinate him. The Gorgon's troops, well outside their normal range, found the assassins and tortured them to death.

ENEMIES: Boris Tetchayav, a young boy yet but growing fast, is learning his weaponry skills and prays diligently to Kriesha to deliver the Raven to him. Boris is the last son of the Tetchayev clan that controlled the southern provinces of the Raven's domain, and he wants revenge for the death of his family and its power. The Raven hardly considers the boy a threat, and allows his tutoring in priestly orders and battlecraft to continue, hoping to meet a worthy opponent in decades to come.

SPECIAL CONDITIONS: There is a particular ancient tree within the estate grounds of the Raven's fortress at Yanskia that appears dead and rotted from within. Its trunk has an irregular fissure in it, and folk say that they see glowing eyes looking out from inside the tree. In truth, this tree contains a portal to the Shadow World, though accessing it is possible only by the following method: On a moonless night, carry an iron key over your heart, walk around the castle three times, always turning to your left, approach the tree and step in with your left foot first. If these steps are followed, a portal to the Shadow World is temporarily opened within the hollow of the enormous dead oak. This entryway was used by Tsar Lenski and Warlord Tusilov to reach the Shadow World and bring back the Raven, though they knew it not at the time.

rhuobhe manslayer

I Rhuobhe Manslayer, once trusted others— but never again. I trusted humans in our joint conquest of the goblins. We elves tried to rid ourselves of the constant menace and plundering of those gods-forsaken creatures. When the humans first set foot here, we saw them as an arriving fortune. We petitioned for their assistance, and they readily joined us in our battle. They'd fought thieving goblins in their homeland, and they didn't want to play victim to them any longer.

"Once the goblin threat was removed from our forests and valleys, the humans became the next menace. I thought the goblins were bad, but the humans were far worse in their own tyrannical ways. The humans loved to rape the land for its resources, whether in the ground or above it. Our forests were defoliated faster than they could repair themselves, and the humans could not begin to care, given the shortsightedness of their brief lives. All in the name of commerce and industry, the forests were chopped with axes and saws, then converted into homes and heating lumber. The land was stripped of game for clothing and sport. War with the humans was inevitable.

"We fought the humans with little success at first—they bred almost as fast as the goblins, and they were far tougher and more stubborn. In response, we created the *gheallie Sidhe*—the Hunt of the Elves, for you simpletons who cannot learn our language! This special team of elves was extremely effective in killing the encroaching humans. I joined its ranks and underwent more battle training that I thought possible. After the education, I became what was needed of me: I was now a machine of war and a verifiable enemy of the human plague that racked our lands. I knew my enemy well, and I knew it feared me.

"Mission after mission, we hunted the intolerable humans with a fervor, promising ourselves and the citizens of every elven nation that we would never cease until each and every lying human on Cerilia was killed or forcibly removed from our homelands. After my 100th confirmed kill, I became known as Rhuobhe Manslayer, a name I carry as a badge of honor among our people to this day.

"The Hunt was approached by that which was called Azrai with a plan to cull the humans. I joined his entourage eagerly, and he led us to further victory against the humans. At Mount Deismaar, many of my people abandoned Azrai and all that had led us close to dominating the cursed humans, and I felt betrayed once again! When Azrai was destroyed by the traitorous humans and elves alike, my hatred and fury gathered some of his essence, and it fuels my rage yet today.

"Today and forever, my followers hunt our lands, looking for hated humans to kill. Not only do humans continue to despoil the lands, their presence has distracted the elves and thus caused the return of the goblins again. Once I hated goblins more than anything, but humans caused goblins to return, and therefore I hate humans more. I shall not rest until each human, be it man, woman, or child, is slaughtered. And then shall come the goblins' day of reckoning."

As a young elf in southern Aelvinnwode on the banks of the River Maesil, Rhuobhe Manslayer met his first humans. Hoping to find peace with the humans in a common enemy, the elves sought their aid in neutralizing the rising goblin tide. Human and elf worked together for a short time, and they learned much about each other. As the humans and elves pushed the goblins back, Rhuobhe found himself fascinated by the humans and the way they fell into war so easily.

After the goblins were beaten, the humans began to settle in larger numbers on the Cerilian shores. Rhuobhe saw little problem with this, and even befriended a few newcomers, showing them Cerilia's secrets.

But once the forests began to fall at a rapid pace to the humans' axes, Rhuobhe went to his friends and pleaded with them to cease their damaging ways, but to no avail. Bitter and angry, he joined the *gheallie Sidhe* and began hunting humans with a zeal unseen by any elf, soon gaining the label of Manslayer.

When Azrai came to the elves with his plan to destroy the humans, Rhuobhe and hundreds of elves eagerly allied themselves with the god. Although the elves deserted him upon finding what Azrai stood for, Rhuobhe remained with the god of evil. He was astonished that his fellow elves could forsake their hatred of the humans so quickly. As a result of his loyalty, Rhuobhe was

bathed in Azrai's power at Deismaar. Rhuobhe Manslayer has used his power to further his agenda of human extermination. Moving west of his homelands, Rhuobhe placed himself in an important pass between the Seamist and Stonecrown mountain ranges where he has harried humans for centuries.

INTELLIGENCE: 18 (Genius)
ACTIVITY CYCLE: Night
DIET: Special
ALIGNMENT: Neutral evil
MOVEMENT: 15
SIZE: L (7' tall)
ARMOR CLASS: 6 (base), -8 (with armor)
HIT POINTS: 88
SAVES AS: Best of F16 and W15
THAC0: 5 (base), -2 with sword or bow
NO. OF ATTACKS: 2
DMG/ATTACK: 2d4+7 (sword) or 1d8+3 (bow)
SPECIAL ATTACKS: Create arrows
SPECIAL DEFENSES: +3 or better weapon to hit, immune to launched missiles.
MAGIC RESISTANCE: 25%
MORALE: 20 (Fearless)
BLOOD: True (Azrai) 95
BLOOD ABILITIES: Awareness (Minor), Bloodform (Major), Enhanced Sense (Major), Fear (Major), Regeneration (Minor)
XP VALUE: 21,000

S: 19 (+3, +7)   D: 18 (+3, +3, -4)   C: 15 (+1)
I: 18   W: 14   Ch: 17
                                      (8/non-elves)

Rhuobhe Manslayer appears as a tall, regal elf, but his skin is now a shadowy gray, and he looks more like a marble statue than a living being. His eyes have become cold, solid-white orbs that blaze with fury when Rhuobhe is mad.

The Elf has a mighty arsenal of magical weapons and armor at his

command: *Glaivebreaker*, a suit of *elven plate mail +4*; *Anger's Turning*, a *shield +3*; *Heartspiller*, Rhuobhe's primary weapon, a *bastard sword of life stealing +4*; and *Winged Death*, a *longbow +3*. Rumors say that he might even have a tighmaevril weapon in his hoard!

Rhuobhe does not carry a quiver of arrows with him, because he can conjure arrows of energy at will. The radiant blue arrows have no attack bonus, but cause normal sheaf arrow damage and are +5 weapons for the purpose of hitting creatures resistant to normal weapons. When they hit, the arrows cause an additional 1d6 points of damage unless the target saves vs. spell.

The blood of Azrai has altered Rhuobhe's skin, darkening and toughening it. The elf can no longer be hurt by arrows and other bow-launched missiles. Though daggers, thrown stones, and axes still affect him, arrows and crossbow bolts bounce off his skin harmlessly.

Nothing invisible escapes Rhuobhe's pearly eyes. They uncover all subterfuge and illusions, forcing his enemies to fight him on even ground. However, his sensitive eyes can't abide bright light; when in highly illuminated areas (normal daylight or brighter), Rhuobhe attacks with a -4 penalty. As a result, he can no longer operate during the day; he's a creature of dusk who he hates those who enjoy the sun.

Rhuobhe is also a potent sorcerer. He can cast spells in combat while wearing his plate armor, though he must have his hands free to do so. His most common memorized spells are:

1st-level: *Charm person, chill touch, jump, magic missile (x2)*
2nd-level: *Blindness, fog cloud, levitate, stinking cloud, web*
3rd-level: *Blink, dispel magic, fly, haste, lightning bolt*
4th-level: *Fire shield, ice storm, minor globe of invulnerability, plant growth, polymorph self*
5th-level: *Animate dead, conjure elemental, contact other plane, dismissal, telekinesis*
6th-level: *Disintegrate, Otiluke's freezing sphere.*
7th-level: *Prismatic spray*
Realm Spells: *Demagogue, dispel realm magic, mass destruction, raze, scry, subversion, warding*

REALM NAME: Rhuobhe
LOCATION: North of Avanil and south of Boeruine
STATUS: Not available for PC use
ALIGNMENT: Neutral evil
PROVINCES/HOLDINGS: This is a single province (2/6) with no developed areas beyond the camps of Rhuobhe's forces and his fortress Tower Ruannoch, a castle (5). Rhuobhe controls all law and source holdings within his domain, and he is especially careful to guard access to the magical sources, which are centered near Ruannoch. As an "uncivilized" elven area, there are no guild or temple holdings within its borders.

REGENCY GENERATED/ACCUMULATED: 17/35 RP
GOLD GENERATED/ACCUMULATED: 8/12 GB

ARMY: Rhuobhe now spends his time in Tower Rhuannoch plotting humanity's removal from Cerilia. He has gathered a force of hundreds of elves to him and is training them to destroy the neighboring kingdoms. In all, Rhuobhe has four units of elven infantry and two units of medium elven cavalry.

REGENT: Rhuobhe Manslayer
LIEUTENANTS: Rhuobhe has no direct lieutenants, as he puts great faith and trust in all of his loyal band. His favorites and constant companions include a female named Gwyn and the young hotheaded elf Nhoun, whom Rhuobhe nicknamed "The Butcher" after his last bloody encounter with human loggers.

IMPORTANT NPCs: Rhuobhe has completely cleared his forest domain of humans. If humans enter the area, Rhuobhe somehow senses them, and bloodthirsty culling raids are sent out against such imprudent folk.

One such foolhardy human, an elf-hater named Baracus, calls himself Rhuobheslayer. He is hunting for the Elf, hoping to kill him and thus end the ugly war. Baracus magically disguises himself as an elf to pass through the land safely. He dresses in animal skins in order to keep himself separate from the rest of elven culture and prevent his disguise from being compromised. Those looking to rid the world of the menace called Rhuobhe Manslayer should seek out this human, who sometimes rests in Tuornen. His knowledge of Rhuobhe's domain is impressive, to say the least.

DOMAIN DESCRIPTION: Unspoiled by even the smallest of roads, the domain is among the most undeveloped and wild areas in Anuirean lands. If you did not know elves populate this expanse, you would never believe the forest or mountains were ever touched by even a footprint. There are small elven camps where the trees are shaped and constructed around natural dwellings, but the bulk of the domain is wild and untamed, like its ruler.

Rhuobhe Manslayer's Tower Ruannoch is a tall, blackened spire of wood and stone, which sits on the banks of Clearwater Lake. Its base is a colossal tree stump. Surrounded by a wall of brambles and thorns, the keep can be reached only by a small, well-protected path that leads to a portcullis and gate. Cages dangle off outcroppings along the sides of the spire from the ground to its peak; the cages are occupied by the skeletons of traitorous elves who betray Rhuobhe and humans who foolishly attempt to destroy the Manslayer and his kin. Rumor has it that something truly malevolent—all eyes and teeth, if one survivor is to be believed!—lives within the wall of brambles surrounding Tower Ruannoch, and that creature is linked to the Shadow World.

DOMAIN CAPITAL: Ruannoch
DOMAIN VILLAGES: Elfexult, Sylvan Crater
SPECIAL LOCATIONS: Clearwater Lake
TRADE GOODS: All Rhuobhe and his followers could want is found in the forests and mountains where they make their home. They can create weapons, should they need them, but the elves take pride in wielding weapons forged before man came to Cerilia—and they vow to wield them until mankind has left again. There are no exports or imports for this realm.

ALLIES: Rhuobhe Manslayer has no close allies. The elven nations scattered around Cerilia bear no animosity toward the Elf, but they don't support his hostile ways, either. He's become far too diabolical in his intents for their liking.

SPECIAL CONDITIONS: Rhuobhe has changed over the past 1,500 years with his awnshegh status from Deismaar. In the years since the gods' destruction, he has become more lawful and more stringent in his actions, rather than trusting to the chaos that once ruled his life. He is committed more to preserving and expanding the elven way of living than enjoying his own life, a far cry from the usual elven outlook. Traditionally chaotic, elves are suspicious that he has drifted toward neutrality. Thus, some would say he is unfit for the *ghealie Sidhe* and fighting for the elven way of life, though he still believes in driving humans out of Cerilia.

75

seadrake

I was a merchant, and my wife and daughter had the best things my profits could afford. I loved them more than anything else, and everything I did was for them. That's why I risked my life sailing the Straits of Aerele. I made my trade carrying goods and passengers, and it was profitable for years. My luck ran out the day a green-cloaked passenger booked passage with his weight in gold.

He spoke very little and always in a whisper. I was suspicious, but the gold clouded my reason.

"We embarked in early afternoon with full sails unfurled and good weather. Unfortunately, we were caught in a furious storm. The strange passenger lost his hood, and we saw him in his full, scaled ugliness. He attacked a woman who screamed in terror, and a battle began. Many of my crew fell to the creature before I crept behind the creature and stabbed it with a harpoon. The beast cursed my name and my family as its dark ichor stained my deck.

"I was cursed by the diabolic beast, and I soon took on its characteristics. In desperation, I tried to drown myself, but I found I could breathe water as easily as air. Now, I'm cursed to live my life here in the Straits of Aerele. To this day, I don't know why it was so important for the scaled man to gain passage to Mieres. Still, the time for stories is done, and you owe me two hundred gold pieces for safe passage."

About 600 years ago, while Roeles still ruled Anuire, Garrilein Suliere, an Anuirean merchant, sailed the Straits of Aerele, selling grains, steel, and fabrics to Mieren merchants. In return, he came home with gold, spices, and silk. He and his family lived well off the profits, but he was ever greedy for more. On his trips, he sometimes supplemented his cargo with passengers who wished to visit the other side of the Straits. One mysterious cloaked passenger in particular, who paid his weight in gold, proved to be Garrilein's undoing. That trip and passenger irrevocably changed Garrilein's life.

A storm came up and the wind blew the passenger's cloak from his face. He was scaled and horned, a horrible lizard-creature that slaughtered the crew members where they stood. Though Garrilein was only a mediocre fighter, he couldn't stand by and watch his crew die. Summoning his paltry courage, Garrilein crept up behind the beast and drove a harpoon through its back. The scaled beast perished, cursing Garrilein all the while.

Whether it was the curse or the slaying of the creature that awoke Garrilein's blood abilities, he gradually took on the beast's scales over the next few years. Soon, he could no longer show his face in public and did his business through intermediaries and couriers. His appearance continued to worsen, until at last he slipped into the sea in an attempt to drown himself.

He found that immersion in water didn't kill him; instead, the salt water of the Straits sped up his transformation, and he swiftly became a sea serpent. The years have seen the creature become larger and more powerful. Despite the fact that he isn't evil, his evolution continues.

The Seadrake currently appears as a 50-foot-long serpent with a large, fan-like crest adorning his back. He is mottled green and blue, and he blends easily with the turbulent waters of the Straits. Fangs fill the Seadrake's mouth, and he moves powerfully through water with great speeds. He is no longer even remotely human except for his morals and his ability to speak; sailors of the Straits speak of the Seadrake as "he," not "it."

The Seadrake can breathe either water or air with no difficulty, but he has difficulty moving on land. He has, in the past, pursued enemies onto shore, but he prefers the water, where he can maneuver.

Although he has little use for it, the Seadrake still collects treasure, taking it from the captains of vessels that navigate the Straits of Aerele. He's terrorized merchant ships for the past 500 years. After the first few years, rumors rendered the brave weak; few now dare to deny him the treasure he seeks. He doesn't take life when it can be avoided. He kills only in self-defense or when he attacks pirate ships that disrupt his tribute. Apparently, he feels some obligation to earn the money he takes from the traders.

INTELLIGENCE: 10 (Average)
ACTIVITY CYCLE: Any
DIET: Omnivore
ALIGNMENT: Neutral
MOVEMENT: 6, Sw 24
SIZE: L (50' long)
ARMOR CLASS: 0
HIT POINTS: 100 hp
SAVES AS: F15
THAC0: 5
NO. OF ATTACKS: 1 (bite) or 2 (flukes)
DMG/ATTACK: 3d10 (bite) or 2d8/2d8 (flukes)
SPECIAL ATTACKS: Crushing coils, Swallow
SPECIAL DEFENSES: Ink cloud, regeneration
MAGIC RESISTANCE: Nil
MORALE: 17 (Fanatic)
BLOOD: Great (Azrai) 80
BLOOD ABILITIES: Bloodform (Great), Major Regeneration (Great), Regeneration (Great).
XP VALUE: 14,000

Ship captains rarely resist giving their tribute to the Seadrake, since he is quite well equipped to destroy their small ships. His bite causes 3d10 points of damage with his razor-sharp teeth. Alternately, he can make a crushing attack with the two flukes of his tremendous tail, each causing 2d8 points of damage. Breakable objects with a victim must save vs. crushing blow when hit by either attack or be shattered.

The Seadrake has grown to a sufficient size where he can swallow man-sized enemies. If attacking with his bite, the Seadrake can swallow his victim whole on an unmodified roll of 19 or 20. The victim takes an added 1d20 points of damage from its teeth. When a victim enters the Seadrake's gullet, he has 1d6 rounds to cut his way free—by causing 20 points of damage to AC 5—before he drowns and is consumed in the stomach. Only small slashing and piercing weapons can be used inside the creature to cut a way out; there's no room for larger weapons, and bludgeoning weapons have no effect.

The Seadrake can wrap his length around a ship that's smaller than 20 feet across and crush it by tightening the coil. If the wood of the ship cannot save vs. crushing blow, the hull is pulverized and the ship sinks into the ocean, taking 1d4+2 rounds to submerge. If the Seadrake chooses to

remain wrapped around a foundering ship, the hulk sinks at the end of the round as the Seadrake's weight drags it to a watery grave.

If his life is in serious jeopardy, the Seadrake can emit an inkcloud from under his flukes to escape. This defense mechanism acts as a *darkness* spell with a 50-foot radius underwater; this protection is ineffective above water or on land.

The Seadrake regenerates two hit points per round. If a wound is exposed to air for more than three rounds, it must heal normally. If reduced to -10 hit points, the Seadrake dies.

The Seadrake patrols the Straits of Aerele, eating sharks and whales. If these are not available, he can eat plankton or seaweed just as easily. His home is a grotto under Baergos Isle, where he drags the tribute left by sailors eager to avoid his wrath; at this time, the Seadrake has accumulated over 50 GB worth of treasure in his grotto. A few brave souls have stolen from this grotto, planning carefully to enter when the Seadrake is away — but this is a chancy venture, for the Seadrake keeps no set schedule and might return at any instant. Despite a generally pacifistic nature, he will kill anyone he finds tampering with his treasure. Though he has no use for it, he still enjoys its presence. Some suggest the Seadrake collects treasure to remind him of his lost humanity.

Prospective travelers on the Straits are warned: Though the Seadrake can be bargained with, he always demands tribute and is angered if denied it. There has never been a recorded case of someone escaping from the Seadrake by promising to return later with gold. Though he is greedy, he is not stupid. No one escapes an encounter with the Seadrake with purse intact.

serpent

I am the Voice of the Serpent, and you will heed my words and despair. The Serpent is a god unto his followers, and a fiend unto his enemies. Those who do not bow down and worship the Serpent as a new god coiled upon our lands and seas will learn, much to their quaking terror, that he is the true heir of Azrai, and not some petty tyrant as some fools would hope and suppose.

"The Serpent alone of the awnsheghlien born at Mount Deismaar can assume the form of the Great Snake, which all truly wise folk know to be divine. In this form, he can consume whole villages, or strangle the life out of the world, but in his munificence he chooses not to do so. The Serpent is a true god, and he will reward those faithful who serve him with their whole bodies and spirits.

"Take heed! The Masetian people live on under the Serpent's watchful gaze! The Sons of the Serpent gain their righteous powers from his holiness, and their true faith is rewarded by his favor. The Priest-Lord Lakial rules the Sons and pays homage to the Serpent, and I, who was once Ekila, speak with his true Voice. Even the Basarji, who have not yet fully accepted the true faith of the Serpent, pay tribute to him, that they might deter his righteous wrath.

"The day is not long in coming when the Sons of the Serpent shall go forth into the world and spread the true word of their god to all the peoples of Cerilia. Already, the Serpent confers with the Celestial Brotherhood of Serpents, and he foretells the approaching time of the great crusade. All resistance shall be swept away before his devoted, and the Serpent shall bring order to all peoples. Bow down to his holiness now and spare yourselves from his wrath. . . ."

Known alternatively as the Serpent's Voice, the Serpent's Tongue, or the Voice of the Serpent, Ekila is an apparently young Masetian woman. She is the spokeswoman for the Serpent, and she supposedly has his voice speaking through her to all the Serpent's subjects but the select few actually admitted into the Serpent's presence. In recent years, it has been reported that only the High Priest (a wizened old man named Thatio, who calls himself the "High Son of the Serpent"), a few of his High Clerics, and Ekila herself have actually seen and spoken to the Serpent in person. Anyone else who has met the Serpent has not lived to tell the tale.

The Sons of the Serpent devoutly believe that the Serpent has stopped showing himself to the people he governs because he has ascended to a heavenly throne and now comes to the mortal world of Cerilia in his tangible form only when it pleases him to do so. They profess that the Serpent, now a god in a pantheon of all serpent gods, rules over his domain from the heavens.

Those who doubt the Serpent's divinity have a more pragmatic explanation: The Serpent has

"invented" his own pantheon of gods and has inducted himself as a member. Whether he truly believes himself to be a creature of divinity is something no one but his closest advisors can say—and if Ekila and Priest Lord Lakial believe this self-concocted myth, the Serpent can fool anyone in his domain.

But there are still a few questions that trouble the Serpent's detracters. What is this "Celestial Brotherhood of Serpents" the Voice speaks of, and why has no one else ever recorded the existence of such a pantheon? Has the Serpent made contact with some divine powers other than those previously known to Cerilia? Has he made some unholy bargain with them? If the Serpent is only an awnshegh and not a god, how can logic explain the spells that the Sons of the Serpent, the Serpent's worshipers, are able to cast? If the Serpent himself is not divine, what power fuels their magic?

For centuries, the only news and stories that made it across the waves of the Baïr el-Mehare about the Serpent were ones that spoke of his utter cruelty, savagery, and inhuman ruthlessness in enslaving his once-noble people. One can only hope that whoever—the Serpent himself, the Voice, or another among the Serpent's Chosen—has of late tempered the awnshegh's legendary cruelty and man-eating tendencies will continue to do so. While this makes his followers that much more loyal, and many now seem to serve him out of reverence rather than fear, it may also mean that the Serpent could be undergoing another metamorphosis—perhaps one less dangerous to his Khinasi neighbors and Cerilia in general, or one even more startling than the changes wrought at Deismaar.

INTELLIGENCE: 15
ACTIVITY CYCLE: Night
DIET: Carnivore
ALIGNMENT: Lawful evil
MOVEMENT: 12 (all forms)
SIZE: M (6½)' tall), L (9' tall), or G (50' long)
ARMOR CLASS: 2 (human/serpent-man) / -4 (serpent)
HIT POINTS: 130
SAVES AS: F18/W12
THAC0: 3 (base)
NO. OF ATTACKS: 2 (human); 3 (serpent-man); or 1 (giant serpent)
DMG/ATTACK: By weapon; 1d6/1d6/2d8 (claw/claw/bite); or 4d8 (bite)

SPECIAL ATTACKS: Spells (human &
  serpent-man), Poison (serpent-man & giant
  serpent), constriction, swallow (serpent)
SPECIAL DEFENSES: +2 or better weapons to hit (all)
MAGIC RESISTANCE: 25%
MORALE: 20
BLOOD: True (Azrai) 77

BLOOD ABILITIES: Bloodform (Great), Charm Aura
  (Major), Divine Aura (Great), Fear (Major),
  Long Life (Great), Major Regeneration (Great),
  Major Resistance—Magic (Minor), Regeneration
  (Great)
XP VALUE: 28,000

Human Ability Scores
S: 19 (+3, +6)   D: 16 (+1, +1, -2)   C: 19 (+5)
I: 15   W: 18 (+4)   Ch: 21

Serpent-Man Ability Scores
S: 23 (+5, +11)   D: 18 (+2, +2, -4)   C: 21 (+6)
I: 15   W: 18 (+4)   Ch: 17

The Serpent is an awnshegh that stands out as
something truly extraordinary, something more
than half-monster and less than half-man. He is
also something of a deity, at least among his own
people on the Isle of the Serpent, and this worries
many of his neighbors. These outsiders deny his
divinity, yet they cannot refute the evidence that his
priests, who worship him, can cast spells. Either the
Serpent has become something far more powerful
than an awnshegh, or there are a multitude of
secrets about him and his people that no mainlan-
der can begin to guess.

Whether he is a deity or just an awnshegh, the
Serpent is a dangerous, reclusive foe. If he is
forced into
combat, he
can fight as a
serpent-
headed
humanoid,
using claws
and fangs, or
he can
shapechange
into a giant
constrictor
serpent, the
likes of
which have
never been

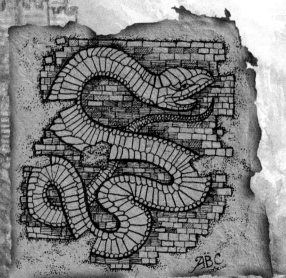

seen before in Cerilia.

As a humanoid, the Serpent appears
as a tall, well-proportioned man with the head of
a giant snake; the Serpent has not shifted back to
his original form of a Masetian male in over 400
years, but whether he chooses not to or cannot
change is a mystery. As a serpent-man, his body
motions are smooth and precise, but his head darts
about like that of a hunting snake—back and forth,
his forked tongue flicking in and out continuously.
In this form, the Serpent disdains the use of weapons. His claws and fangs can act as +4 magical
weapons in terms of which targets they affect.
Quick and agile, the Serpent is almost impossible to
hit, and his smooth, almost perfect skin is harder
than the densest plate mail. The Serpent wears only
a silk loincloth and a loose ornamental collar. He
might also wear a weapons' belt with a pouch
attached, but what he keeps in that pouch is
unknown. Perhaps it is where he keeps spell components—many people have forgotten that the Serpent
is a powerful wizard as well as an awnshegh and a
warrior.

If a character is bitten by the Serpent in either
his humanoid or serpent form, a saving throw versus poison is required at a -4 penalty. If the character succeeds, he takes 2-8 hit points of damage
along with the bite damage. The poisoned character fights at a -2 penalty on all rolls until a *neutralize poison* is cast on him or he gets at least 24
hours of rest. If the character fails his saving
throw, he takes the damage listed above, and, if he
survives, the Serpent decides the character is
"worthy" to serve him. In one round, the victim
will then either change into a constrictor snake
(see the MONSTROUS MANUAL™, Snake) under the
Serpent's total control, or he will retain human
form and be subject to a powerful *domination*
spell. Either magic lasts until the victim is killed or
a full phase of the moon passes (about a week). At
this time, the Serpent will either consume the victim or release him—there is no telling which the
Serpent will choose at any given time. A *wish* spell
is all that can free a character from the Serpent's
control before the poison wears off.

The Serpent can also cast spells while in humanoid (or human) form, and he casts them at 12th-
level of ability. Commonly memorized spells include
the following:

1st Level: *Color spray, grease, magic missile (×2)*
2nd Level: *Darkness 15' radius, ray of enfeeblement, scare, web*
3rd Level: *Dispel magic, fireball, haste, slow*
4th Level: *Confusion, dig, Otiluke's resilient sphere, shout*
5th Level: *Animate dead, cone of cold, domination, monster summoning III*
6th Level: *Monster summoning IV*

Should the Serpent choose to change into his constrictor form, the danger will only increase. Over the past few centuries, the Serpent has become more animalistic in his habits—he used to be lawful evil, and now he is almost completely chaotic in his monstrous form. He fights as an animal, squeezing the life out of his foes, then swallowing them whole. He can shapechange in one complete round of combat.

If the Serpent hits a character with his coils, that character takes 1d8 points of damage and must successfully save vs. paralyzation or be trapped in the Serpent's coils. Each round thereafter, the character takes 2d8 points of damage automatically and is allowed another save to try to escape again. If the character has a Strength score of 19 or higher, he can add half of his Strength damage bonus to his saving throw. The Serpent can hold and constrict up to six man-sized characters at once. Characters held in the Serpent's coils are virtually immobile—they cannot attack, defend, draw weapons, or cast any spells that require movement or the use of components. However, they are protected from other external attacks by the Serpent's own armor class.

The Serpent, like a few other awnsheghlien, has become more animalistic and less human over the years. He has taken to a snake's habits: He is primarily nocturnal and dislikes going outside during the daytime. In fact, the Serpent is uncomfortable in open spaces or in broad daylight; if put in these situations, the Serpent's morale drops to 13. This may be the reason he speaks to his followers only through the Voice.

A final irony: Once a great Masetian sea captain, the Serpent is building a great armada to invade his coastal neighbors, but it is highly unlikely that he will captain any of his ships himself, even on a nocturnal voyage.

All of the Serpent's blood abilities can be used in any of his forms and in conjunction with any other abilities. The Serpent can speak in either form, though he is difficult to understand because of his spitting and hissing. If the Voice is nearby, she usually speaks for the Serpent, or reiterates in clearer language what he relates.

REALM NAME: Isle of the Serpent
LOCATION: East of Ghamoura in the Ajari Deeps
STATUS: Unavailable to PC use
ALIGNMENT: Lawful evil
PROVINCES/HOLDINGS: The two areas on the Isle are Calliana, province (1), and Masetium, the civilized province (6). No matter where you go, the Serpent's presence is everywhere.

Law: The Sons of the Serpent are the awnshegh's police force, and control all the law holdings but yield the regency to the Serpent.

Temples: The Sons of the Serpent have a large series of temples throughout the island, and worship at these is mandatory. Attempts have been made at expanding the Serpent's worship, and there are one or two small temples on the islands off the coast of Ghamoura and Khourane with small enough followings to not attract the attentions of the region's political and religious leaders.

Guilds: The Society of the Serpent, the thieves' guild of the domain, dominates the guild traffic of the island and much of the coastal lands along Baïr el-Mehare; if anyone seeks to do trade, whether honest or illicit, they must first deal with the Society of the Serpent. This Isle is the only area where they operate openly as a true trade guild; anywhere else, their home is among the shadows while their presence is felt everywhere.

Sources: The northern province is almost totally uninhabited as per the Serpent's centuries-old orders, and this provides him with a powerful level 8 source for magic.

REGENCY GENERATED/ACCUMULATED:
21/100 RP, plus an added 30 RP/turn from vassals and 25 RP/turn from the Society of the Serpent's scattered holdings and influence.

GOLD GENERATED/ACCUMULATED: 10/35 GB, and an extra 15 GB/turn from vassals.

ARMY: The Serpent's army is 10 units strong, containing 6 infantry units, 3 elite units of Serpent Guards, and a unit of artillerists. In addition, the Serpent's navy has a complement of 4 dhows, 8 Serpent galleys, and 5 dhouras, all complete with full crack crews.

REGENT: The Serpent
LIEUTENANTS: Little is known of Ekila, the Voice of the Serpent (FKh/P2/?/N). She seems to have given over her entire identity to the service of her master. Everything she says is attributed to the Serpent, though it is unlikely that they have some sort of telepathic bond. Likewise, Ekila does not seem to be *dominated* by the Serpent—she serves him for other reasons. She is the youngest of the Serpent's inner circle, but is accorded a great deal of respect despite her youth.

Thatio, the High Son of the Serpent (MKh/P6/Vo10/LE), runs the Sons of the Serpent cult and is dominant in its priestly hierarchy. He and his clergy control much of the day-to-day business of the Serpent's domain; in his words, "A god need not

be troubled by these petty concerns of mundane, mortal life."

Thatio's Sons of the Serpent worship the Serpent completely, and they are rewarded for their devotion. They make up the Serpent's ruling bureaucracy, and those that progress in the priestly arts can cast up to 5th-level priest spells. Of course, those who violate the Serpent's or Thatio's rules of order and compliance find themselves serving their god in another way—human and demihuman sacrifice are common punishments on the Serpent's Isle.

IMPORTANT NPCs: Darius Asparta (MKh/T13/Br23/NE) is the native Masetian leader of the Society of the Serpent, the deadliest guild of assassins and thieves along the Baïr el-Mehare and beyond. He is a master of poisons, which is how he came to his position of power. He secretly plots to slay his master, the Serpent, but delays for fear that he may be found out. He continues to plan, though, and waits for the right time to strike.

DOMAIN DESCRIPTION: The Isle of the Serpent is a lush, warm island covered with mountainous forests, steep gorges and waterfalls, and the overgrown remains of the fallen Masetian Empire. Aside from the Serpent's worshipers, there are no people of Masetian descent throughout Cerilia. In decline as a sea power, the Masetian culture and people died out roughly 500-600 years after the destruction of Mount Deismaar and the last and greatest outing of the entire Masetian fleet.

The ruins of the Masetian Empire are high in the mountains as well as just outside the city of Masetium. Rumors of lost treasures and ancient

magics lead many to explore the ruins all over the island, and hidden traps and other dangers still active after a thousand years claim the lives of most such fortune-hunters. With the bulk of the population limited to the southern half of the island, many of the former roadways, buildings, and small outposts of the Masetians have become lost amid the rapid growth of the jungle. What was once a center of learning 1,400 years ago is now a vine-wrapped ruin and home to a wide variety of large apes. Folk also talk of various creatures that wander the northern jungles of the island, from wandering ghosts of bygone days to giant vampire bats or invisible apes.

DOMAIN CAPITAL: Masetium; This city is built over the ruins of the earlier seat of the empire, and the Serpent's palace is one of the few surface buildings that survives intact from the days of empire. Under the palace and the city are miles of labyrinthine tunnels and dungeons that the Serpent now uses as his lairs rather than occupy the above-ground structure, which houses his lieutenants and guards.

DOMAIN TOWNS: Calliana

TRADE GOODS: The Serpent does not import or export any goods to or from the island.

ALLIES: None

ENEMIES: The surrounding isles of Ghamoura and Suiriene have kept the Isle of the Serpent and his fanatical populace under close scrutiny for centuries now. While the Serpent is one of the least active of the awnsheghlien, residents of his two closest neighbors say it's only a matter of time before he (or his servants, in his name) goes on a rampage. Both countries maintain small naval forces in addition to normal trade vessels to protect their coasts against the Society of the Serpent's raids.

SPECIAL CONDITIONS: Many mainlanders believe that the Serpent's bulk and fierce fighting capabilities have dulled its wits, turning it more into a true snake. However, when in human or humanoid form, the Serpent is one of the most meticulous and far-sighted planners this world has ever seen. While many Anuireans quake at the multilayered intrigues of the Gorgon, the Serpent's plans and strategies are best described as coils within coils within coils.

the siren

Given the known power of the Siren's voice, our team of sages found it rather odd that she would not speak with them, but the facts about the Siren have always been cloaked. All that was previously known about her south of the Aelvinnwode was that she was a lovely woman from Talinie who had the power to charm or destroy with her voice. The following testimony was apparently written by the Siren herself and delivered to our sages to place within this text.

"My true name is Jerusha Fjoldan, though my title and power is that of the Siren. All throughout the early part of my life, I wanted only one thing—to sing. I was orphaned at birth—found crying, I am told, in a derelict cabin in the Aelvinnwode just north of the Black River—but I was raised well as the daughter of a merchant and his wife in Nowelton. My early years were uneventful, spent mostly in childish pursuits, though I always enjoyed and excelled at singing.

"On the day of my fifteenth birthday, we were visited by an old friend of my father—a half-elf man named Jobhel. After hearing me singing softly while preparing dinner, he made us an offer. Jobhel ran a traveling show that went from town to town in Talinie, Boeruine, Taeghas, and Tuornen, and, after some study, he wanted me to join them as a singer of tales and ballads. With my parents' blessing, I joined Jobhel's Illustrious Minstrels' Consortium.

"Within months, I learned every song in Jobhel's repertoire and performed with the troupe at waysides, in taverns, at circuses and fairs, and even out of our own wagons under the stars. While we were hardly famous and even less rich, everyone thought it was a wondrous time. Until a fateful night near Chalktop Hill in central Talinie, all was well within the Minstrels' Consortium.

"We had camped for the night in the woods, but I was restless. The clear summer sky beckoned to me. I roamed by myself, not expecting danger for none of us had ever heard of trouble within this part of the woods. Jobhel had mentioned that he knew of some nearby ruined elven towers, and he planned on showing them to us the next day. I came upon such a ruin in my walk, finding an old tower with a hooded figure leaning against it and looking directly at me!

"To this day, I curse my boldness and wish dearly to change what happened, but I stood my ground that night, curious to find a person in these ruins. He threw back the hood of his cloak, and his perfect features and broad smile drew me forward. Then he began to sing. It was the most beautiful, haunting, and powerful ballad I had heard, and it was in a tongue I did not know but somehow understood. The singer sang of sorrows of loss and the hope to rise again from defeat, and I began to cry in sympathy. The stranger dried my tears and began another song, an elven ballad of which I had heard only pieces before. Without a thought, I began singing along, even the parts I did not know before, astonishing myself and amusing my partner with our perfect harmony. The night went on forever, it seemed, and I sang better than I ever had before. To this day, I remember the melodies perfectly, but the words are lost, blurred by the veil of memory.

"The last thing I remember was my partner leaning over me and staring deep into my eyes. He spoke, for the first time not in song, and his voice was rich and powerful as he said: 'My darling woman, you know not what legacy lies within you. There is power to be awakened, and that power is song. Your father learned well from me, and you too have learned my song this night. We will never meet again, but song shall always bind us together.' My next memory was awakening at sunrise at the camp with no recollection of having traveled there.

"I said nothing of that night, but when I next took the stage, I chose a song I learned from the stranger. Singing to a group of woodsmen at their camp, I felt a spark ignite within my heart and grow to crescendo with the song. My audience and friends all sat as if charmed. When I hit the high note of the song, my song became a furious force of energy, killing many who heard the devastating sound!

"I fled from that carnage, little realizing until later what had caused such destruction. Luckily, a few survived hearing my fledgling Siren's Song, but they organized parties to hunt me down, and I had to flee. Every time I tried to speak, the

sound of my voice would cause the utmost destruction, preventing me from speaking in my defense. So, I ran and continued to run for months, heading north, then following the coast along Tael Firth west and north until I reached the farthest point west on Cerilia—an isolated area devoid of people who would hound me for what I had done.

"As I made my way toward a secluded cabin I had spotted from a nearby hilltop. I heard the sounds of battle. I crept around a snow-covered pine to see what was happening, when four small children burst through the branches and barreled into me in a panic, followed soon after by their pursuers—two gnolls brandishing axes. Forgetting my need to remain mute, I screamed at the gnolls to stay away from us. There was little left of either gnoll or two surrounding trees after my power tore them all apart with surprising force.

"Collecting myself and leaving the children hidden beneath another tree's branches, I faced yet more attackers. My power and spirit built up to raging. The children's parents were set upon by three more gnolls led by a dark-skinned awnshegh I later learned was the Dusk Man: a thief, marauder, and creature of power who had tormented the folk of Svinik and Halskapa for years. Flush with rage and power, I sang a battle hymn that sent out waves of force and killed the advancing gnolls almost instantly. The Dusk Man weathered the fury of my song, however, closing with me and forcing me down into the snow.

"Though in pain from my song, he clamped his hand over my mouth, recognizing my powerful blood ability. He swore he would claim it upon my death. While he ranted about my being tainted by Azrai's touch but remaining so pure, I pulled my dagger and stabbed him. Energy spilled out of him as I watched the light drain from his eyes, and I felt a rush of power rise within me. My slaying of the Dusk Man and protection of an innocent family gave me power to mitigate but not cancel my Siren's Song, and it also gave me many loyal friends who have awarded me a crown to rule them. I do not rule or use power to conquer, only to protect those who wish to be left alone. That is the Siren's true wish."

Upon further investigation of the incidents mentioned above, we have concluded that this story is truthful and sheds new light on the awnshegh known as the Siren. Unfortunately, no one can confirm or find who Jerusha's mysterious mentor and stranger was, though some colleagues suggest that she slipped into the Shadow World for the night and was corrupted by one of the evil denizens of that realm. Minor magical examinations reveal that Jerusha's unknown parents had the blood of Azrai, which is responsible for her power.

In Jerusha's flight north after her power emerged, she caused a number of smaller, local disturbances (accidentally destroying a barn with a cough, creating a crater in the forest of western Thurazor with a shriek, slaying an entire goblin tribe, etc.). When word of the Dusk Man's death spread, she found herself attracting a large following. Several months later, the people appealed to her to be their ruler, and she accepted, if only to have a secure place to live and use her power to protect those few friends she made here.

With the help of seven advisors, the Siren, as Jerusha was called due to her power, laid down a loose set of laws, levied moderate taxes, and started work on reconstructing the stronghold of the Dusk Man to become her home. Within a year, Siren's Cry was completed and the small peninsula soon became known, as it has for 27 years now, as the Siren's Domain.

A year after the Siren's arrival, Halskapa sent a company of 50 soldiers and dignitaries to Newtonor, the domain capital. They falsely petitioned for a lasting peace; the only power that kept Halskapa away before was the Dusk Man, and they believed they could claim large portions of land from this untried woman in return for a nonaggression pact. The contempt and spite the Halskapans had for her and those she ruled

was maddening to the Siren, though she and her advisors held firm.

During their stay at Siren's Cry, the Halskapans attempted to slay Jerusha and her advisors in a bloody coup. She destroyed them all in a furious display of power. To this day, no Halskapan has ever walked the halls of Siren's Cry, nor has any great attempt been made to annex the small territory by military force.

INTELLIGENCE: 16
ACTIVITY CYCLE: Day
DIET: Omnivore
ALIGNMENT: Neutral
MOVEMENT: 12
SIZE: 5½' tall
ARMOR CLASS: 6
HIT POINTS: 48
SAVES AS: F6
THAC0: 15
NO. OF ATTACKS: 1
DAMAGE/ATTACK: 1d4 (dagger)
SPECIAL ATTACKS: Siren's Song
SPECIAL DEFENSES: Nil
MR: Nil
MORALE: 12
BLOOD: Minor (Azrai) 29
BLOOD ABILITIES: Divine Aura (Major), Healing (Minor), Regeneration (Major)
XP VALUE: 5,000

The Siren cannot speak at all without loosing her *Siren's song*, a powerful blast of sound and force shaped like a cone 100 feet long in a 90° arc in front of her. All creatures in it must make a saving throw vs. death magic, while objects need a saving throw against crushing blow. Anyone outside the area of effect hears a high-pitched blast but is not harmed by it. Living beings who fail their saving throws are subject to 3d10 points of damage, but damage is halved with a successful save. Physical objects either survive the *Siren's song* with a successful save or are blasted to pieces by its fury.

The Siren's other blooded abilities manifested more recently, after the power she assumed from the Dusk Man gave her slight control. By humming various tunes, Jerusha can use her other listed abilities. While

many believe she has much more power than exhibited, she and many sages believe that the bulk of her power keeps her *Siren's song* from overwhelming her.

The Siren and Radnor, her chamberlain and one of her chief advisors, developed a complex series of hand signals so Jerusha could directly communicate with her advisors despite being effectively mute. Anything of great detail is written out, and the library at Siren's Cry is filled with an elaborate collection of documents (and many songs) written by the Siren.

REALM NAME: The Siren's Realm
LOCATION: South of Halskapa
STATUS: Not available for PC use
ALIGNMENT: Neutral
PROVINCES/HOLDINGS:

Province	Law	Temples	Guilds	Sources
Callanlars (2/4)	Sr (2)	—	Can (2)	—
Dantier Island (1/6)	—	—	BA (1)	—
Gigha (2/5)	Sr (2)	—	Wis (2)	—
Newtonor (3/3)	Sr (2)	CTN (2)	Can (2)	—
Port Helen (1/4)	Sr (2)	CTN (1)	Wis (1)	—

Abbreviations: Sr=the Siren; Can=Cannock; BA=Bannier Andien (Andien and Sons); CTN=Coastal Temple of Nesirie (Ahrek); Wis=Wisbeck.

Law: The Siren controls all the law holdings within her domain through her militia and the Elite Guard.

Guilds: While the Siren taxes the people to maintain the Elite Guard and pay the militias, much of the commercial and mercantile power is in the hands of Cannock and Wisbeck, two of her advisors and the owners of the primary trade fleet and the shipbuilding company that made the fleet.

Sources: All the magic is currently uncontrolled, though three of the Siren's advisors are looking into tapping the power of their rough land to further defend itself against Halskapa.

Temples: There are two temples within the domain, which have been built since the Siren took power; both are dedicated to Nesirie, and the high priest is one of Jerusha's closest confidantes outside of her advisors, Ahrek j/P9/Ne14/NG). Aside from the two temples at Newtonor and Port Helen, there are only small personal or familial shrines to Erik and Vorynn dotting the domain.

REGENCY GENERATED/ACCUMULATED: 16/20 RP
GOLD GENERATED/ACCUMULATED: 8 GB/2 GB

ARMY: The Siren has a loosely organized army assembled from among her sparsely populated provinces, consisting of some heavily trained Rjurik soldiers (known as the Siren's Guard) and levied irregulars from the outlying provinces. Included with their statistics are those for the individuals who reside with her in her stronghold at Newtonor:

Advisory Council (7): Int 17-18; AL LN or N; AC 8; HD 1 or 2; hp 6 or 12; THAC0 20; #AT 1; Dmg 1d4 (dagger); Save F1; SZ M (6' tall); MV 12; ML 18; XP 35 or 65/ea.

Elite Guard (75): Int 12-15; AL LN; AC 4; HD F2; hp 18; THAC0 19; #AT 1; Dmg 1d8; SZ M (6' tall); MV 12; ML 16; XP 45/ea.

Irregulars (200): Int 9-11; AL LE; AC 6; HD F1-1; hp 4; THAC0 20; #AT 1; Dmg 1d6; SZ M (6' tall); MV 12; ML 12; XP 15/ea.

Militia Leaders (5): Int 17-18; AL LE; AC 0; HD F4; hp 32; THAC0 16; #AT 1; Dmg 1d8; SZ M (6' tall); MV 12; ML 18; XP 175/ea.

Household Services (12): Int 8-12; AL N; AC 10; HD 0; hp 2; THAC0 20; #AT 1; Dmg 1d2 (tools); Save F0; SZ M (5½' tall); MV 12; ML 8-10; XP 7/ea.

REGENT: The Siren

LIEUTENANTS: The members of the Advisory Council help the Siren make all decisions, though the final word is hers even if all disagree with her. So far, the Siren has listened to them and considered their words. The members' names are Birkenhead, Cannock, Hanley, Radnor, Thorpe, Wisbech, and Wolds.

IMPORTANT NPCs: The five militia leaders, Bardsey, Govan, Hugh, Ryde, and Shanklin, are the primary military minds of the domain. All former members of the Elite Guard, they act as constables, policing the domain and helping lead the army in war. All are older, patient men and serve the Siren with respect; Govan's family was saved from the Dusk Man by the Siren, and he and his sons will defend her with their very lives.

The Captain of the Elite Guard is a burly, honorable man named Rolf Junnarson. He keeps the Guard and its equipment in peak shape, ready to repel attacks on Siren's Cry at any moment. He hoped that this would help him gain the affections of his ruler, but he realizes he has lost her to another (whom he now jealously plans to murder).

DOMAIN DESCRIPTION: The Siren's Domain is a relatively happy place to live. Many of her citizens are here to avoid persecution in other countries, or they simply like the hardy life the stormy coast has to offer. Little more than a collection of insular towns and fishing or hunting villages, the Siren's Domain is perfect for those seeking quiet and solitude.

The windswept hills and rocky cliff-ridden coastline that form much of the domain are harsh terrain for living, even in midsummer. The Rjurik folk who have dug out meager lives here are grateful for the protection of the Siren and are glad to be free of the oppression of the Dusk Man, but most have few concerns about the politics of whoever has the throne. They worry more about feeding and housing their families through the winter.

DOMAIN CAPITAL: Newtonor
DOMAIN TOWNS: Callanlars, Falkart
DOMAIN VILLAGES: Arkaig, Clyden, Gigha, Grangemouth, Port Helen
SPECIAL LOCATIONS: Miere Rhuann, Siren Peak
TRADE GOODS: The Siren currently has a solid sea trade route set up between Port Helen and Dantier Island, and a trade triangle with Dantier and Nowelton in Talinie. The Siren exports crafts, arms forged by the master smiths in Newtonor and Grangemouth, and various herbs and fish. Imports include Talinien goods and rare seaweed from Dantier that is a spell component for an improved *divination* spell used by some of the Siren's advisors.

ALLIES: Dantier Island operates solely as a trading partner and offers little aid as a military or political ally.

ENEMIES: Due to the incident over 20 years ago, Halskapa is an enemy in all but name.

Officially, Halskapa is deemed a reluctant ally, held in check by fear of the Siren using her power against it. Superstitious Halskapans actually believe she could decimate the city of Odemark from the walls of Siren's Cry. Should they gain a chance to remove the Siren, Halskapa would overrun the domain swiftly and decisively. This, of course, is understood and guarded against by the Siren at all times.

SPECIAL CONDITIONS: Newtonor is the largest of the settlements in the Siren's domain, and it is the main trading port for all the provinces. Many mines in the hills of the domain smelt their ores close to the mines and travel to Newtonor with raw metals to trade to the noted blacksmiths for forged weapons and tools. Over half of the domain's people live either inside the city or within three miles of its center, the citadel called Siren's Cry.

Siren's Cry, to the surprise of some, is not a high castle like those in Anuirean lands, but a large three-story stone villa surrounded by a stone wall; two stories extend below ground to provide barracks for the guards, prisons, and storehouses. Should any danger come to the domain, the people's best place for protection would be Siren's Cry.

Set on the large island off the mainland from Newtonor, Grangemouth is the shipbuilders' port, sporting a tall lighthouse that is the pride and joy of its citizens. The lighthouse brazier at Newtonor is kept lit at all times during the autumn and winter, when the Sea of Storms is at its worst. On clear nights, the light from the Grangemouth tower can sometimes be seen on Dantier Island.

The Advisory Council is quite pleased with one recent development: The Siren has fallen in love with a recent arrival to her domain. His name is

Dhaelrik, a wandering ranger of Rjurik blood. Little else is known of him, and the Siren is refusing to allow the advisors or others to badger him with questions. What little can be found out about Dhaelrik is that he worships both Nesirie and Erik, and he has spent much of his time adventuring in the Blood Skull Barony. His reasons for arriving in the Siren's domain are as yet unknown.

There is a mysterious mountain at the southern tip of the outer island, close to the lesser isle of Gigha. It has a jagged hole that runs through the peak; when wind blows through it at certain times, a high-pitched cry is heard for miles. Long before Jerusha was even born, this mountain bore the name Siren's Peak, though some superstitious folk claim the mountain called to her and that is what brought her here.

the sphinx

I was hunting somewhere near the Tarvanian Hills. I was searching for the lost great cats that reportedly killed wantonly and crept into pole-houses to attack women and children. They were believed extinct, but I knew better. I could feel in my heart they still prowled the savannah, and I wanted to hunt one and bring it down. I had something to prove, but wouldn't admit that for the world. I wanted to search the plains for one, sight it with my bow and kill it before it did so to me. I was in touch with my primitive self, and it made me feel more alive. My friends told me I was crazy with a death wish but they didn't understand. I didn't want to use my magic—for I was a spellcaster—but the instruments of our ancestors to prove the cat's mortality.

"The savannah is a big place. It stretches far beyond the horizon and it all looks the same: soft, rolling hills with a few twisted trees to break the monotony, and these trees were my only hiding place. I stealthily made my way up to one of these trees, threw my bow over my shoulder and started my ascent. I climbed about 10 feet when I grabbed a tuft of hair. My heart sank as I looked up in time to have a huge forepaw slice my face. It caught me below and through the left eye and I fell, landing on my back with a huge savannah cat leaping upon me with unsheathed fangs and claws.

"I don't recommend being mauled by claws and torn by fangs, nor do I recommend having your skull crushed by the canines of a large predator. The feeling is indescribable, as I was mysteriously still cognizant and feeling every bit of this in the worst way. As the beast chewed and swallowed my dead body, I still retained consciousness. I remember the warmth of its stomach, the pounding of the beast's heart, and an odd clarity as my consciousness finally came to rest in the creature's brain.

"For the first time, I saw from the great cats' point of view. The colors were dull, muted, and grey, but my ability to detect motion and heat were uncanny. I don't know how it happened, but my awareness overpowered that of the lion that originally bore this body and had consumed my own flesh. When I saw the delicious irony of it, the savannah heard for the first time the sound of a lion's laugh."

The Sphinx originated from the happenstance coalition between a lion and a human named Danil the Inquisitive. *The Scrolls of the Tainted*, an Anuirean collection of scrolls with information on the awnsheghlien as they were seen decades ago, tells a version of the Sphinx's origin that differs slightly from the above interview. The scrolls state that Danil the Inquisitive was on a exploratory mission to determine if the much-feared savannah cat was extinct or not. For decades, the domain of Zikala tried in vain to kill off the savannah cat and prevent the loss of any more of its peoples to their savage appetites. Only in recent years did it appear successful. Zikalan provincial leaders wanted to determine if any cats still prowled their lands and the nearby domains, so they sent a number of sages into the wilderness to find the cat, if it still existed, and direct where hunters could return to destroy them.

This account makes it appear that Danil was there only as an observer, not as an antagonist. If this is true, Danil probably wouldn't have been attacked, since the savannah cat is not known for its attack on humans and elves without provocation (rabies, *charm* spells, and other mental-debilitative effects notwithstanding).

Theocrats of Mystical Forces, a tome of large parchments within a heavy leather-wrapped wooden cover and bound in iron, is a wellspring of information on magic and blood abilities (and the awnsheghlien). The original book rests in the tower of Khufu the Mad, a wizard long believed dead, though something keeps people out of his tower in the city of Zikala. There are copies of every section of the book all over Cerilia, though only five sages have access to the complete text. It gives a small account of the Sphinx gained, as the book states, from a telepathic link engaged several years ago: "A strange duality existed within the Sphinx. An intelligent, knowledgeable being was the vanguard consciousness, but a primitive, violent, savage, and instinctive force waged a mild but constant war against the more civilized mind. This conflict often forced the intellect into submission and made the Sphinx prone to fits of anger and rage that resulted in catastrophe and death for those around him."

The violent side to the Sphinx's temper is also documented in the *Scrolls of the Tainted*. An account by a now-deceased Khinasi negotiater states, "We had never seen such a horrible display in all our lives. The awnshegh drew itself into a red-eyed frenzy of wrath when we refused to give it the concessions it asked for. The Sphinx grabbed our lead negotiator and removed her head from her shoulders with nary any trouble. It threatened 'war far more savage and as deadly than you can ever imagine' and came forward as though to kill us all. We had no choice but to concede to its demands. (Unfortunately, our leaders reneged on these agreements several months later and lost three counties in the process as a result.)"

This reference pertains to a short-lived skirmish along the border between the Tarvan Wastes and the Domain of the Sphinx. This battle saw the defeat of the Tarvan's Rioters and the loss of three counties to the Sphinx. This battle is known as the Carnegaua Resolution in the Sphinx's domain, and as the Carnegauan Massacre nearly everywhere else. The people in the Tarvan Wastes will not allow this atrocity to continue for long. War is inevitable.

INTELLIGENCE: 17
ACTIVITY CYCLE: Day
DIET: Carnivore
ALIGNMENT: Neutral evil
MOVEMENT: 24
SIZE: L (9′ long)
ARMOR CLASS: 2
HIT POINTS: 84
SAVES AS: W12
THAC0: 9
NO. OF ATTACKS: 3
DAMAGE/ATTACK: Bite (2d8); Claws (2d6/2d6)
SPECIAL ATTACKS: Control Cats, *Roar*, Spells
SPECIAL DEFENSES: Nil
MR: Nil
MORALE: Elite (17)
BLOOD: Major (Azrai) 47
BLOOD ABILITIES: Bloodform (Great), Charm Aura (Great), Create Fear (Major), Divine Aura (Major), Regeneration (Great)

First, the Sphinx's huge paws make such a lethal assault, they can kill an average man with a single swipe. This attack form can be made once per round and involves a double-strike with both paws. This attack affects its target like a *vorpal blade* attack, severing limbs with a solid hit. The Sphinx rarely uses this attack, but if he does, he often removes his prey's legs to immobilize them.

Second, the Sphinx has a unique ability to *roar* and use the abilities of *fear* and *divine aura* against any creatures within 200 yards (saving throw vs. wands or face the effects of either particular blood ability). In addition, anyone within 30 feet of the Sphinx when he uses his *roar* power falls over unless it is a large creature (8′ or taller) and needs to make a successful saving throw vs. breath weapon to avoid falling unconscious for 1d6 rounds.

Third, the Sphinx's form has shifted slightly more toward humanoid form within the past few decades, and he can now cast spells as if he were a 12th-level wizard again. These spells are those commonly memorized by the Sphinx.

1st-Level: *charm person, detect magic, hypnosis, magic missile*

2nd-Level: *ESP, know alignment, ray of enfeeblement, web*

3rd-Level: *fireball, hold person, lightning bolt, non-detection*

4th-Level: *fire shield, monster summoning II, polymorph other, stoneskin*

5th-Level: *cone of cold, false vision, monster summoning III, wall of force*

6th-level: *mass suggestion*

Finally, the Sphinx's other power is the ability to control any and all types of felines, from domesticated cats to lions. This power works as a combination of the *charm aura* and *divine aura* blood abilities, giving the Sphinx an immediate range of control of 150 feet.

REALM NAME: Domain of the Sphinx
LOCATION: North of Zikala, East of Binsada
STATUS: Unavailable for PC use
ALIGNMENT: Chaotic evil

PROVINCES/HOLDINGS:

◆

Province	Law	Temples	Guilds	Sources
Agradíl (2/3)	Sx (1)	—	Sx (1)	Sx (3)
Akhada (3/2)	—	—	—	—
Beïr el-Tehara (1/4)	Sx (1)	—	—	Sx (4)
Birbeg (0/5)	—	—	—	Sx (5)
Facessin (0/5)	—	—	—	Sx (5)
Irbouda (2/3)	Sx (2)	—	Sx (1)	Sx (3)
Khousaba (2/3)	—	—	—	Sx (2)
Meid Aïn (2/3)	Sx (1)	—	Sx (2)	Sx (1)
Meid Tarvai (1/4)	Sx (2)	—	Sx (1)	Ada (4)
Meid Zhirgen (3/2)	—	—	Sx (1)	Sx (2)
Seïf el-Avarra (2/3)	Sx (1)	—	—	Sx (2)
Sérifel (3/2)	Sx (1)	—	Gho (1)	Sx (1)

Abbreviations: Sx= the Sphinx; Ada=Adara of Shoufal (a local sorceress of growing power who has managed to avoid the Sphinx so far); Gho=the Ghoudaia Coster (local trade guild).

◆

REGENCY GENERATED/ACCUMULATED: 49/100 RP
GOLD GENERATED/ACCUMULATED: 12/25 GB

ARMY: The Sphinx's subjects are cutthroats and marauders. If the Sphinx raises a militia, the units are treated as if they were irregulars. Gnolls, goblins, and human brigands make up the units—four to ten might be active at any given time. The Sphinx keeps a standing bodyguard of elite infantry at Irbouda. The Sphinx's progeny from both human and leonine mates are a mixture of semi-sentient felines that can speak, albeit in broken sentences, and slightly feral humanoids that are intelligent though dangerously temperamental.

They take orders from the Sphinx (and no one else) and are willing to fight for "the cause," but not slavishly fight to the death.

All the cats below are listed as having a morale of 20, though they will not fight to the death. Once death is imminent, the beast turns tail and runs from the battle to find a secure place to rest and lick its wounds. Once healed, regardless of the amount of time necessary, it returns to the ranks of the Sphinx's army. As an army, the cheetahs, jaguars, and leopards fight as one unit, as do the great cats.

Cheetah (50): Int 1; AL N; AC 5; HD 3; hp 18; THAC0 17; #AT 3; Dmg 1d2/1d2/1d8; SA rear claws 1d2; SD surprised only on a 1; SZ M (4-4½′

long); MV 15, Sprint 45; ML 20; XP 175/ea.

Jaguar (50): Int 2-4; AL N; AC 6; HD 4+1; hp 25; THAC0 17; #AT 3; Dmg 1d3/1d3/1d8; SA rear claws 1d4+1; SD surprised only on a 1; SZ L (5-6′ long); MV 15; ML 20; XP 420/ea.

Leopard (50): Int 2-4; AL N; AC 6; HD 3+2; hp 20; THAC0 17; #AT 3; Dmg 1d3/1d3/1d6; SA rear claws 1d4; SD surprised only on a 1; SZ M (4-4½′ long); MV 15; ML 20; XP 270/ea.

Lion (50): Int 2-4; AL N; AC 5/6; HD 5+2; hp 32; THAC0 15; #AT 3; Dmg 1d4/1d4/1d10; SA rear claws 1d6+1; SD surprised only on a 1; SZ M (4½-6½′ long); MV 12; ML 20; XP 650/ea.

Savannah Cat (25): Int 1; AL N; AC 6; HD 7+2; hp 44; THAC0 11; #AT 3; Dmg 1d4+1/1d4+1/2d6; SA rear claws 2d4; SD surprised only on a 1; SZ L (8-12′ long); MV 12; ML 20; XP 1,400/ea.

REGENT: The Sphinx

LIEUTENANTS: The most direct and obvious minions of the Sphinx are the great cats; his animalistic nature links it to these mighty predators, and no such animal can resist the awnshegh's command. A few rare lions and savannah cats have semi-sentience through their association with the Sphinx, as do a number of rumored half-human, half-lion humanoids. Together, the intelligent cats are the Sphinx's agents and assassins throughout its domain, and the lionine humanoids aid him in his ruined capital at Irbouda.

The only humans with any real influence within the Sphinx's domain are the *khourseti alif*, the Hands of the Sphinx. As its cat allies are not capable of managing his holdings, the *khorseti alif* control all law and guild holdings in the Sphinx's name. This small cadre of servants is widely known and feared within the domain, but exists only in rumors outside its borders.

Most human or humanoid servants of the Sphinx tend to be short-lived; sooner or later they displease their master, and his bestial temper brings lethal results from his vexation. However, the leader of the *khourseti alif*, the priestess Tuara min Mesire, seems to have some influence over the beastly awnshegh and has avoided death for some time. She sometimes acts as the Sphinx's voice, speaking for the monster.

IMPORTANT NPCS: The strongest allies of the Sphinx are the Yezdaga gnolls, a savage band of raiders who attack the surrounding lands from their citadel in the Meid Tarvai. A powerful witch-chieftain known as the Yezd (MM/F6/—/CE) leads them; he is a clever war-leader who wishes to replace the Sphinx as ruler of these lands, but he is cunning enough to conceal these plans from anyone.

Iuri Ilyich (MVo/ F7, Dr8/—/N) is currently the man most hated by the Sphinx. This Vos druid and warrior wanders the northern range of the Sphinx's domain, challenging his control over the great cats with his own spells. His lone war has wreaked havoc in the north, leading to a 5,000 gp bounty on his head for his death.

DOMAIN DESCRIPTION: The domain is a range of dry, broken badlands—the least hospitable part of the entire Baïr el-Tehara. The Khinasi domain of Irbouda once dwelt proudly here, but the Sphinx's growing power led to its fall centuries ago.

Few honest people live in the Sphinx's lands, due to both fear of the creature and its bestial subjects and a relatively rough environment. The awnshegh abides a few hill-tribes and herdsmen, and they build their settlements with high walls to deter the entrance of any great cats. Only the awnshegh's true followers—the felines—are truly at home here. In recent years, the Sphinx has augmented his armies by pressing more of the hill-folk and nomads into service, as well as recruiting gnoll mercenaries.

DOMAIN CAPITAL: Irbouda
DOMAIN CITIES: Akhada, Meid Aïn, Seïf el-Avarra
DOMAIN VILLAGES: Agradíl, Beïr el-Tehara, Birbeg, Facessin, Khousaba, Meid Tarvai, Meid Zhirgen, Sérifel
SPECIAL LOCATIONS: Adel-Esa Oasis, Dongala Oasis, Jalo Oasis, Khaybar Oasis

TRADE GOODS: The Sphinx's people produce few goods and barely manage a subsistence survival in the harsh environment. The gnolls frequently raid surrounding lands, and live quite well on the booty. Some raiders sell loot to their neighbors, only to steal it back later.

ALLIES: The *khourseti alif*, or the Hands of the Sphinx, serve the monster by controlling the erratic humanoids and brigands of the domain. Most Hands are warriors or thieves, but there are some priests who worship the Sphinx and the savannah cats of the Baïr el-Tehara. Since few subjects know who may be one of the Hands, they live in fear of these agents.

OTHER INFORMATION: Over the years, the Sphinx has been increasing its forays across the Baïr el-Tareine. Thus, many trade routes across the steppes have been abandoned as the awnshegh has made them untenable. This threat to the livelihood of Binsada, Sendoure, and Zikala has the three realms talking of ridding themselves of the awnshegh by any means possible.

According to a Sendouran traveling minstrel, the Sphinx has also undertaken a massive excavation effort in the Tarvanian Hills, but the reason for this exercise is unknown at this time.

Within the Sphinx's domain is a strictly held social structure, starting with the Sphinx at the top and the humans on the bottom of the social order. The exact layers are: the Sphinx, the paw, the slept, the purr, and the tuft.

The tuft is the largest group. It consists of every living creature in the Domain of the Sphinx that is not feline and has no special skills for the Sphinx to exploit. This includes humans and humanoids and is the largest caste group. Those in the tuft do not have any rights and are often killed without fear of punishment.

The purr is the lowest caste group of felines. The common cats all reside in this caste. This consists of over 92% of the felines.

The slept caste consists of the upper-class citizenry. Over 7% of the population fits into this caste. The few humans in it are business owners, spellcasters, and the *khourseti alif*.

The paw caste consists of the Claw leaders (equivalent to clans or bloodlines among the feline inhabitants) and the Sphinx's offspring. Less than 1% of the felines fit into this caste.

spider

The elves are elitists who think they're the only beings worthy of the gift of life. Bigoted attitudes like that must be exterminated, and I dedicated my life to removing fanatics from my land. I became a master of hunting and trapping the murderous elves, never allowing them to escape with their lives. The Dark Woods that became my home soon was called the Spiderfell—like a spider's web, once you've entered, there is no escape, and I was henceforth nicknamed the Spiderlord.

"Though you may recognize me already, I am the goblin king Tal-Qazar. As the leader of the greatest army of goblins and gnolls to ever scar the earth, it is my responsibility to make their voices heard and never suppressed, and I have accomplished that, but at the expense of my body and my spirit."

"How many centuries ago it was I know not, but I stood with the so-called forces of darkness at Deismaar, and I and my troops slew our share of nobler-than-thou elves and their comrades. The only time our forces faltered was when the world shattered about us with the deaths of the gods. Out of that destruction, I and a handful of my troops survived to return to our citadel and tend to our wounds. Since that time, I've changed mightily. I think the gods were pleased with my achievements, and they spared my life and my people so I could continue exterminating the vicious elves.

"I soon discovered, following that awful day, that the death of the gods granted me great powers. I started using these abilities to bring my people—goblins and gnolls—together into one house. Some formerly loyal henchmen turned on me, using power of their own they garnered at Deismaar, but my wits and superior power allowed me to slay them and claim their power as well. After a few 'examples' of what happened to those who turned on Tal-Qazar, my plans began to work. Goblin and gnoll worked side by side, coordinating their strikes and raids, meeting with incredible success.

"Unfortunately, these successes all came with a price, and I paid that price. As I used my powers, my body started to change. If I didn't use my power, the changes ceased but didn't reverse. I tried to refrain from using my new abilities, but others rose up from the ranks to challenge my position, and I was forced to use the powers to retain my station. After killing the last subchieftain who stood with me at Deismaar, I noticed a great change in power and shape—my body was actually shifting to earn me a new nickname—the Spider!

"After the changes slowed to a crawl, I was no longer goblin, but much, much more. I had the multiple legs and pedipalps of a spider, with my own legs converted into spider legs as well. My torso was now more strongly muscled and powerful, and it sat upon this stable frame like a proud beacon on a shoreline. My hands became claws so massive and sharp, I could trim small trees, disloyal goblins, and spying elves with a second's effort. I control the giant spiders of my woods as easily as I command my goblins, and I now literally spin the webs of intrigue that gained me the name Spiderlord at the beginning.

"To hear those whining fools in surrounding Anuire say I am mad and a corruption of nature makes me smile at their hypocrisy. They covet this power; if they could have it, they would welcome the changes that come with it. I believe it rankles them that they cannot conquer Tal-Qazar's stronghold."

The Spider is one of the most gruesome-looking awnshegh still alive today and the least sane creature in Anuire. Its spiderlike frame, its cunning, madness, and its abhorrent need to kill elves and anyone who stands in its way makes it even more repellent than it ever was when it was simply Tal-Qazar the Goblin King. The above interview was transcribed over 200 years ago; it was the last civil audience given by the Spider before his mind was lost. Certain questions and rumors regarding this dangerous awnshegh, however, have been raised recently.

A small number of tomes, including one called *Theran's Torment* which was recently found in Endier, mention the Spider as a corrupt, evil elf out to assassinate the Goblin King Tal-Qazar. They say Tal-Qazar returned from

Deismaar flushed with power and overconfidence and he easily fell to the killer's knife. During the murder, this unnamed elf was invested with the Spider's Azrai-tainted blood and energy, and the power swiftly shifted him into the form of the Spider as it is known today.

In his research and studies of awnshegh bloodlines, a scribe named Thesselonius of Bindier discovered a tattered and dry-rotted bundle of scrolls in a cave near the Straits of Aerele. The original scrolls are preserved, but they are incredibly old and fragile—some associates estimate the bundle is at least 400 years old—so Thesselonius copied their contents into a journal. This transcript is the only existing copy of this writing.

The document, now known as the *Aerele Scroll*, seemed to be a collection of information on early shipping and trade along the Straits of Aerele and the Gulf of Coeranys, including a few notes on where certain ships sank. Its interest to Thesselonius (and to us) lies in a short reference to a human named Tal-Qazar, the widely accepted original name of the Spider. According to this chronicle, Tal-Qazar was an avaricious and ruthless spice merchant who sailed along the Southern Coast of the continent looking for the quickest profit possible. His greed caused him to swindle a haphazard magician self-named the Impeccable Borderf out of a great sum of money and a sizable shipment of herbs and spices. The miffed magician retaliated by placing a very powerful curse on Tal-Qazar that turned the wretched, miserable, and selfish Tal-Qazar into his present form as the Spider.

Other undocumented stories and rumors about the Spider attribute just about any ill or bad happenstance around the Spiderfell to it: Plagues in Ghoere, Medoere, and Roesone are caused by its breath; the fishing is bad in the Spider River because the Spider fouled it in the spring. Almost as many ills are blamed on the Spider as are blamed on the Gorgon.

INTELLIGENCE: Very (11)
ACTIVITY CYCLE: Any
DIET: Carnivore
ALIGNMENT: CE
MOVEMENT: 15
SIZE: L (7′ tall, 7′ long)
ARMOR CLASS: -2 (carapace)/4 (underbelly)
HIT POINTS: 81
SAVES AS: F13
THAC0: 7
NO. OF ATTACKS: 3 (claw/claw/bite) or 1 (web)
DAMAGE/ATTACK: 1d10/1d10/1d6 (claw/claw/bite)
SPECIAL ATTACKS: Jump, poisonous bite, web
SPECIAL DEFENSES: Spittle, regeneration
MR: 15%
MORALE: 20 (Fearless)
BLOOD: True (Azrai) 95
BLOOD ABILITIES: Animal Affinity—Spiders (Great), Bloodform (Great), Invulnerability (Great), Long Life (Great), Major Regeneration and Regeneration (Great)
XP VALUE: 14,000

The Spider is not the most powerful Anuirean awnshegh, but it is still a powerful foe. With its spider legs, it can move quickly from side to side, easily dodging attacks. Its primary attacks are its powerful claws followed by the bite of its razor-sharp teeth. If the Spider successfully bites an enemy, the target must make a saving throw vs. poison at a -2 penalty or die immediately. Successful saves prevent death, but the target still takes 20 points of damage.

The Spider is able to jump up to 30 feet in the air; with a successful attack roll, it can land on a target 50 feet away, causing 3d6 points of damage. This is usually not a combat tactic but a maneuver for ambush or escape.

The Spider's altered body has spinnerets in its tail to emit a single strand of web behind it or actually spin a full web. The web covers a 40′×40′×40′ area and holds any creatures in that area with the effectiveness of a *web* spell. This web cannot be burned away, but it dissolves after 1d20+20 hours. If the Spider's life is in serious danger, it uses a spray of

blinding spittle to escape. This can hit three individuals up to 15 feet away with a successful attack roll for each victim, and it blinds them for 1d6 turns. If a save vs. poison is failed, the spittle also causes 1d6 points of damage after one round. The eyes can immediately be flushed with water to prevent the damage but not the blindness.

The Spider's blood abilities let it regenerate one hit point per round, even below -10 hit points. It can also regenerate entire limbs; with its *invulnerability*, it is almost impossible to kill. It is said that the Spider's death is ensured only by performing the following rituals: Reduce its body to scattered remnants and keep them separated; use wood from a dryad's tree to burn the pieces of its body; and, after a day of burning, extinguish the fire and generously sow the earth where the ashes lie with salt, plowing all remains of the Spider into now-barren soil. Obviously, this series of activities is not likely to happen unless someone is able to destroy all the Spider's followers—hundreds of gnolls and goblins, and thousands of normal and giant spiders!—who will all aid their ruler.

REALM NAME: The Spiderfell
LOCATION: South of Ghoere, north of Diemed.
STATUS: Not available for PC use.
ALIGNMENT: Chaotic evil.
PROVINCES/HOLDINGS: This realm is only a single province. Nearly all holdings within the Spiderfell are tightly controlled by the Spider itself. The magical sources, which it cannot tap, it jealously guards. However, the mage Caine has nonetheless seized control of some of the magic.

REGENCY GENERATED/ACCUMULATED: 7/10 RP
GOLD GENERATED/ACCUMULATED: — / 20 GB.

ARMY: The Spider's armies are feared by all the surrounding realms, since they pillage without cause or reason and none can tell where they will strike next. Beyond its armies of goblin and gnoll raiders, it has a strange control over spiders. No one knows what the full extent of this power is, but many believe it works like a standard *animal affinity* blood ability over spiders. This phenomenal control over spiders keeps the Spider's goblins and gnolls from harm by the many poisonous denizens of the Spiderfell.

Gnoll Raiders (50)
Int 5-7; AL CE; AC 5; HD 2; hp 9; THAC0 19; #AT 1; Dmg 2d4 (Weapon); Save F2; SZ L (7½)′ tall); MV 9; ML 11; XP 35/ea.

Goblins (400) Int 5-10; AL LE; AC 6; HD 1-1; hp 4; THAC0 20; #AT 1; Dmg 1d6 (by weapon); Save F1; SZ S (4′ tall); MV 6; ML 10; XP 15/ea.

Goblin Spider-Riders (100) Int 5-10; AL LE; AC 6; HD 1-1; hp 5; THAC0 20; #AT 1; Dmg 1d6 (by weapon); SA Ranged weapons-bows (1d6) Save F1; SZ S (4′ tall); MV 12; ML 12; XP 35/ea.

Giant Spiders of Spiderfell (100) Int 3-6; AL CE; AC 4; HD 3+3; hp 15; THAC0 17; #AT 1; Dmg 1d8 (bite); Save F3; SZ L (8′ diameter); MV 12; ML 13; XP 975/ea.

Note: The mounts for the Spider's goblins are a type of giant spider indigenous only to the Spiderfell. They act as steeder spiders (see the MONSTROUS MANUAL tome) for the goblins.

REGENT: The Spider.

LIEUTENANTS: Two goblins and gnolls stand with the Spider at all times, taking orders from the insane awnshegh and translating the ranting into recognizable orders for the troops. This assignment rotates among the spider's many minions.

IMPORTANT NPCs: Rumors from Ghoere talk of an elf assassin, Denin the Mutable, who has infiltrated the Spiderfell. A master magician, he can alter his shape to match his surroundings. He is apparently so good at hiding himself that rangers are unable to track him or discover his whereabouts. Since no one has found this elusive elf, even those interested in helping his cause, there is no knowing this story's accuracy. If an adventuring party or team of assassins could ever find this elf and gain his trust, assuming he exists, they might discover exactly how he plans on a successful execution of the Spider.

DOMAIN DESCRIPTION: The Spider controls the Spiderfell, a forest that lies in the midst of the lands of Anuire. It's one of the most dangerous, deadly, and foul forests in all Cerilia, filled with natural pitfalls and traps, and crossed by game trails that lead into bogs, quagmires, and webs spun by the spiders or their monstrous ruler. The forest is filled with spiders, goblins, and gnolls, all ready to do the Spider's bidding.

Centuries have passed since anyone tried to usurp the Spider's position or power; tales that still circulate around the campfires do well to keep any insurgents quiet. The Spiderfell is a legacy to the Spider's cunning in that it has survived this long among so many realms hostile to its existence.

DOMAIN CAPITAL: The Web

TRADE GOODS: The Spiderfell exports nothing. Imports include whatever the raiding parties find in their assaults on nearby territories.

ENEMIES: The realms of Ghoere, Roesone, Medoere, and Diemed are all fearful of the Spider's power, but they do not attack the Spiderfell itself. They do keep heavily armed patrols around the forest when the raiders make themselves known outside the treeline.

SPECIAL CONDITIONS: The Web would hardly be seen as a city, let alone a domain capital, in any other land in Anuire, but this settlement of goblins is the seat of the Spider's power. Nestled among the trees at the center of the Spiderfell, the Web is a collection of dwellings carved out of the living trees themselves, with platforms and huts attached to the trees. These dwellings are connected from tree to tree by rope bridges.

the vampire

The Sinister and my battle with it signalled both the end and the beginning of my life. When I was simply young Britter Kalt, I was eager to please those in power, including my liege. He requested the aid of any heroes of power in ridding his lands of the ravages of an awnshegh known as the Sinister. For years, I and my companions had hunted the lesser awnshegh in Rohrmarch and Kiergard. This time, we answered the call and faced the abomination in its own lair.

"It was truly a simple matter to slay the Sinister, as it had become powerful but lazy and used to slaying foes at a distance. It was unprepared to face one of my bravery and strength, for when I closed with it to fight with my sword, he quickly fell. Even his mighty gaze that turned other men to vapor was ineffectual in stopping my killing blow! Finally, I had met a foe worthy of my ability and I had slain it, gaining much of its power. As I had been angry beyond belief and partially transformed to mist when I was struck by the dying Sinister's energies, my corporeal form reconstituted itself in a form that was anger personified.

"After that, I looked around to find that I had always been willing to sacrifice all for the good of my liege lord, but he was not willing to sacrifice anything for me. I saved his land from the Sinister—I performed his regal duties of protecting his people! If I was to bear a ruler's responsibilities, I was due a ruler's crown. Therefore, I slew my former, undeserving lord and claimed the territory as mine.

"Now, everyone in my domain gains what they work for and what they deserve. If they do what I deem best for them, they live happy and prosperous lives. I alone know what is best for my people, and that is what is best for me." Kalt slew the Sinister and became an equally dangerous awnshegh that was soon known as the Vampire. While my sages' interview with the Vampire was a little sparse in detail on its rise to power, recorded histories within Kiergard tell us the beginning of the tale and a journal of one of his surviving comrades sheds some light on the birth of the Vampire.

Approximately 1100 years ago, a Brecht warrior named Britter Kalt was honor bound to kill the being that slew his father. The being that murdered his kind and noble father was the Sinister, a three-eyed being of unimaginable fright and ruinous power. When his prince beseeched warriors to gather and slay the Sinister, Britter knew he had to slay the beast in order to regain his family's honor and some recognition of his own heroism and bravery.

It took Britter and his companions two years to finally locate the location of the awnshegh, as the Sinister survived by staying mobile at all times. Britter became obsessed in his search for this evil being, and he was quite ruthless in using every means at his disposal to reach his goal and kill the Sinister. As he readied himself for the battle at the Sinister's refuge in the Vicissitude Mountains, he seemed a man possessed and on the verge of madness now that his goal of many years was within reach.

Acromeire, a long-time acquaintance of young Kalt and his father and one of his companions on the quest for the Sinister, was the only other surviving member of that expedition. He lived for 15 years after the encounter, and he penned the only written account of Britter Kalt's battle with the Sinister. The excerpt below, in Acromeire's own words, gives some startling details about both the Sinister, the Vampire that was once Britter Kalt, and the effects of bloodtheft.

"Though we had heard stories of the Sinister and its malevolent power, we had never seen its effects at hand, and only knew we had our mission to slay this foul abomination. Britter had stopped talking to anyone days before, just after we left the city, and there was nothing in his stance or his eyes but burning hatred. When we arrived at the noisome cavern that allegedly housed the Sinister, Britter dashed inside immediately without regard for his own or anyone else's safety. We were to pay for that.

"I fought alongside the elder Kalt and his young son against many evils that terrorized the forests of Kiergard, Rohrmarch, and Massenmarch. I was never so afraid as when we hastily entered the lair of the Sinister. The cold dankness and gloom of the cave was heightened by the sight of shattered swords, rent shields, and the rotted remains of those who came before us.

"Suddenly, without warning or fanfare, it was upon us. To this day, I shudder as I remember poor Runthar, a hearty ranger with a rumbling laugh, screaming pitifully as he dissolved into a

fog and swirled upward and out of sight overhead. As I later found, the Sinister's main power was to turn its opponents to mist and absorb them into itself for added strength and vitality. All but three of us fell to the the deadly gaze of the Sinister, as it cattily loomed over us in the darkness of the cavern's high ceiling. When my enchanted arrows finally brought it to ground, it was only slightly wounded. It managed to knock me out with a backhanded slap that sent me into a rock wall. As my eyes clouded over, I saw him mercilessly tear our wizardess companion to pieces.

"When I came to moments later, Britter Kalt was toe-to-toe with the Sinister, his magical blade glowing brightly against the gloom and illuminating his enrapt face and that of the furious Sinister. The awnshegh appeared to have forgotten all others and was now bringing his gaze to bear on young Kalt. Britter's legs began to become hazy and mistlike, and the Sinister laughed; it was its final mistake, as the enraged Britter Kalt buried his father's enchanted sword into the cackling creature even as his arms lost their solidity.

"As the body of the Sinister fell to the floor of the cave, the mist that was once Britter Kalt was inundated with wild energies that exploded from the collapsed body of the awnshegh. A shrick of agony echoed off the cave walls, louder than the crackling energy of the Sinister's birthright emanations. I shielded my eyes for but a moment,

and when I looked again, what I saw turned my hair white and shook me to my very core.

"Britter Kalt stood with us once again, but he was changed, poisoned by the touch of Azrai's blood from the Sinister. While he still appeared as Britter, his teeth and ears had grown sharp points, his skin was like alabaster, and his metal armor was replaced by armor made of shadow that glistened most unnaturally. I did not know at the time exactly what had overcome my young friend, but he helped me return to the city and report the Sinister's death to the prince. Had I known then what he had planned in his obsessive mind, I would have tried to slay him myself before we returned.

"He had seemed a bit distracted on our return trip, but I attributed that to a usual reticence after such a brutal battle. When we arrived and were granted audience with the king, we were offered much gold and high honors. Britter ignored all of it and stalked up to our ruler; after easily batting away four personal guards, he executed our helpless ruler, threw his body to the floor, and sat down upon his throne. That was the last day the sun shone brightly in what is now the Vampire's Domain."

INTELLIGENCE: 14
ACTIVITY CYCLE: Night
DIET: Hemovore (blood)
ALIGNMENT: Chaotic evil
MOVEMENT: 12, Fl 32 (B)
SIZE: M (6½)' tall)
ARMOR CLASS: 2
HIT POINTS: 116
SAVES AS: F10
THAC0: 11
NO. OF ATTACKS: 1
DAMAGE/ATTACK: 3d4 (claws) or by weapon
SPECIAL ATTACKS: Life draining attack
SPECIAL DEFENSES: Darkness, immune to normal weapons.
MR: 15%
MORALE: 18
BLOOD: Major (Azrai) 49
BLOOD ABILITIES: Bloodform (Great), Regeneration (Minor), Shadow Form (Great), Travel (Great)
XP VALUE: 15,000

S: 18/00 (+3/+8) D: 17 C: 20 (+6 hp/level)
I: 14 W: 12 Ch: 15

The Vampire is totally ruthless and has no honor—it will do anything to destroy a foe. The Vampire's most common attack is its claws, which cause 3-12 points of damage. If it chooses to wield a weapon, it wields it with 18/00 Strength and adds bonuses accordingly; its primary weapon is the *long sword +3* that slew the Sinister—its once silver-white metal has turned black over the years.

If the Vampire makes two successful attack rolls in one round, he inflicts no damage but grabs his target and bites its neck. After one round, during which the Vampire only holds and bites its prey, the held victim is dead, its body a dessicated husk, and the Vampire gains one permanent hit point per level or Hit Die of the victim. Blooded victims are drained of blood abilities as if he has used a tighmaevril weapon to slay them. Victims can attempt to break free when first grabbed (Strength check at -4 penalty against the Vampire's hold); if still held, they need a successful saving throw vs. death magic to resist the Vampire's bite. If successful, they only suffer 2d4 points of damage and are stunned for 1d6 rounds.

For defenses, the Vampire's form naturally attracts darkness, keeping him in an almost eternal twilight. During nighttime hours, the Vampire's cloak of shadow grants it a +3 Armor Class bonus and a +3 bonus against any light- or vision-based attacks and spells.

The Vampire has batlike wings that fold against its back, and can use them only at night; if his wings are unfolded outside of his aura of darkness in sunlight, they begin to burn, dealing 1d12 points of damage to the Vampire per turn and preventing him from using the wings for 1d6 hours.

Finally, the Vampire's most dangerous ability is its combined *shadow form* and *travel* blood abilities. Unlike the standard forms of these abilities, the Vampire can reduce his form to a dark mist three times a night or once during daylight. It uses this form to flee by transporting itself to the Shadow World at any location, creating his own portal with this variant power. If used during the day, it cannot teleport, only fly slowly (9 Move rate, Maneuverability E) but is immune to attacks of any less than +2 enchantments, though spells affect it.

REALM NAME: The Vampire's Realm.
LOCATION: South of Massenmarch.
STATUS: Not available for PC use.
ALIGNMENT: Chaotic evil
PROVINCES/HOLDINGS: The three provinces of the Vampire's Domain are Bloodshroud (4/3), Landsborough (3/4), and Ruapacht (1/7).

Law: The Vampire controls his three generals and the armies through them, thus holding all law powers in his domain.

Temples: Cults to Haelyn and other gods are growing in the domain, but the only temples are dedicated to Kriestal and Alenecht. All the Vampire's soldiers are worshippers there, and the high priest is among the Vampire's highest ranking lieutenants.

Guilds: The Vampire allows his minister of finance to control trade and internal taxation.

Sources: All magical sources within this domain are currently uncontrolled.

Province	Law	Temples	Guilds	Sources
Bloodshroud (4/5)	Vp (4)	Al (2) Kr (2)	Vp (3)	—
Landsborough (3/6)	Vp (3)	Al (2)	Vp (1)	—
Ruapacht (3/6)	Vp (1)	Kr (1)	Vp (1)	—

Abbreviations: Vp=the Vampire; Al=Black Church of Alenecht (Gustaf Kremler); Kr=Temple of the White Hand of Kriestal (Karyana Darnov).

REGENCY GENERATED/ACCUMULATED: 16/40 RP
GOLD GENERATED/ACCUMULATED: 8/8 GB

ARMY: The Vampire keeps a standing army within his domain to crush any internal dissidence. While it might normally equal three units of human infantry and one cavalry unit, they are never collected as an army to invade other domains or protect the entire domain. The units are scattered among the settlements of the domain, keeping nearly every person that lives within the domain borders under strict martial law. The army enforces the implied law of the land: The Vampire, your deserving ruler, wishes you to be happy. Be happy or be dead.

The only army the Vampire wields against outlying domains is a swarm of bats that he commands through the use of a special amulet. He only resorts to this tactic if he hears rumors of troops massing against him; he *travels* through the Shadow World to scatter the assembling armies, and his bats lend additional

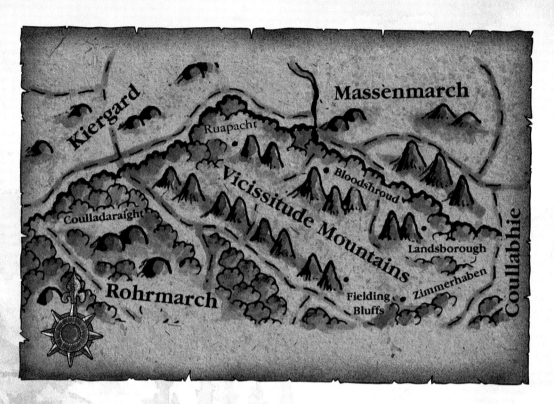

confusion and fear. This warning served him well in deterring two campaigns against him.

REGENT: The Vampire
LIEUTENANTS: The Vampire has three generals who maintain the order in his domain by their local control of the military personnel in each province: General Karl Haasen of Bloodshroud, General Henricht VonStaffel of Landsborough, and General Josef Bellshauf of Ruapacht. The three men work well together, supporting each other's actions along provincial borders whenever necessary, making their efforts successful and bloody.

The high priest of the Black Church of Alenecht is Gustaf Kremler (MAw/P11/Az9)/CE), and he frequently makes trips through each of the provinces with the generals, "converting" the people to the worship of darkness. Most often, he conscripts the farmers and peasants into work on his major temple at the capital at Bloodshroud.

IMPORTANT NPCs: Two new champions are gaining public popularity, though not such widespread popular support as to bring them to the Vampire's notice. These champions hail from Zimmerhaben and Ruapacht.

Zimmerhaben's champion, Roe Se'ame, is a young woman of fine standing who returned to her Zimmerhaben home after a five-year conscripted stint in the Vampire's army. She's gathered a small following, mostly the young (25 years of age and younger), who are tired of living under the tyranny of the Vampire. They want to see a ruler who does not wage war and injustice against his own people. Landsborough, a town in the same province, has been showing signs of support for this beautiful champion, who regularly convenes dissident meetings late at night in some of Zimmerhaben's taverns.

Ruapacht's champion, Josef Bladesmith, is an elderly man in his 70's, an unusual lifespan for a human in this area. He wants to change his homeland from its basis on military might and violence to one based on education and knowledge. He believes that by creating a land of peace in the midst of the current chaos, the domain will flourish and nearby provinces from other domains—or even full domains—will flock under its banner.

but these are unsubstantiated. Others talk of an alliance with Massenmarch, though those close to the Swordhawk laugh at such a suggestion.

DOMAIN DESCRIPTION: The Vampire's domain contains three mountain ranges that cut across the land from northwest-to-southeast. Heavy, deciduous forests cover the rest of the land. Small pockets of cleared land and trails between them allow the few towns and villages of this domain to survive.

The people living in the larger towns and the cities are now expanding the land for crops by cutting down the trees and using the timber to build new homes, and to continually improve the capital city of Bloodshroud.

Bloodshroud, though it contains about 2,000 people, has wood-slat streets, elevated sidewalks, and beautifully reconditioned homes and buildings; the smell of cedar still is strong. It is a growing city, despite the oppression of the Vampire's centuries-old regime, though what grows quickest in it are thoughts of rebellion. These pockets of rebellion and their champions, thus far, have been suppressed, but they have yet to be totally eradicated.

DOMAIN CAPITAL: Bloodshroud.
DOMAIN CITIES: Ruapacht.
DOMAIN VILLAGES: Fielding Bluffs, Landsborough, Zimmerhaben.
SPECIAL LOCATIONS: Vicissitude Mountains.

TRADE GOODS: The Vampire must import at least one-third of the consumed food in his domain from outside, and much of his trade comes from Massenmarch. The greatest export the Vampire has is minerals. The unstable Vicissitudes are unusually rich in gold deposits, iron, and a sulfurous mineral called uxoricore. When put in contact with liquids like water or blood, uxoricore heats up very quickly, causing incredible burns to anything touching it. This deadly mineral is stored in ceramic jars far away from the mines. The Vampire uses captured goblins to shape arrowheads from this soft ore. When used in weapon construction, the uxoricore adds 1d6 points of burn damage on top of normal weapon damage (no saving throw allowed).
ALLIES: The Vampire has no allies, though he has several domains that "tolerate" him because of the threat they fear he poses. Rumors tell of a planned movement to overthrow Kiergard,

SPECIAL CONDITIONS: The Vicissitudes are the southernmost mountain range of unstable peaks in the Vampire's Domain. In one human lifetime, they've expanded, grown, and altered in response to great earthquakes reported in Rohrmarch to the south. Bloodshroud is a constantly-remodeled, beautiful, yet dark town nestled among these mountains that serve as the home of the Vampire.

Permits for intercity travel are needed wherever one goes. Permits are also needed for hunting, fishing, and trapping. Anyone traveling the roads (especially at night) is stopped and checked for papers. If they're not in order, the traveler is immediately incarcerated and put to work in the mines by Fielding Bluffs or as the labor for the official buildings in Bloodshroud.

The Vampire has uncovered the dissident Josef Bladesmith, but is currently studying the exact threat he poses. Rumors state that the Vampire plans to crush the life from this frail man only when he becomes a true nuisance or when the Vampire is in need of a diversion.

Recently, alchemists and magicians from across the land have petitioned the Vampire for permission to study the Vicissitudes. This unusual mountain range is highly active and these wise men believe that many questions regarding nature and its effects on magic can be answered here. The Vampire has allowed this, but he charges extraordinary fees for "protection" during their stays. This money has been most recently used to procure high-quality and (relatively) trustworthy mercenaries for deeds unknown to all but the Vampire. Little information has been made public by these Kiergardian and Binsadan sages, though news is expected within the year.

the white witch

I am the White Witch. That is all anyone truly need call me. Do not concern yourselves with where I come from and from whence I gain my awesome powers—only those of the blood of royalty and the gods need to concern themselves of such things.

I am the mistress of one of the largest realms in all Cerilia and that, in itself, is a great responsibility. I am the most beautiful creation on the face of the land—that, too, carries with it great responsibility. I must always deal with suitors who feel they are qualified to spend their mediocre lives in my presence, though very few are worthy of such a boon.

"I am a great leader and my children have never felt the invasive forces of an enemy since my uncle's weak-spined rule was overthrown. My financial genius and my magic have ensured that my children have never felt hunger. I am a shrewd arbitrator and I never lose when it comes to negotiation. I am constantly looking for ways to expand the borders of my domain in order to more properly provide my children with whatever they need or desire. Soon, the entire northern half of this continent will belong to the children of the White Witch. For they, and I, deserve it."

The White Witch is egotistical and arrogant beyond many of the other awnsheghlien. She believes she's the best at everything, and to some extent, she's correct. As the leader of one of the largest realms on the continent, she has some support toward her thoughts of greatness.

She claims to be a great leader, and it's impossible to prove this allegation wrong, unless the leader is absolutely tyrannical. Some in her realm believe she is a great sovereign, while others disagree. Despite this split, she has maintained the safety of her sovereign lands. She or her underlings have kept the borders clear of invaders for years; in fact, the White Witch's forces have expanded into nearby domains, on occasion without the knowledge of the invaded domain's leader.

The White Witch is a financial genius. If one considers that she receives very little in taxes but manages to wage war and infiltrate guilds in nearby domains, it's frightening to think of what she could accomplish with the monetary diet of a country like Ghoere or Mhoried. Thus far, she controls much of the guild activity in Hogunmark, Red Skull Barony, and Lluabraight.

She takes credit for the lack of starvation in her country, but she really has no part in feeding her people. Most of her provinces contain self-sustaining individuals who sustenance hunt and fish, and gather and store food during the warmer months. They often sell furs and jerked meats from their kills in order to pay the taxes demanded from them. These hearty folk also protect their personal lands jealously from any intrusion. Often, the arrival of a tax collector is considered an intrusion; given the retribution associated with the death of an official of the domain ruler, few resist the light taxes, though they do not relish them.

Stories and tales about the White Witch are numerous, and a number of written sources in Anuire and parts north and east of it have conflicting accounts of who she is and what she looks like. The only facts that agree across most accounts are that she is the niece of a usurper jarl named Gunnar, though none can trace a given birth name to her. Upon her ascension to rule, she became the White Witch. Since ascending to the throne, she has emerged from her castle at Mandal only twelve times, and only to go to war.

Some talk of the White Witch as the most beautiful woman in personality and form. Standing over 5 feet tall, she has a long mane of frost-white hair and the lithe figure of a young girl, even though she has ruled her domain for over 30 years. She reportedly prefers elegant silk dresses that cling to her shape as clothing.

Other sources tell a different story of the Witch, reporting her to be a very ugly old woman. This disgusting, twisted crone was summarized as being highly vindictive, using magic to infiltrate the minds of men and to bend their wills to her bidding.

Both forms are reported to be powerful priestesses, though the young, beautiful White Witch is more inclined to use items of power, and the crone is more apt to use spells. Well, our research has discovered that both the crone and the beautiful winter maiden are one and the same—the White Witch shows her young face and form to her public, and she only reveals her twisted, true form to her immediate lieutenants and military advisors.

According to the recently penned *Theocrats of Mystical Forces* (a definitive tome on practitioners of magic in Cerilia), the White Witch uses magical items and spells of her own device to change her appearance. The items can be used to make her appear as a captivatingly beautiful woman. The side effect of these items, however, also alter her personality, making her several shades kinder. With this benign attitude, she can't negotiate with her usual ruthlessness, so she refrains from it. The White Witch realizes this fallacy when the items and spells are in effect, and she can refuse to negotiate under these terms as well.

When the spells and items are not in effect, the White Witch is a shrewd negotiator. When negotiating a treaty, haggling for hunting or logging rights or bargaining in business deals, she's always in cloaked in darkness and hidden from direct view. Her most effective tactic is to appear as her young self, flatter guests and negotiators over dinner, and excuse herself early, but invite a negotiator to her chambers for further discussions. Once there, she drops her illusions, keeping her voice the same and hiding behind bed curtains and darkness, and continues a harsher negotiation while her guest is off-balance and distracted by the setting.

The White Witch, in her normal nonillusory form, is psychotic and must always get her way. When she doesn't, she uses her *charm aura* ability or spells to increase her effectiveness. She has grown to rely on her *charm aura* in all her dealings, making her extremely successful. When this tactic fails (against elves, half-elves, and people and awnsheghlien with a natural immunity to *charm*), she threatens with spells and military might, in hopes of forcing them into submission through threat of widespread harm and *curses*.

Without Illusion		With Illusion
20	INTELLIGENCE	20
9	CHARISMA	19
Any	ACTIVITY CYCLE	Any
Omnivore	DIET	Omnivore
Neutral evil	ALIGNMENT	Lawful good
12	MOVEMENT	12
M (5′ 1″ tall)	SIZE	M (5′ 6″ tall)
3	ARMOR CLASS	6
45	HIT POINTS	45
P14	SAVES AS	P14
13	THAC0	13
1	NO. OF ATTACKS	1
By weapon	DAMAGE/ATTACK	By weapon
Charm, Spells	SPECIAL ATT	Charm, Spells
Nil	SPECIAL DEF	Nil
Nil	MR	Nil
13	MORALE	10
13,000	XP VALUE	13,000

BLOOD: Minor (Azrai) 20

BLOOD ABILITIES: Charm Aura (Major), Heightened Ability (Minor), Major Resistance—Charm (Great), Persuasion (Major), Unreadable Thoughts (Minor).

The White Witch abstains from physical combat and allows her guards to contain and remove any physical threat to her person. If necessary, she carries a small jewelled dagger in an ankle scabbard that's hid by her long gowns. She supports her guards by casting spells, if trouble arises. The White Witch can cast spells as a 14th-level priestess of Karesha, and the spells she often receives are listed below.

1st-level: *Bless/curse, command, cure/cause light wounds, detect evil/good, detect magic, invisibility to undead, magical stone, protection from evil/good, purify/putrefy food & drink, remove fear.*

2nd-level: *Augury, enthrall, fire trap, heat metal hold person, resist fire/cold, silence 15′ radius, spiritual hammer, wyvern watch.*

3rd-level: *Call lightning, change self, dispel magic, feign death, glyph of warding, magical vestment, meld into stone, prayer.*

4th-level: *Cloak of bravery, control temperature 10′ radius, divination, free action, imbue with spell ability, improved invisibility, produce fire, reflecting pool, tongues.*

5th-level: *Atonement, communion, divination, plane shift, quest.*

6th-level: *Blade barrier, weather summoning, word of recall.*

7th-level: *Confusion, exaction.*

MAGICAL ITEMS: The White Witch has one of the largest collections of magical items in Cerilia, and she uses them to maintain her rule over her large domain.

Wintering: The White Witch always wears one item, a ring of artifact status called *Wintering*. Upon her ascension to the throne of this domain, the priestess who is now the White Witch was visited in a dream by Karasha and granted a gift to further her power in Cerilia. When she awoke, the *wintering* was on her finger, where it still remains today. The ring has the following powers at 12th level:

✦ all the powers of a *ring of warmth*;
✦ Immunity to cold-based damage;
✦ *Flashfrost*, an effect identical in effect to a *fireball* spell but with a wave of cold;
✦ *Ice storm*, three times per day; and
✦ *Weather summoning* to call a blizzard, once per week.

The Ring of Beauty: The other most constant item she uses is her *ring of beauty*, which is responsible for her transformation from crone to beautiful maiden. Not simply an illusion, but a limited *polymorph self* that alters any being to the brink of perfect physical beauty. In terms of game mechanics, it adds a +8 Reaction bonus for the Witch and +10 Charisma from the character's normal base score. The *ring of beauty's* only side effect alters the wearer's alignment to lawful good and renders the wearer incapable of deceit; the wearer is aware of the personality change, and can avoid any circumstances that might reveal any deception. If the ring-wearer wished to steal something or behave in other than a lawful or good manner, he or she would have to remove the ring.

REALM NAME: Realm of the White Witch.
LOCATION: North of Giantdowns.
STATUS: Not Available for PC use.
ALIGNMENT: Lawful evil

PROVINCES/HOLDINGS: The White Witch keeps a firm grip on all holdings in her domain, whether controlling the fur trade through taxes or the law with her armies. She covetously guards her magical sources, though one in Vejle was claimed by a new settler there, a Rjurik mage called Ohlaak the Dragon; the White Witch plans on removing this usurper soon. Aside from small shrines on the tundra or personal shrines to gods in peoples' homes, the only temples in the domain are the grand temple to Karasha by the Witch's castle at Mandal, and the lesser temples at Oulu and Boden.

REGENCY GENERATED/ACCUMULATED: 44/20 RP
GOLD GENERATED/ACCUMULATED: 20/5 GB.

ARMY: The Witch Witch's army is split into two groups. The first group consists of her personal guards, which equal one unit of elite foot soldiers. The other group in the army is five units of soldiers. The Witch can collect an additional three units of levied troops within one month's time in her domain.

Elite Guard (50): Int 13-14; AL LN; AC 7; HD 2; hp 12; THAC0 19; #AT 1; Dmg 1d8; SZ (M 6' tall); MV 12; ML 16; XP 65/ea.

Rjurik Irregulars (500): Int 9-12; AL LN; AC 9; HD 1; hp 7; THAC0 20; #AT 1; Dmg 1d6; SZ (M 6' tall); MV 12; ML 13; XP 35/ea.

REGENT: The White Witch.

LIEUTENANTS: The Witch has no immediate lieutenants save her personal guard, Captain Haghar. He is a mountain of a man, and he is one of few who does

Province	Law	Temples	Guilds	Sources
Bjornoya (1/6)	WW (1)	—	—	—
Boden (2/3)	WW (2)	Kar (2)	WW (1)	—
Folda Fjord (1/4)	WW (1)	—	WW (1)	—
Halten (0/7)	—	—	—	—
Innherad (0/7)	—	—	—	—
Kandalask (1/4)	WW (1)	—	WW (1)	—
Mandal (4/3)	WW (3)	Kar (4)	WW (4)	—
Nordcapp (0/5)	—	—	—	—
Oulu (3/4)	WW (2)	Kar (3)	WW (3)	—
Pitea (2/3)	WW (1)	—	WW (1)	—
Rovan (1/6)	—	—	—	—
Solung Bank (1/6)	WW (1)	—	WW (1)	—
Soroya (1/4)	—	—	—	—
Torne (0/5)	—	—	—	—
Vejle (1/6)	WW (1)	—	—	Oh (4)

Abbreviations: WW=the White Witch; Kar=Great White Church of Karasha (the White Witch); Oh=Ohlaak the Dragon.

not flinch from the White Witch in either form. Haghar has the respect of his Rjurik brethren and is a capable leader, though he dislikes the Witch's excesses. He loathes the Blood Skull orogs and relishes any chance to lead troops over their borders.

DOMAIN DESCRIPTION: The White Witch's domain is a frigid and wind-blown landscape of permafrost and sweeping glaciers in the north and tundra in the central and southern areas.

Each county has one fairly-large community and at least one other tiny settlement with at least a trading post, a lodge that often serves as an inn and a tavern, and two or three other buildings for housing of animals or vagabonds, a slaughterhouse, or food storage for the clan.

DOMAIN CAPITAL: Mandal.
DOMAIN CITIES: Boden, Oulu.
DOMAIN VILLAGES: Bjornoya, Folda Fjord, Halten, Innherad, Kandalask Guba, Nordcapp, Pitea, Rovan, Solung Bank, Soroya, Torne, Vejle.
SPECIAL LOCATIONS: Folda Fjord, Kandalask Guba, Solung Bank.
TRADE GOODS: The domain's major exports, and the only ones widespread enough to merit attention, are furs and meat. The domain imports grain goods from the south.

ENEMIES: The White Witch is not on friendly terms with any nearby domain, though open hostility only crops up during the summer when travel is feasible across the northern plains. She plans on annexing independent domains that surround her borders one province at a time. Over the past 20 years, she's been successful at adding seven provinces to her domain.

SPECIAL CONDITIONS: A few centuries ago, rumors of the existence of a strange awnshegh circulated throughout the northern realms. These rumors claimed that an alluring shadow of inky blackness flowed across the land. This darkness was the supreme ruler over all it surveyed, and no other ruler could dare annex the land. This sable vapor would sap the strength and the health from whomever it surrounded. The onyx cloud never killed anyone outright, but its touch would leave a person bedridden for days after contact (3d10 days). The people who lived in the area learned to avoid the mist when possible.

Sages still argue over whether these accounts were either completely fictitious or not. Those who believe these stories now hypothesize that the jet mist was either an early version of the Apocalypse or another evil gas form of malevolence. Few think that the two creatures are one in the same, as accounts and rumors of the effects matching those of the Apocalypse have never been reported further north than the Sielwode. Since the appearance of the White Witch perfectly followed the disappearance of the life-tapping cloud, many believe she knows something about it and its withdrawal from activity. There are those who believe the black cloud still exists, but is currently dormant. If this is true, it should be interesting how the White Witch and the nearby domains react to it when it arises and terrorizes their territories anew after 30 years.

the wolf

The Wolf is a mysterious and shy beast that is rarely seen outside its current territory; its range of movement is known to change with the seasons and the encroachment of elven and human settlers, but there has been little change in its territory in decades. Wolfgaard, the official name for the Wolf's territory, can be found in the inhospitable terrain south of the Hag's Domain and north of Grevesmühl, bordering on the eastern edge of Krakenspiel Bay. Wolfgaard, while mapped and referred to as a distinct and separate domain, is simply an independent group of provinces under the regency and control of Hjorig.

Our interviewer, an Anuirean named Shaeron, and her guide, Naple of Grabentob, were among the first recorded people to ever encounter the Wolf in a nonaggressive manner. Shaeron was chosen for her rogue talents of telepathy and empathy; as advised by Daznig, she kept a complete diary of the trip. This journal has her thoughts, her feelings, and experiences while on this tour into Wolfgaard.

Day 33: For over one month, we've made an intensive search for the Wolf, but have found no trace of the beast whatsoever. Could the existence of this creature be merely a rumor?

Day 42: Naple found a large scat pile from a predator about an hour before camp (bone chips were found in it). Two-day old tracks from a large canine lead from the deposit and head to the north.

Day 47: We've followed the tracks for five days into progressively denser woods. Naple thinks the beast is hunting—tracks show signs of jumps in speed and erratic movements.

Day 50: Today, the tracks are very fresh, and they lead right up to a large crag of rock. We found a bedding that appears to have been used just a few hours ago. Naple has been finding territorial markings on trees and outcroppings, so he thinks we're very close to the creature's den.

About an hour before we set up camp, Naple suddenly felt very uncomfortable. I could see the color drain from his face, and he complained of being watched. We searched around after five terrifying minutes, and we found fresh tracks of a canine beast—the Wolf was watching us! It may have been watching us for hours, or even days.

Day 51: Today we spotted the creature's den. It was about one mile away from last night's camp site, and we decided to set camp within sight of the cave opening. We were very conscious of the noise we made because we didn't want to disturb or irritate the Wolf.

Day 60: We've seen the Wolf several times each day since our arrival. Last evening it spent about 45 minutes staring at us. I think it was wondering what we're doing here and if we pose a threat.

Day 72: The Wolf was in our camp last night. It ate some food, stole a pack of supplies, and marked the entrance to our tent. Its tracks come up to the fire—I thought all animals were frightened of fire.

I later established an empathic link with the beast for the first time and was surprised at the result. The Wolf seethes with emotion and seems capable of a full range of emotional responses. The emotion from this creature was far stronger than any I've ever felt.

Day 100: I've come to the opinion that the Wolf is a highly emotional creature. Sometimes the emotions are so strong that I get pulled into their continual ebb and flow. I'm going to try a telepathic link next, to find out more.

Day 130: I haven't yet telepathically linked with the Wolf, but there's still so much to learn. Naple and I haven't been agreeing recently, and he complains that I've become obsessive. I think he's jealous, and I find that so irritating. I've stopped trying to explain the situation to him. He just doesn't know.

Day 138: Today I tried a telepathic link with the Wolf and I was amazed. He is intelligent, but his thought processes are very different from our own. A refreshing innocence pervades his mind. His only concern is with "the now" and he lives with more vigor and amazement than a young child.

Day 156: I've linked telepathically with the Wolf every day for several weeks. I can't believe the simplicity of his thoughts when compared to the complexity of his emotions.

Note: After this point in the diary, the narration is executed by Naple.

Day 177: I think Shaeron has lost control of her wits. I considered forcing her from the area but I'm afraid she's got some link with the Wolf and might convince him to attack. I've stopped talking with her, as she makes less sense each day. She speaks of things that either don't matter or about things I don't understand. Shaeron's even talking in a guttural language at times, and I've no idea what she says.

Day 191: The Wolf and Shaeron ran into the woods together. Very late in the evening, they came back dragging a moose carcass. I moved to cut a piece off for my supper but was met with two pairs of devilish eyes and bared teeth. I ended up waiting until they were done with their binge and asleep before I ate.

Day 202: I can't tell who's more the beast anymore—Shaeron or the Wolf. It shows more human qualities than she does now. I decided to leave her, as she's attached to the Wolf in many ways. Maybe someone smarter can save her, but I am only able to watch her become a madwoman who wishes to be a wolf.

INTELLIGENCE: Low (7)
ACTIVITY CYCLE: Any
DIET: Carnivore
ALIGNMENT: Neutral
MOVEMENT: 18
SIZE: L (9′ long)
ARMOR CLASS: 5
HIT POINTS: 46
SAVES AS: F6
THAC0: 15
NO. OF ATTACKS: 1 or 2
DAMAGE/ATTACK: 2d6 (bite) or 1d8/1d8 (paws)
SPECIAL ATTACKS: Nil
SPECIAL DEFENSES: Nil
MR: Nil
MORALE: Elite (13)
BLOOD: Tainted (Azrai) 11
BLOOD ABILITIES: Bloodmark (Minor), Heightened Ability—Intelligence (Minor), Major Resistance—Nonmagical Attack (Minor).
XP VALUE: 1,400

The Wolf is not the fearsome beast that everyone suspects it is. When it's hungry, it kills, preferring to kill things with less intelligence than himself: Intelligence tends to bring out caution in the creature.

The Wolf either consumed a being with Azrai's blood or was infected in an unknown way. It is a blooded awnshegh, but all this taint has done is increase its size and intelligence.

The Wolf is content in the security of the woods uninhabited by humanity. It prefers to move to a different spot rather than share its territory with a large number of humans or humanoids. The Wolf has moved its territory three times. First, it was located in southern Drachenward, but it left the area when a dragon attacked it. The Wolf moved to the eastern part of the Hag's territory, but a forest fire forced it west into Grabentod. The Wolf stayed there until its territory was invaded by humans, who established a settlement to mine gold from the mountains. The Wolf then moved into its new location, the westernmost provinces of Hjorig. The Wolf seems to like this current home, as it has fended off three human and one goblin incursions into its territory.

If attacked or threatened, the Wolf can attack with its paws, striking opponents for 1-8 points of damage per forepaw, or its bite, which deals 2-12 points of damage. There is no threat of disease from the Wolf's bite unless the wound is left open and exposed to dirt or other substances. The Wolf only turns tail and tries to escape its opponents only when there is an overwhelming force against it.

Shaeron is a 5th-level diviner with minor access to the enchantment/charm and abjuration spheres, and she has talents of empathy and telepathy. She's willing to trade perusal of her spellbooks for a *polymorph* spell (or its equivalent) with a *permanency* spell.

PROVINCE NAME: Wolfgaard
LOCATION: South of Drachenward and west of Hjorig
STATUS: Provinces of Hjorig
ALIGNMENT: Neutral
PROVINCES/HOLDINGS: Holde, Nourne, and Sorfeet are the western provinces of Hjorig currently considered part of Wolfgaard. It is sparsely populated with hunters and fishermen, and the small settlements herein are each little more than a trading post, a tavern, and a bunkhouse for those far away from their own shacks in the mountains.

ARMY: The Wolf travels in a pack with eight normal wolves, as per the MONSTROUS MANUAL accessory. Five are males and three are females, and all are subordinate to the Wolf and follow its every lead. They share in the hunting, denmaking, and protecting the den from predators. The Wolf is the breeding male and as such, it is the leader (alpha) of the pack.

Wolves (8): Int 5-6; AL N; AC 7; HD 3; hp 18; THAC0 18; #AT 1; Dmg 1d4+1; SZ (S 3'-4' tall); MV 18; ML 10; XP 120/ea.

IMPORTANT NPCs: Shaeron was a woman with empathic talents who was sent by Daznig to study the Wolf. After her initial stay in Wolfgaard, her companion Naple had to leave her and return with the journal to Alamie for Daznig to study. Shaeron lives two miles from the Wolf's den. She has been trying to change herself into a wolf, but she has no access to alteration spells. Her love for the Wolf runs so deeply that anyone passing close to the Wolf must deal with her first. However, she will befriend spellcasters by giving them food, water, and a place to keep warm. Once she's made friends, she will try to buy a *polymorph* spell.

DOMAIN DESCRIPTION: Wolfgaard includes three provinces—Holde, Nourne, and Sorfeet—and Hjorig has not received the Wolf well. When it first appeared in their western provinces, many soldiers were dispatched to rid Hjorig of the enemy. Apparently, the Wolf decided to make a stand. After nearly 30 deaths, Hjorig ceded the territory to the Wolf and set up ley lines leading back into Hjorig to tap the magic the land naturally carries.

Because the Wolf is so feared, the area has been cut off from the rest of Hjorig. Taxes are sometimes taken from the human populace, but this is infrequent at best. Few taxmasters willingly journey to the area, choosing instead to say they were robbed in the Wolfgaard woods.

At this juncture, I, Daznig, have taken the liberty of collating and organizing a wide number of legends, tall tales, eyewitness accounts, and other reliable or questionable sources to provide the kind reader with a wide range of knowledge on a number of other blooded scions that roam Cerilia. These entries are little more than rumors and tales, for that is all that could be ascertained about these persons without even more grave risks by my associates. Needless to say, they were sufficiently rattled by interviewing the Gorgon, Lamia, and other such notables that no amount of coercion could convince them to continue their researches on these beings noted below. As such, it is imperative that the reader understand that these notations are a combination of my own theories, what few facts we know about each being, and the few tales that seemed to hold true over a number of tellings. Not everything within the entries can be assumed as true, but neither can one assume that everything is false. Simply judge for yourself, and should you find out more about any of the following creatures of evil or the rare good beings, pray tell you should take steps to reach me at the Imperial City and enlighten me to your new intelligence. And should you bring one to its doom, I should like to know of that as well, for such things are of import to all in Cerilia.

Entries are noted in alphabetical order by their most common name or title. Names are followed by a classification as awnshegh ("Blood of Darkness" for corrupted, inhuman evil creatures), ehrshegh ("Blood of the Light" for altered, nonhumanoid creatures of good), or simply Blooded (for characters and beings of varied bloodlines who have a certain stake with the awnsheghlien or ehrsheghlien).

Binman: (Awnshegh) This grisly being is the result of a horrible experiment conducted over a century ago by a mad wizardess from Sendoure named Danita Kusor. This creature was created by grafting various body parts and limbs from elves, dwarves, and humans together into one form, but it remained inert despite the intense magics used on it. When Kusor was interrupted at

her gruesome work by a wandering awnshegh seeking power, she slew it with spells; as a result, she and what is now known as the Binman each absorbed some of the attacker's fleeting birthright. The Binman became animate, if not quite alive; after an initial period of adjustment, the mute Binman gained control over its body. Having retained some basic warrior's abilities, it attempted to kill Danita Kusor, but only succeeded in forcing her to flee for her life; she now resides in Chimaeron as its namesake awnshegh, the Chimaera. The Binman left behind the ruined tower in the Iron Peaks and headed through Rohrmarch to Binsada.

The Binman currently still wanders the lands of Binsada, Zikala, and Sendoure, seeking a true purpose and more power. It generally kills anyone who challenges it, but it also has befriended thieves and honest folk alike (though said friends are few and far between). The Binman sometimes lends itself out as a mercenary. It has fought against the invading forces of the Sphinx, helped Sendoure ward off an attack by a coalition of orog tribes from Coullabhie, and has worked with adventurers and other awnsheghlien alike in short-term quests of power and gold. Few know or can gauge how much power the Binman wields, and fewer still can guess how it will react in any given circumstance; it is my theory that its component parts had conflicting natures and certain parts of its past lives come to the fore at random. It may be this chaotic nature that protects the Binman from clashes with other blooded creatures, but a battle between the Binman and the Sphinx is inevitable.

lesser awnsheghlien & other npcs

Black Princess: (Awnshegh) Known in varied texts as "First Consort," "Raesene's Lady," or "The Gorgon's Queen," the Black Princess is one of the least encountered yet most fabled of the awnsheghlien. The first wife of the Black Prince Raesene, this raven-haired beauty was called Tara, and she was the sole daughter of a highly placed noble family of Anuire. She was present in her pavilion near the battle of Deismaar, and was thought buried under tons of rock in the final explosions that rocked the mountain. Legends say that she survived the fall of Azrai and the rise of her husband, though no historical accounts tell of her rise from the rubble of Mount Deismaar. Believers of the legends say she has grown to loathe the creature her husband has become, and she bides her time in marshalling her power and learning magic to destroy him. Few speak of how she changed over the years, though one legendary account describes her as an exquisite female whose flesh appears made of solid onyx, her hair and eyes flashing blue and white with lightning. If she still lives, she will be one of the main agents to rally against the Gorgon to bring about his downfall.

Borelas the Badger: (Ehrshegh) Borelas is a human ranger who wanders the great northern woods in Rjurik lands, seeking to protect the lands and people from suffering at the hands of awnsheghlien and other rampaging monsters. A rare, emerging ehrshegh, he has just recently begun a transformation into his totem animal: a badger. His face and left arm are the only parts of him that have been affected. If encountered, he is very soft-spoken, distrustful of strangers to a point, and very careful to leave his hood up and his cloak wrapped around his left arm, keeping his changes hidden. He is uncertain why the changes are happening, but he is confident that his path is true and so maintains his course.

Dame Wither: (Blooded) Within the southern regions of the Coulladaraight in Rheulgard, rumors talk of an old crone who lives deep in the woods with her three sons. Dame Wither, as she is called, acts as a seer, midwife, and minor wizardess for those willing to pay for her services. Where her power comes from, none know, though it is certain she has been alive for nearly 200 years.

Her sons are identical triplets, all three huge, barrel-chested woodcutters with wild manes of flaming-red hair and beards. They are all nearly a century old, but none looks older than his mid-twenties. Known as Bori, Molor, and Tynnos, these men are never without their heavy axes or knives.

If rumors are to be believed, it is best not to cross either Dame Wither or her sons. She may have the *wither touch* of Azrai's blood, though she is not corrupted in body by this taint. Her sons apparently have a peculiar ability to see through each others' eyes and think as one. "All the better to protect Mother," they say.

Diabolyk: (Awnshegh) One of the first true awnsheghlien, the Diabolyk was an enemy of all blooded scions who lived, and he remained nearly equal to the Gorgon in power for centuries until the death of Michael Roele. Originally, the Diabolyk was Daryn Theros, an assassin and spy within Prince Raesene's entourage, and as such he was present at the battle for Mount Deismaar. His *blood-form* abilities became immediately apparent after he slew a number of retainers, absorbing their power; his own body began to run like quicksilver, allowing arrows and swords to pass wholly through him. With this power, Daryn Theros became the Diabolyk, a faceless humanoid whose solidity changed at will. While inherently one of the most dangerous of the early awnsheghlien, he apparently fell victim to the Gorgon over 400 years ago; the Gorgon's then-new ability to paralyze folk with a gaze overpowered the Diabolyk's ability to shift around killing blows. One account describes the final blow that "shattered the Diabolyk into a thousand razor shards of stone that swiftly melted into a pool and drained away into a running stream."

There are some that believe the Diabolyk still lives today and is biding its time and planning revenge against the Gorgon. However, little activity of anything resembling the shifting form of the Diabolyk has been reported in centuries. Of course, the awnshegh was always crafty, even when he was human.

Fae: (Ehrshegh) This stunning woman was once known as Ryllimahr, a elf of such magnificence "that no man of any race could bear to part from her presence once he saw her beauty." She also was a high-ranking elf—some even say she was their queen—in a clan that formerly lived in the Forest of Thuringode. According to legend, her magic grew after the battle at Deismaar and she began to change, her hair shifting to silver and eventually to shining reflective crystal. These changes did not alter her demeanor, which was always agreeable and kind. Eventually, she grew "wings of mist, morning dew, and frost" and flew away over the Krakennauricht, apparently to her death, over 700 years ago. But recent tales from the Hoarfell Mountains tell of a dazzling figure that walks the mountains at moonrise and sings ancient elven ballads. The few elves who claim to have seen her believe this creature of living crystal is the Fae, though those who set out to seek her have never returned.

Faun: (Ehrshegh) Little is known of this particular blooded creature, save that its form is that of a Rjurik man's body with the legs of a goat; many suspect that the Faun is a former druid of Erik. It apparently resides somewhere within the great northern forest that covers the Blood Skull Barony just north of the Silverhead Mountains. Tales tell of the Faun's singing being irresistible to any who hear it. Apparently, those who dance and drink with the Faun "for a night" return to their homes days later but are years older for their diversions.

Garak the Glutton: (Awnshegh) This evil dwarven mercenary fought on Azrai's side at Deismaar and gained much power with the battle's conclusion. This power has cost him much, though, as he has been consumed by a ravenous hunger for over 1,000 years. Garak is a fierce, disagreeable creature to be near, as he still resembles a dwarf only in stature; his jaw and mouth have widened to mirror his hunger, and his skin has adopted a leathery hidelike appearance the color of coal. His hunger drives him to consume everything within reach: food and drink, rock and raw ore, gold and precious stones, or even his own fallen enemies.

Golden Unicorn: (Ehrshegh) An ally and retainer of Haelyn at the battle for Mount Deismaar, Bhaervas

Whyrven was a high priest and healer dedicated to Anduiras. Upon his assumption of power, Bhaervas allowed his *bloodtrait* to overwhelm him to aid him in healing the sick and wounded, as well as protecting his allies from the Black Prince's power-hungry forces. Within a year of Deismaar's fall, Bhaervas had become the Golden Unicorn, and a mere lock of its mane could cure illness while a touch of its horn restored a person's total health and youth. The last record of its presence

within Anuire lands was in a ballad first sung at the height of the Empire; it says the Golden Unicorn galloped off across the waves of the Gulf of Coeranys, vowing to return only after all of Cerilia knew peace and did not need its healing powers. The now-ruined tower of the Whyrven family in northern Aerenwe is still held as a holy place for those pilgrims seeking miracle cures.

Green Man: (Awnshegh) Once a minor elven warrior among Rhuobhe's forces, this young elf held a minor taint of Azrai's power in his blood. Recently, on a raid into Boeruine, this unnamed being slew two human guards (each with a taint of Vorynn's blood) and assumed their power. His entire body took on green hues, and many say his mind shattered that day. Now called the Green Man, this awnshegh is a totally unpredictable hazard to those traveling anywhere within the Aelvinnwode. While his power hardly contests Rhuobhe's, each elf covets the other's power and they have clashed twice in the past year with no apparent result. The Green Man's most unique ability involves travel by leaping into a tree and appearing out of the trunk or branches of another tree, allowing him a quick escape at all times within his own territory.

Hoarfrost: (Awnshegh) No one knows if he still roams the northern coasts of Vosgaard, but mothers still frighten their children with horrific tales of Hoarfrost, an awnshegh that, according to current tellings, kidnapped naughty children and fed them to his pet varsks.

In truth, Hoarfrost was a descendant of one of Kriesha's retainers and a strong bloodline continued through till nearly 50 years ago. The true name of the bloodline is now lost, but the last remaining member of that line became the awnshegh known as Hoarfrost. A burly Vos warrior of enormous height, he had grown a tail and his legs resembled a varsk's; his skin was the color of glacial ice and frigid to the touch; and his scalp and beard were thick with snow at all times. Anything he touched froze, and his icy footprints were once a common sight to natives of Hjorig and Drachenward.

According to a local legend in Icemarch, Hoarfrost fell prey to a giant bird of fire, and he melted away somewhere on the northern plains off Leviathan's Reach. Most Vos believe this to be false, since the Phoenix (the only known creature to fit the description) would not

stray so far from home, and there are recent reports of overflowing spring streams suddenly icing over in Berhagen and Kal Kalathor and freezing sleet falling in a forest in Molochev at midsummer. Hoarfrost himself has not been seen in more than 50 years, but few believe him to be gone entirely.

Kiras: (Awnshegh) Kiras Earthcore, and old dwarf from Mur-Kilad, has proved his worth and loyalty to the Gorgon enough to have been granted the infamous title and position of the "Hand of the Gorgon," the Gorgon's primary enforcer within the Crown. At last sighting eight years ago, Kiras still retained most of his dwarven features, though his hair was falling out at an exaggerated pace. Like the former Black Prince, he is arrogant, takes offense at the slightest hint of insult, and shows a remarkable aptitude and desire for causing others pain.

Current rumors tell of Kiras' fall into awnshegh status. His body now resembles its original shape, but has no features aside from smooth granite skin, a wide fanged maw, and razor sharp talons where fingers once were. It is astonishing to hear of an awnshegh transformation happening so swiftly; one suspects the Gorgon may be punishing him for treasonous plotting. A terror within the Gorgon's Crown, Kiras would certainly be a danger should he go on rampage.

Languis the Protector: (Blooded) While I believe this to be little more than folklore, a number of sources talk of a being most often known as Languis, whose abilities mark him as a scion of the blood. If the stories are held as true, Languis never ate, slept, or drank, but simply acted as a guardian and provider. They say he survived off the goodwill his kindness fostered, and that tragedies force him to move on to another village or family. The last known legend of such a protector placed Languis near the lands of the Basilisk, where the legend mentions the ransacking and destruction of a nearby farming community by a tribe of gnolls. Languis either couldn't fight the gnolls or was lax in his duty. This happened over 40 years ago, and no current tales are told of Languis the Protector.

Meson the Wolfman:

(Awnshegh) This creature stalks its prey in the Coulladaraight, most often near Treucht and Rheulgard, but he was once spotted as far afield as Kiergard. The best account on Meson is given to us by a militiaman from the realm of Justina Heulough, also known as the Banshegh's Domain:

"The wolfman stands at the height of a normal man, and he wears a finely-crafted suit of armor with wolf motifs all over. All I saw other than the armor was his face and hands, and they were covered with a fine, glossy brown fur, finer than a wolf's pelt, but his fingers ended in huge claws.

"We were fighting Rheulgardian invaders in a clearing when the wolfman burst out of the woods and started tearing everybody apart. Within minutes, we're the only ones left standing—and he just bowed, said a polite how-do-you-do, gave his name as Meson, and bounded off. His accent placed him from somewheres east of here, but I can't say that his features looked human at all."

"Maybe he's not half-wolf and half-man, but he was obviously dangerous. I still don't know why he left us alone, but I'm grateful. Maybe he's just out to kill Rheulgardians too, like us, do you think?"

Pegasus: (Ehrshegh) This skittish beast is a powerful horse with wings, and it makes its home somewhere within the Seamist Mountains. At the fall of Deismaar, Haelyn rose up to godhood, and his charger gained power, too: intelligence and its wings. Since Deismaar, the Pegasus has aided the forces of good, though only the Roele bloodline could call on it. None have seen the Pegasus in years.

Phoenix: (Ehrshegh) Many details on this being's life are steeped in legend, but it is known that the Phoenix was once the daughter of a prominent Khinasi house and a priestess to Avani. She became so peaceful and so close to the gods that she burst into flames and became the firebird known as the Phoenix. That is all that can be corroborated in texts. Oral traditions of southern Cerilia offer over 200 versions of the Phoenix's tale, each tied to the teller's family or a friend's family. While she has not been officially sighted in over 300 years, the Phoenix might roost at the peak of Ras Deissid on the island of Ghamoura.

Prikesk: (Awnshegh) Prikesk was a young Vos squire with the troops at Deismaar, and he and his master were among the few who did not abandon Azrai. Invested with power upon the gods' destruc-

tion, Prikesk stopped aging. After 700 years, he still appeared as a boy of 11, though his mouth was filled with razor-sharp fangs and he could climb walls like a spider. Often taken in as an orphan to work as a castle squire, Prikesk fed on unwitting blooded scions within reach of his venomous fangs. While the Gorgon claimed to be Prikesk's final master and slayer, tales of a young lad with similar abilities still filter out of Vosgaard.

Quickfoot: (Blooded) This honorary title is granted to the eldest son of the Rhurfoot halfling clan of Avanil upon the investiture of power from father to child. The current Quickfoot is the 40th halfling to hold this title and the position as Special Messenger for his Grace, the Duke of Avanil. Each Quickfoot for centuries has been granted this ability (usually from father to son, though there were 12 females who bore the Quickfoot name in the past) to run as swiftly as a riding horse for three full days without tiring. Quickfoot once ran more swiftly and for longer periods—Quickfoot the 3rd allegedly ran from Vosgaard to Avanil in four days!—but the powers were lessened by the 19th title-bearer, who invested half of the power into each of his twin sons. One fell

to the power of the Hydra, and only the other remained to ensure the survival of this bloodline, which continues today as a proud and noble lineage.

Rage of the Sea: (Awnshegh) A new menace in the waters off the coast of southern Anuire, the Rage of the Sea appears to be a mixture of Anuirean woman and shark. Nothing is known about her, other than the fact that she is consumed with anger, and she has attacked a number of ships in the waters off Medoere and Ilien. Tylas, a scribe in the city of Ilien, cited her name as the Rage of the Sea, for that is her popular name among seafarers. Tylas also suggested that a link to her origins might be found in an old seaman's tale of a lonely young wife losing her man to the sea, and longing for any way to swim out and bring him back. As this awnshegh has been spotted only twice in the past two years and the story he quotes is a centuries-old folk tale, little stock is put in it.

Ruovar the Red Bull: (Awnshegh) Ruovar, one of Rhuobhe's lieutenants, was always an elf of fiery temper and brash actions. As the power of Azrai twisted his form toward an unearthly crossing of elf and bull, Ruovar increasingly lost his self-control and staged many frequent raids against nearby human "encroachments." By the time his transformation was complete (as a red-pelted bull with sharp, horn-like ears and a slimmer but muscular form), he was nearly mindless. Over four centuries ago, Ruovar and Ruobhe parted company, and the former began a decades-long trek across

the land, killing anyone or anything that crossed his path, including a few possessors of blood abilities. Ruovar's hunger for power was inestimable, and it is unknown how much additional power Ruovar gained from these kills. The beast was reported missing over seven decades ago near the land now known as the Magian's Domain, and there is only idle speculation as to Ruovar's current whereabouts and status.

Shadows: (Blooded) This devious little halfling is known only as Shadows, and no halfling clan across Cerilia lays claim to his birth, so one can only wonder at his origin. It would be hard to mistake this halfling for another, as he is an albino, with pure white hair, red eyes, and a very pale complexion.

Tales are told of him waylaying lone travelers or small groups on lonely roads during the nights of the new moon, stealing valuables and lives. Given the generally affable nature of halflings, this is quite a disturbing image for most, especially halflings (though Shadows has never been known to harm his own . . . yet).

Some legends suggest that this malevolent little being spirits folk away to the Shadow World, whether in broad daylight or deepest night, by enveloping them with thick tendrils of shadow. They say this is why there are rarely more than a few scraps of bloodied cloth left at the scene when Shadows strikes. As few survive meeting Shadows, only he knows his true motives and abilities for certain. It is almost certain, given his proclivity toward death and ill will, that Shadows draws his power from the blood of Azrai and not a little power from a very direct tie to the Shadow World.

Stag of Sielwode: (Blooded) This creature is guaranteed to pique the curiosity of any blooded scion. It is a veritable questing beast, as it is seemingly immortal and ageless. Thirteen times this black-haired stag with a rack of pure silver horns has been brought to ground, and thirteen times has it gotten up and escaped while being dragged out of the

Sielwode. It is fast, cunning, and nigh-impossible to kill—it'd even test the forest god Erik's skills at the hunt!

Swordhawk: (Awnshegh) The current ruler of Massenmarch, Karl Bissel has only begun his transformation towards his ultimate form and powers. Wild rumors float about Massenmarch and the surrounding lands about Bissel's actual appearance, announcing anything from eyes on the sides of his head and wings on his back to blades sprouting out the length of his arms. The only guaranteed facts are that he keeps his face and body hidden beneath armor (including full gauntlets and basket helm) almost all the time he is in public. Despite this transformation to awnshegh form, Karl Bissel is still one of the most ruthless, cunning, and capable leaders within the Brechtür lands on the Krakennauricht. His appellation as the Swordhawk is a self-proclaimed title from his days as a bandit and assassin, and he uses it now as a badge of distinction, warning all who cross his path that the Swordhawk is on the road of power, and shall not be stopped.

Synnith the Wraith: (Blooded) Many believe Synnith is currently allied with the Magian, though he has spent the past 30 years traveling the continent as a mercenary. While short and wiry, he still appears as an Anuirean human, though his eyes are wholly black with no irises or pupils—some say his gaze freezes a man's blood cold with terror! He is also well known by a habit of chuckling evilly from shadows before he strikes. His name stems from his particularly strong blood ability to *travel*. If accounts are to be believed, this man has enhanced that ability to allow himself to teleport between our world and the Shadow World at will, despite time of day or location. It is this ability that has both saved him from assassination and aided him in killing other blooded foes.

Terror: (Awnshegh) They say the Terror is only a shadow, but this shadow has more substance and power than most. If the rumors are to be believed, this creature was once a trusted emissary and sometime spy for the ruler of Elinie, but he gave in to his greed and his tainted blood, swiftly becoming the living silhouette known as the Terror. He now stalks the nighttime lands surrounding Elinie, seeking out folk of the blood to increase his power in the hopes of conquering Elinie someday soon.

Tollan: (Awnshegh) A new lieutenant of the Gorgon, Tollan is a far less powerful awnshegh at this stage in his life, for he is less apt at combat

and claiming the blood abilities of others and more apt at skulking and intrigues involving money. Tollan manages the Gorgon's few trade routes and oversees the latter's spies and assassins. He is changing slightly and is certainly no common human, as his skin and fingernails have taken on a gold hue, and his teeth have become ruby fangs. Tollan considers taking on an appellation to underscore his *blood-form*, but he has yet to create one to his and his master's satisfaction (and he has killed the insolent spy who dared nickname him "The Living Hoard").

Treant: (Ehrshegh) A former Grand Druid, Gunnar Svorjinn now lives an immortal life as the Treant, a true part of nature. His form is that of a monstrous oak with a discernible bearded face within its bark. The Treant has not moved or spoken to anyone other than his dryad companions in over 250 years, though a number of druids make a trek to his clearing within the Aelvinnwode in Cariele in hopes of gaining wisdom from him. Tales say he can uproot every tree within a mile of him to send it on the march, though such a thing has never been seen, and it is doubtful a creature of nature would ever resort to such tactics, no matter what the provocation.

Warlock: (Awnshegh) Allegedly one of the surviving children of Prince Raesene's early attempts at founding his own dynasty, the Warlock lives a life of paranoia and distrust, always believing his power-mad father seeks his death at every turn. The Warlock is not without his own power, and after 1,000 years, he is one of the premier wizards on the face of Cerilia, surpassed only by the Magian. He plans on facing his father some day, but not before he has the might to bring the Gorgon down.

Water Maiden: (Ehrshegh) The Water Maiden was a half-elven wizardess and consort to an elven lord in the forests of Lluabraight. She could perform amazing magic with water, though she had no power over ice or mists. According to a poem found in Hjorig, she could transform her body into water and flow to safety when threatened. The last time she was seen, she used this transformation to escape the pursuit of the Gorgon, but with no prominent water sources nearby, sages believe she evaporated and died somewhere within the foothills of the Stonecrown Mountains of Markazor. A diviner who inspected the area recently claims that an immense aquifer lies relatively close to the surface. Could this be the Water Maiden or simply a new well?

White Goblin: (Awnshegh) The White Goblin is a vile beast that barely resembles its former hobgobilin status. It stands a full three feet taller than the average goblin and has double the weight, and has a deathly white pallor—even its bristlelike hair is wan. It possesses the tusks of a boar and razor-sharp claws that it uses to shred prey and opponents. A potent leader of a renegade band of thieving and murdering goblins and gnolls, the White Goblin is worshiped by its followers as a god (just as its great-grandsire, the Spider, has been worshiped for centuries). It is quite powerful, having slain many minor blooded persons within its short 40 years as a known awnshegh, though its life span is considered to be coming to a close now that the White Goblin is encroaching on the Massenmarch lands of Swordhawk (whose power is evidently on the rise, with the swiftly fading humanity of the ruthless Karl Bissel).

The *Rulebook* of the BIRTHRIGHT campaign set details bloodline abilities for all scions of the ancient gods, including those bloodlines descended from Azrai. These abilities are the basic core gifts, but there are many more available to awnsheghlien and heroes alike, as will be shown in this appendix. However, differences between heroes of Cerilia and their monstrous counterparts affect how their abilities manifest. The new abilities given here demonstrate how and why much of the power of the awnsheghlien is placed in their transformed bodies.

power or curse?

Some awnsheghlien in this book have new abilities, but not all new abilities are included in the tables below. The powers wielded by the Basilisk or the Siren, for example, are unique. Why are these beasts given such power? Why can't the heroes tap such might? Simply put, drawing upon such power most often comes at a high cost: the person's humanity.

To summon an old adage: "Power corrupts, and absolute power corrupts absolutely." A large proportion of an awnshegh's power actively alters that being's original form, feeding it power but simultaneously forcing it to become more like the base creature the being is in spirit. Given the penchant of those with the blood of Azrai for selfishness, greed, or unabashed evil, those beings tied to Azrai become the horrific awnsheghlien. The majority of the power adapts and maintains the changes wrought on a body, keeping it in monstrous form. Awnsheghlien still have access to the standard and new blood abilities, but it is more likely for them to have unique skills tied to their altered forms.

Though most blooded heroes are loathe to allow their powers to build up enough to change them physically, a select few advanced their blood abilities beyond the norm in the cause of good. These rare beings are collectively called the Ehrsheghlien, "blood of the light," and are mentioned in the "Lesser Awnsheghlien and Other NPCs" section.

appendix I: blood abilities

new blood abilities

This section details new powers, along with any limitations or consequences. A chart provides the Dungeon Master with a random way to assign these powers to future NPCs or to PCs as further birthrights.

Blood Abilities II Table

d%	Ability
01-25	Bloodform (Major, Great)
26-28	Bloodtrait (Major, Great)
29-33	Charm Aura (Major, Great)
34-40	Detect Life (All)
41-45	Death Touch (Minor, Major)
46-48	Invulnerability (Great)
49-60	Long Life (Major, Great)
61-63	Major Regeneration (Great)
64-70	Major Resistance (All)
70-72	Wither Touch (All)
73-00	Roll on Standard Blood Abilities Table*

*Table 13: Blood Abilities can be found in the *Rulebook* of the BIRTHRIGHT campaign set.

Bloodform   Major, Great
Derivation: Azrai

This is the power that causes an awnshegh's form to shift toward its most corrupt state; from the character's perspective, he is achieving power that ultimately suits his nature (if not his aesthetic wishes). An uncontrolled power, *bloodform* manifests whenever a character invested with the blood of Azrai (and this ability) taps his powers.

In many ways, *bloodform* is more a curse than an ability, but many awnsheghlien look at it as a mixed blessing. Initial changes are small but noticeable; for example, a human female with Azrai's bloodline is wounded, and when she uses her *regeneration* ability, her body heals over the wound with different skin, almost a scaled hide. Continual use of blood abilities brings these physical changes more to the forefront until they totally alter the original creature, creating an awnshegh; our example of the human female could eventually become the Naga or some other suitably scaled creature of nightmares. Depending on the amount and frequency of powers used, as well as the character's bloodline strength, the transformation to awnshegh form could take as little as three years or as many as six centuries.

When a character with the *bloodform* ability receives any additional power, through bloodtheft or other channels, there is a 75% chance that the new ability will manifest as a physical change in his body which allows either a new attack (claws, beak, fangs, etc.), a new defense (armored or furred skin, increased speed, etc.), or a new physical ability entirely (the Gorgon's paralytic gaze, the Vampire's mist form, etc.).

The ultimate transformation of a character to awnshegh status should be carefully planned by the DM, so there is a logical progression of the creature's form, attack and defense modes, and final powers based on the character's personality and nature. If this is a player character, discussions with the DM on the character's drives and goals can help to divine how the PC's *bloodform* will be manifest.

Bloodtrait   Major, Great
Derivation: Any except Azrai

Blooded characters can change their physical forms to access their blood abilities more evocatively. In effect, a character can use this gift to alter his body to accurately reflect his powers. This is very similar to the uncontrolled *bloodform* ability that creates awnsheghlien, though the characters partially control the power changing them. The exact form of these *bloodtrait* transformations is not controlled by the blooded character, but the timing of the change is. Therefore, these characters choose to exhibit their special legacies openly. An NPC with a *bloodtrait* is unsettling to normal mortals, though, and results in a +1 to +4 encounter reaction penalty, depending on circumstances.

Examples: A character with Vorynn's bloodline might choose to change her entire head to resemble that of an owl in order for her to more easily tap her *animal affinity* talent. Another blooded character might shift his hand from appearing as solid flesh to something crystalline that glows

when the *healing* talent is used. Unlike the *bloodform*, this change does not advance uncontrollably; it advances and alters a character further only if so willed by the character.

It is rare that any regent or scion of any bloodline would choose to significantly change his form, as this sort of alteration of form is most closely linked in many peoples' minds with the awnsheghlien. Within the first eight centuries after Deismaar, though, circumstances forced this ability into use in order for the forces of good to vanquish the growing evil of rampaging awnsheghlien. While no one in the public eye has actively used this power to change himself in recent centuries, a few ancient heroes embraced this ability to become servants of good who moved beyond humanity. Known ehrsheghlien (elvish for "blood of the light") that still exist within Cerilia include the Pegasus, the Phoenix, and the Treant.

Charm Aura   Major, Great
Derivations: Azrai, Basaïa, Brenna

Similar to *divine aura*, *charm aura* projects an invisible shroud of power around the blooded character. Rather than enthralling onlookers with awe and majesty, this aura also mesmerizes and controls those within 50 feet. As a major ability, the character can *charm* 1-6 nonhostile creatures or *scare* enemies. As a great talent, *charm aura* inflicts either *mass charm* on nonhostiles or *confusion* on hostiles within 75 feet. This power, regardless of its rank, is usable only three times per day and affects only nonblooded creatures of six or fewer hit dice.

Charm aura, when used with a *divine aura*, can extend the range of either *aura* to 100 feet.

Death Touch   Minor, Major
Derivation: Azrai

A character afflicted with this ability can exude a virulent poison in some manner. Contact with this toxin results in disease or death, depending on the strength of the ability. With the slightest contact, *death touch* can spoil food and drink, or pollute a small well or enclosed pool of water. This ability manifests in a wide variety of ways, such as a skin-contact poison (emitted through pores on hands or other appendages), injected poisons (introduced through fangs or another piercing implement), or a spray or cloud (anything from a mist-like breath weapon to an underwater ink cloud). At its widest dispersal, the *death touch* affects only those creatures within a 25-foot radius of the emission point.

At minor levels, contact forces a victim to save vs. death magic or else contract a disease and lose 1d4 hit points per day until a *neutralize poison* or a *cure disease* is cast on the victim. A major *death touch* is more virulent, and an immediate save vs. death magic is needed to stave off death in 1-10 rounds; if successful, the effects still operate as per the minor ability.

Obviously, some awnsheghlien have even more dangerous variants of this ability, exuding natural poisons of extremely virulent natures. While they are listed as having this ability, their particular poisonous touches (or effects) are unique and detailed under each specifically empowered awnshegh.

Detect Life   Minor, Major, Great
Derivation: Any

The blooded character can sense all living creatures and things within a particular range. At minor ability, the character can sense animal life in general amounts (little to a lot) and the exact amount and location of living plant life within 100 yards per Intelligence point. Major ability grants the character a range of 300 yards per Intelligence point, the power focused to detect exact amounts of animals and a general amount of sentient life. At great ability, *detect life* can pinpoint exact numbers of all forms of life (sentient or not) within 500 yards per Intelligence point.

Invulnerability   Great
Derivations: Azrai, Basaïa, Vorynn

The blooded character that possesses this blood ability is not fully immortal, but he cannot be killed except under specific circumstances. This ability renders him immune to all spells and effects that use the Death Magic saving throw matrix. He is also immune to the effects of all poisons, no matter how virulent.

A character with *invulnerability* can be killed only under a particular set of deadly conditions which are unique for each blooded scion. If an NPC has this ability, the DM must decide what procedures must be accomplished for it to be slain. As an example, a being might need to be slain like so to bypass its *invulnerability* and end its life: "It must be reduced to less than -10 hit points, the head must be severed, and its heart must be removed from its chest. The parts must each be burned separately on open fires."

If even one of the proscribed steps is not done properly, the character regenerates one hit point each hour until it reaches one hit point. The normal healing process for that individual then takes over at that point. Unless it is truly destroyed, the blooded character does not lose any of its birthright or regency.

Long Life   Minor, Major, Great
Derivation: All

With this ability, a blooded character enjoys a greatly increased life span, as the aging process is vastly slowed down. This does not protect a character from normal damage from combat or poisons, but simply postpones the ravages of age. A character with the minor ability ages only one year for every five that pass. A major *long life* sees a character age one year across 25 years. Characters with this great ability, like the Gorgon, are aging at a rate of only one year each century.

Major Regeneration   Great
Derivation: Azrai, Reynir

This ability is available only to those blooded scions who also have the standard *regeneration* ability; this is simply an extended version of that ability. With this ability, an awnshegh or scion of

Reynir can regenerate lost limbs, damaged organs and senses, and heal wounds much faster than normal or blooded beings.

The character regains lost hit points at a rate of one per round. If limbs, organs, or senses were lost, they are restored in weeks (30 days, reduced by one day per Constitution point).

This power, when used by a blooded character of Azrai, dramatically increases the speed of the transformation to awnshegh status, as restored limbs and senses are rarely those of the character's original race.

Major Resistance   Minor, Major, Great
Derivation: All (see below)

The *resistance* ability in the core rules outlines only the most common resistance to attacks or spells prevalent in each particular bloodline. Like the original ability, *major resistance* at minor rank affords 25% immunity, major rank allows 50% immunity, and a great rank *major resistance* grants the blooded scion 75% immunity to the noted effect. Again, this ability is most similar to the resistance an elf has to *sleep* and *charm* spells.

Below are additional resistances, and under each resistance are those bloodlines that have access to this *major resistance*.

Charm: This ability is identical to the elves' resistance to *charm* spells and spell-like effects or the standard *resistance* ability of the Anduiras bloodline. This further conveys resistance to the *fear* blood ability. New derivations: Azrai, Brenna, Reynir.

Magic: Like a number of rare creatures, this scion of the blood is naturally resistant to the effects of magic, whether from spells or items. This ability applies to all types of magic except blood abilities. *Note:* This ability is only accessible to those of Great bloodline rank or higher, and can be accessed only at Minor rank (25% magic resistance). New derivations: Anduiras, Azrai, Reynir, Vorynn.

Nonmagical Attacks: Unlike the other *major resistances*, this ability does not immediately prevent attacks or effects from happening, but it does lessen their impact. Those same immunities per rank (25% / 50% / 75%) mark the amount by which damage from normal weapons or natural attacks is reduced. For example, an awnshegh with this ability at minor rank is damaged for 8 points of damage, but only 6 points are subtracted from its hit-point total (25% of 8 is 2). New derivations: Azrai, Brenna, Masela.

Poison: If a character with this ability is exposed to any type of poison (by gas, venom, poisoned weapon, potion, etc.), he rolls to neutralize the poison outright according to his rank ability. If that roll fails, he still gains his saving throws vs. poison, at a +1 bonus per rank (+1/+2/+3). New derivations: Azrai, Basaïa, Brenna, Masela, Reynir.

Bear in mind that blooded scions may have other types of *resistance*, but these abilities are currently limited enough to be considered unique to one family or bloodline.

Wither Touch   Major, Great
Derivation: Azrai

Just as *touch of decay* ruins and destroys inanimate objects, *wither touch* desiccates and withers living tissue on contact. The scion affects only extremities like arms or legs, but its effects are the same no matter the target.

When touched by this major ability, a victim must save vs. polymorph or suffer 1d8 points of damage; the affected limb is emaciated, and full use of it is impossible for 1d6 days. A character's Strength is reduced by an amount equal to the damage to a minimum score of 2. If the blighted limb is not removed, *healed*, or *regenerated* by blood ability in 2d4 days, the victim permanently loses the ability to fully use the limb, and a character's Strength remains permanently reduced.

At great rank, *wither touch* emaciates an entire creature and initially reduces Strength and hit points by 1d12 points each. It also forces victims to save vs. death magic once each day. If this saving throw is failed, the victim dies. This blight can be cured by *healing* or *regeneration*, but if this isn't done within 2d4 days, the creature is permanently emaciated and reduced in Strength. At that time, no further saves vs. death magic are needed as the curse has run its course.

Both ranks of *wither touch* are usable only once per week.